The Strangely Interesting Story
of Morris Figg

Hereford Books

1

To Morris's way of thinking, waking up next to a dead body was not a good start to the day.

As the dim winter sunlight filtered through the thin curtains and dragged him into today, he could tell he wasn't alone. He knew the difference in the feel of the bed, those mornings he woke with a woman. The way the mattress dipped, on account of it being a cheap one his landlord, Morris suspected, bought second hand.

And this morning it had that feeling. He racked his brains to try and remember what had happened last night, but it wouldn't come. Still, a woman in your bed is not to be wasted and you never know, she might be up for a quick one before she went, whoever she was.

Only, when he stretched out his hand to feel her thigh it was strangely cold. He couldn't compute cold. He ran his hand up her leg to her waist, passed that and onto her breast. Cold, stone cold. Morris closed his eyes and tried to pretend it wasn't, but it was. Cold was wrong. Cold was definitely wrong, Morris knew that, even after last night, and last night had been, he remembered now, pretty heavy.

He tried to decide if it was a better idea to climb over her to check this out or get out of bed and go round. Climbing over, he thought, could be very unpleasant if what he was thinking was true, but on the other hand getting out of bed was something he never did if it could possibly be avoided, before at least one roll-up. He fumbled on the bedside table but couldn't find his tobacco, so he closed his eyes just in case it worked this time and when he opened them it would all be different, and this horrible thing would just go away.

But when he opened them it hadn't. It never sodding did, not in Morris's experience. Not dead bodies, which of course he hadn't yet confirmed and in any case had never been a problem before, but bad things in general. No, bad things in general were usually still there, being as bad as they liked, when you opened your eyes again.

Well, there was nothing for it. He had to know. He put one foot on the lino and then the other. Bloody hell, it was cold. He wanted to wrap the bedspread round him but that would have meant exposing the person next to him which he didn't want to do, not on account of his feelings for her which he wouldn't have had even if she hadn't been dead but because it would mean he would have to face the truth a few seconds sooner.

So ten seconds later he stood stark naked on the cold floor and lifted the blanket carefully and yes, there was indisputably a dead woman in the bed, his bed. He groaned. His hands started shaking, and he knew he needed a fag. He pulled the bedding up and covered her face, not out of respect so much as so he wouldn't have to see it.

Ten minutes later he sat at the table in his kitchenette wrapped in a motley assortment of clothes and warmed his hands on a brew while he lit his second cigarette. It normally took two, at least, before he could face the day with anything like equanimity. Today was different, though. He didn't want to start today, if it could possibly be avoided. On days like this he usually went back to bed, only there had never been a day quite like this before, and going back to bed was not the solution, it was the problem.

For a moment he felt irritated. Who was this person lying inconveniently dead in his bed, stopping him getting back in?

On second thoughts, who was she anyway, really, who was she?

No, it wouldn't come. If she had a name, and his experience with women told him she almost certainly did, it wouldn't come into his head. Of course, maybe it hadn't been there in the first place. Maybe he had forgotten to ask. Well, a bit bloody late now.

It was about then that a light came on, not in the room but in his head. Something he had seen but not registered when he looked at her, something, if his memory served him right, he didn't like the thought of. He sipped his tea and took another long drag on his roll-up, but the thought wouldn't go away. He couldn't avoid it. He had to go and look.

He lifted the blanket gently, out of fear now, and yes, there it was. Shit. What the hell had happened? Now he not only had a dead body in his bed, a body moreover with no name that he knew of, but round her neck was unmistakably a pair of tights, tied, even he could tell, so tightly that now he knew how she met her end. The poor bloody woman had been strangled.

And in Morris's limited experience, women didn't strangle themselves.

2

Notwithstanding the turmoil this created in his head, Morris found himself suddenly and annoyingly hungry. The only item in the fridge that wasn't a health hazard was the milk he had stolen from number sixteen's doorstep the day before, and to make matters worse there were no bloody Frosties to put it on, so there was nothing for it, he would have to go and buy some food. He rummaged through his pockets and came up with thirty three pence, and even in his present addled state he somehow knew that thirty three pence wasn't going to go far, if anywhere at all.

Then it occurred to him. OK, it wasn't nice, and strictly speaking it could be construed as theft, but somehow he didn't think she was going to complain. He crept back into the bedroom and among the litter of women's clothing on the floor he found her handbag. And in the handbag he found something he hadn't been expecting. Morris had never seen that much money before. In fact he could only have taken your word for it that that kind of money even existed. Whoever she was she was rich. He looked at the clothes spread around his feet. No, Morris didn't know much about how rich women dressed but he was pretty sure it wasn't like this. Whoever this woman was, at least now he knew what she did for a living.

He let himself sink to the floor in confusion, and added up what he knew so far. In his bed was a dead prostitute, strangled, for the want of any other suspect, by him. He looked around the room as if another suspect might miraculously appear, but he wasn't surprised when they didn't. No, he was, in some way he couldn't fathom, definitely implicated in this whole mess.

Shit.

Unable to contain his curiosity, he unrolled the banknotes and started to count them. They went into neat piles on the floor, and there were twelve piles by the time he had finished, and each pile was a thousand pounds, and then there was another small pile of three hundred. Morris didn't know how much prostitutes earned but he didn't think it was this much. Not unless she was a high-class prostitute - a very high-class one - and that raised the question of what she was doing in this shithole that he called home.

Come to that had he offered to pay her last night or was it a freebie, and if it was what kind of taste did she have? He looked at the money. Then he looked at the money some more. This was bad, but it did have a good side to it, in that there was a hell of a lot of cash on his bedroom floor. OK, it wasn't exactly his money but for now it was, well, in his possession. There was the small matter of a dead body but that could be dealt with. No it couldn't. What the hell was he thinking of? He got up and looked at her, whatever her name was. She had a nice face, well, apart from the permanent grimace which now, when he thought about it, might have been something to do with being strangled to death.

And then, instinctively, he bent over and relieved the pressure from the tights, as if somehow that would make her feel better. As he felt the nylon slip through his fingers it felt eerily familiar. Yes, he thought, I had these in my hands last night. But for Christ's sake, surely he didn't strangle her? Why would he? This didn't make any sense.

He couldn't face going out to buy food now, so he hunted in her bag and found enough rolling tobacco and cannabis to make a joint. It was about twenty minutes later, eased by the spliff, that his memory came back. Oh yes, he remembered it all. The games they played, her telling him to tie the tights round her neck. He had never done that before but he obeyed her and he tied them to the bedhead too and them he jumped on her and then, and then ... and then she must have strangled herself. That was it! He didn't kill her, she killed herself. OK, he was a party to it, and perhaps if he hadn't been so, well, violent, the accident wouldn't have happened, but it was absolutely definitely an accident.

'Yes, an accident', he sighed, as the smoke curled from his mouth. 'Not my fault at all. It'll all be OK.'

There, he had said it, and he believed it. The only problem was, would the police?

And then, bizarrely, what worried him was not the police but a question. If she had choked to death when he leapt on her, did that mean she was dead when he screwed her?

'Oh shit, oh shit.'

The raw November air helped to wake him up on the way to the Plentiful Goodness Food Store on the corner. The Plentiful Goodness Food Store sold only junk food, plus some fresh vegetables that were a complete mystery if you were unfamiliar with Indian cuisine, which Morris was. Actually Morris was unfamiliar with cuisine of any kind, living, apart from Frosties, entirely on a diet of E-numbers, and even then only if there was money left out of his Jobseeker's Allowance once he had paid for his cannabis and some duty-free tobacco and a packet of Rizlas.

Morris had a policy of never stealing from Mr and Mrs Patel. If he couldn't afford food he went to Tesco and stole from them. Yes Morris was a firm believer in shoplifting only from those stores that could afford it. It was, sadly, one of the factors he had to weigh up as he put some fish fingers under the grill, on account of the local police being called more than once, in fact four times, on account of his shoplifting at

Tesco. Morris was not the most proficient of petty criminals, and had two hundred and seventy hours of community service notched up to prove it, with a threat of prison if he re-offended, something he was determined to avoid. Prison, that is, not reoffending.

He ate his breakfast, and unusually for him he washed up afterwards. In fact he washed up everything he could find that might benefit from the unusual treatment, and when he had done that he cleaned the cooker and only when he ran out of displacement activities did he sit down and face the fact that he had to face the facts. The obvious thing was to call the police. Yes, now he was in the clear, on account of the foolish woman accidentally hanging herself on her own tights, a fact that had, in his own mind at least, been established pretty convincingly, he could with equanimity ring the police and tell them exactly what happened.

'Let me get this straight. You pick up this young woman at a pub, you bring her back here where you both drink a large amount of cheap wine and smoke several joints, then you take her to bed, tie her tights round her neck, you claim on her request, tie the other end to the bed, and she promptly hangs herself. Then this morning you leave the body where it is, rifle through her bag and remove, let me see, twelve thousand three hundred pounds, seven pounds twenty five of which you take down the road to purchase a twenty-five gramme pouch of Old Holborn, some Frosties and a packet of fish fingers. Does that about cover it?'

No perhaps not.

'Well, it's like this, officer ..... um'. No, perhaps not that either. Well the thing to do was just to call them and say whatever came naturally. He looked at the money, and wondered if he should remove some of it first. After all, there was no way they would know how much she had, and she couldn't tell them, so what was the point in not finding a good home for it, his?

He lifted one of the piles and shifted it from his right hand to his left, and then he picked up another one. There, that was easy. He would hand over ten thousand and keep two for himself. Plus the change.

On the other hand, what was the point of giving them all that? What were they going to do with it, give it to some undeserving charity? Well, charity begins at home. He took another two thousand and put it in his pile.

'Eight for them, four for me.' On the other hand, why should they get more than him? Who were they going to return it to? Probably the bloody Chancellor of the Exchequer. No, why should he get more than Morris? Whose need was greater? He took another two thousand. Yes, that looked about right. Each pile was the same size now and Morris was happy. Then he looked at his pile, and he looked at the Chancellor's pile, and then he looked at his pile again.

'What does the bloody Chancellor want it for? Sod it.' And he made one large pile with it again, only this time it was his, all his. Yes his need was greater, and it was natural justice.

After all, who was ever going to know? Which just goes to show how wrong you can be, but then Morris was a past master at being wrong. In any case, he picked up the phone to call the police. Only it was dead. B bloody T had cut him off again.

3

It was no good, he had to make a decision, and that decision had to be to go down to Barton police station. Today was Jobcentre day, so he would go into town and sign on, and then go and confess.

'Have you done any work in the past two weeks?'

He tried not to look shifty, and since Morris looked shifty even when he wasn't this was nigh on impossible. OK, there were the deliveries he helped Marty Finnigan with, but you couldn't really call that work, although in a technical sense, on account of Marty paying him ready cash, he would have to admit it was, strictly according to the law, paid work.

'No.'

'Mm.' Just Mm, and then some intensive looking at the computer, which of course Morris couldn't see, but whatever it was she was taking her time.

Er, excuse me could you hurry that up please because I've got a body back in my flat and I need to deal with it.

She didn't hear his thoughts, thankfully, and carrying on looking and Mming. Whether she was looking up Morris's entire work history, which let's face it wasn't a long one so it shouldn't take much time, or she was booking her holiday on the Internet, he couldn't tell. Mm, as far as he could tell, might just be so he thought she was working. Maybe they had some kind of rule that each 'client', as they insisted on calling him, had to be kept waiting so it looked like something purposeful was going on.

'So Mr, um, Figg.' She said it as if she suspected him of making it up. She must be new here. Everyone else knew him. 'What have you been doing about looking for work?'

'Well, actually, I'm thinking about going away.'

'Away? Would that be for a holiday or are you leaving the area for good?' She looked hopeful that it might be the latter.

'I can't really say yet. I'm in discussion with someone about a deal, you know.'

'Yes, I know.' She had obviously heard that one before. Even if she was new here, she wasn't new to this game. 'Well, you've got another six weeks. After that you will have to take whatever work we find for you. Or of course you will lose your allowance.' She looked like she hoped again that it would be the latter. Today hadn't started well and she wasn't helping it to get any better.

Morris thought about twelve thousand pounds and wondered if he had to take this. He could get used to twelve thousand, but not perhaps just yet.

'No, I'm pretty sure we'll have this deal sown up by then.'

'Good. Sign here.'

What the hell am I doing, he thought as he walked out into the drizzle, prostituting myself for forty-five quid a week? He tried to divide twelve thousand by forty-five to see how long he could live on it but gave up in the attempt. Mental arithmetic had never been his strong subject. On the other hand Morris had never had a strong subject, mental or otherwise. He was the only one in his class who managed to fail 'O' level woodwork.

And there it was, the police station, its neat red bricks shining in the rain, and its cute little blue lamp over the entrance. He walked straight past holding his breath. He wondered, actually, why he did that, holding his breath, but he couldn't find a reason. Just nerves, he supposed. He decided to go round to Marty's place for a cup of tea, and tell him about the body. Or possibly not the last part.

'So, it's you is it Morris?'

Morris had never figured out why Marty had to state the bleeding obvious all the time but imagined it was on account of him being Irish.

'Sure is Marty, your old friend Morris Figg.'

Marty wondered why Morris always said that, but supposed it was on account of him being English. The English, he had always felt, had a strange way of talking, but you had to go along with it.

'Well Morris, I'm sorry but if it's work you're after I'm afraid there isn't any. Things is a bit slow at the moment.'

'No, that's OK Marty. I'm not short this week.'

'No, I shouldn't think so. About the same height as usual, I would say.'

Morris looked at him carefully to figure out if this was a joke and he was supposed to laugh but Marty's face was dead straight. You never could tell with him, because he never laughed at jokes, even his own, and Morris always laughed at his own jokes himself.

'Anyway, haven't you put that kettle on yet? I'm dying for a cuppa.'

Talking of dying reminded Morris of why he had come round, but now he was here and talking to Marty in the flesh he wondered why he had ever thought he would be a good person to give advice.

'So, Morris, what you been up to then boy?' Boy. That was another of Marty's irritating things. Morris didn't know how old Marty was but he reckoned he must be all of thirty-five and Morris himself was thirty-seven, although he looked a lot older on account of his lifestyle which even he would have to admit was not exactly Sunday supplement. Anyway, he was already irritated with Marty, which usually took about ten minutes but today must be a record, and telling about his problem back at the flat was getting less likely by the second, in which case he didn't want to waste time on pleasantries, or not so pleasantries, with his Irish so-called friend.

'Well, you know, this and that.'

'This and that, eh? Well I like a bit of this, and a bit of that, but to be honest I try not to do them both at the same time you know.'

No, Morris didn't know. In fact he was wondering what this stupid git was on about. He sometimes thought the only language Marty was actually fluent in was gibberish.

'And a bit of the other.'

If that was a joke Morris gave it nul points. Marty's sense of humour, he reckoned, was basically schoolboy smut but even then, on account of him never laughing and therefore never giving you a clue as to whether it really was a joke, Marty never actually told a joke that you felt an immediate urge to laugh at, even out of politeness.

This went on for another hour before Morris decided it would be more entertaining to go back home and talk to the stiff.

The reality of his situation hit him like a brick wall, as he stood in his bedroom and saw a real live corpse on his bed and realised he couldn't put off doing something about this. He sat at the kitchen table with a cup of tea and pondered his options. OK, he could go to the police and tell them the truth, the whole truth and nothing but the truth. Or he could go to the police and tell them some of that stuff. Only then, he reckoned, they would take him to a padded room and get the whole story out of him anyway. Morris's understanding of these things sometimes owed more to the films than to any actual experience.

Then it dawned on him. He didn't know who this girl was, which meant there was absolutely nothing to connect him with her. OK, whoever she was someone was probably wondering where she was, and if she was a prostitute, and a high-class one, that might be her pimp. And then there was the money. It might be hers but it might not. There could be a man looking for her right now, and it might be the cash he was more interested in than her welfare. That kind of money usually, he imagined, had someone worrying about it. On the other hand, maybe it was her life savings and she was leaving to set up fresh somewhere and get away from the sordid life she had been leading. Or perhaps not, on account of her spending the night, her last night as it happened, with him. No, none of it made a lot of sense.

On the other hand, which was where he started, there was absolutely nothing to connect her to him, so the one thing he could be sure about was even if someone was looking for her they weren't going to be visiting him for that purpose.

That was when there was a sudden loud knock on the door. Morris's heart missed a beat, or more likely several. He rushed into the bedroom and covered the evidence with the bedding but the feet stuck up so he threw some of the clothes from the floor on top but then he realised they were hers so he pushed those under the bed and threw some of his on instead. Then there was more knocking and he decided it would have to do and he closed the bedroom door firmly behind him before he opened the door of the flat.

'Well I must say, how long does it take to open the door of one small flat?'

'Angie.'

'What, Angie or hullo Angie how are you? And by the way are you going to ask me to come in?'

'Hullo Angie, how are you? And by the way are you going to ask me to come in?' He was trying not to appear breathless.

'Don't get smart with me Morris, I've known you too long.' His sister rolled her eyes up in her head and thought about this. 'Much too long for my own good.' Considering she was four years younger than him Morris thought sometimes she might show some respect. He was doomed forever to be disappointed on that score though.

He tried to look like he had nothing to hide.

'OK what are you not telling me?'

'Not telling you?'

'Morris, if I didn't care about you I wouldn't worry about you, and if I didn't worry abut you I wouldn't concern myself with the mess you get yourself into would I?'

He wasn't sure about this. 'Can I have time to think about that?'

'Look here kiddo, do you want a thick ear or don't you? It's a simple question this time and you've got five seconds to answer it.'

'Um, no.'

'I would have thought the um was unnecessary but even so you got there in the end. It's a start.'

Now it was Morris's turn to roll his eyes up. Why was he blessed with a sister at all, let alone one like Angie? Did she come round just to torment him when her husband wasn't available for the purpose? He had enough woman trouble just now without her contribution.

'Look Sis, this really isn't a good time, you know. You know.'

He didn't think his eyes were looking furtive but nonetheless his sister was inevitably drawn to the closed bedroom door.

'Oho, say no more. Well she can wait, whoever she is.'

Yes, he thought, whoever she is, she can wait. She wasn't going anywhere.

'So come on then, get the kettle on. I come here straight from work to see my little brother and I've been here all of two minutes and you haven't offered me a cup of tea yet. And a digestive biscuit would be nice but I suppose that's too much to ask.'

'Yep.'

'I thought so. Got any milk?'

'Yep.'

14

'Bloody hell, that's a first. Did you buy it or is it stolen? '

'Yep.'

'Thought so. So you're going to implicate me in your criminal life.'

'Yep.'

'Morris ...'

'Yep?'

'If you don't stop saying yep I'm going to go into your bedroom.'

'Shit!'

'Well, that was a success.'

'Angie?'

'What?'

'You wouldn't like to do me a favour and piss off would you?'

'Good God man, can't it wait? She's not going to go cold you know.'

If only she knew. In a moment of weakness and desperation Morris thought of unburdening himself on her but on regaining his sanity decided against it.

'It's just that she's got to, um, go out.'

'And?'

'Well, she's shy.'

'Look kiddo, you and she are not the only ones who do it you know. What do you think the rest of us are doing while you're shagging everything you can get your grubby hands on?'

Morris considered the thought of Angie's husband Roger doing anything of the kind with his sister and decided it was too horrible a thought. Anyway, knowing Roger as he did and knowing Angie as he did he reckoned it probably didn't happen very often, hence the lack of children. She picked up his thoughts.

'Oh yes, you think you're the only one with a sex drive but I can tell you Roger has his moments.'

'Yeh? When was that, 1985?'

Angie reflected for a moment that her husband's sex drive had indeed been running on unleaded for quite some time but decided that if she was going to share this with anyone it wasn't going to be her worthless brother.

She drained her cup. Angie didn't, thank God, hang around. 'Anyway I've got better things to do than sit here having a pointless conversation with you. I'm off, so you get back to her in there and do whatever disgusting things it is you do.'

'I told you, she's got to go.'

'Yeh, whatever. Well kiddo, I won't tell you to be good because I know that's a waste of breath, so at the very least, and I mean this sincerely, don't get caught, just for me eh? Oh, and by the way, that bannister's wobbly. You'd better get your landlord to do something about it or someone's going to get hurt.'

And with that she gave him a loving clip round the ear and slammed the door behind her. Angie was a physiotherapist. She knew how to hurt people. It was only then, as he listened to her footsteps echo on the bare wooden stairs outside, that for no very obvious reason Morris had the sudden realisation that if he hadn't been so overwhelmed by the roll of loot in his guest's handbag he would almost certainly have found something to identify her with. On his way to the bedroom he wondered what he was going to do with that information, but still, now he had had the idea it was an idea whose time had come.

4

Tinkerbelle Sharon Virginia Jagger.

Morris peered under the bedclothes to see which of those names was likely to be suited. Virginia was out, for a start. He checked the address on her driving licence and on the basis that she lived in Warrington, not Essex, he discounted Sharon as well. So Tinkerbelle it was.

And Tinkerbelle was a long way from home. He pulled the blankets all the way back and looked at her. She had, he had to admit, a beautiful body. A bit on the short side, but that was OK. He tried to guess if her breasts were for real and decided the only way to find out was to feel them but he found he couldn't do it. He had never seen a dead body before and he was trying to decide what he felt about it, but while he was deciding he certainly wasn't going to get fresh with it.

On the other hand what had he done last night? Shit. The thought of it made him feel sick. It also made him start to twitch in the trouser department and he decided this was going too far and covered her up again.

He found himself saying sorry to her and then he got embarrassed that he was talking to a corpse and then he realised, really realised, perhaps for the first time since this morning, that he had a dead person in his flat. That's not normal, even Morris knew that. He supposed the normal thing on discovering one was to tell the police and leave it all

17

to them, but he instinctively knew that wasn't an option. They would, he felt, want to know how it got there. He pulled the blanket down again and looked at the tights round her neck, then he carefully removed them and peered at the skin to see if there was a mark that would tell a police pathologist how she had died. Maybe, maybe not. On the other hand, police pathologists weren't easily fooled. He had seen them on television, finding something you would never spot in a million years, and he wondered if that was for real or just the telly.

Either way, he reckoned that death by asphyxiation wouldn't be that hard to spot, and even the local plod would know that the chance of her having asphyxiated herself was on a scale of one to ten about zero, even if they didn't have the tights to go on, which they wouldn't because he might not be the smartest cookie in the jar but he would sure as hell be disposing of that bit of evidence in a hurry. He wondered for a brief moment, a very brief moment, if Angie would like them, but then on second thoughts he thought that was probably a stupid idea, which it was.

He couldn't answer the question about what to do about the police, so he concentrated on what to do about the body. It couldn't stay there, that was for sure, because there was only one bed and it was his and while he didn't mind sharing it with a living woman, in fact he didn't mind that at all, he definitely minded sharing it with a dead one. She would have to be moved.

But where to?

Morris's flat was not by any standards what you would call spacious. The bedroom, which the landlord called a double, might have justified that description for a single person with a split personality but as for two real people it was a no go. He had a double bed in it, that's for sure, because he had once had sex with a very large woman in a single bed and his back had never quite recovered. But that had meant sacrificing the floor, which existed inasmuch as it was under the bed, but it could hardly be seen anywhere else and even the door only opened halfway before it jammed against the side of the mattress.

There was nowhere to hang clothes, which for Morris didn't matter because he had precious few clothes anyway and even if he had had more he wouldn't have known how to hang them up. As for the rest of the flat, well it was a flat in name only. The landlord described it as a studio apartment. He wasn't sure what that meant but he had seen the description in an estate agent's window once and he figured out it was some kind of euphemism for small. Mr Crapovic had arrived from Croatia in 1998 with only the clothes he stood up in and a fake passport and now he owned four houses with a total of twenty two 'studio' flats, as well as a nice line in importing people from various eastern European countries.

He also employed several of the latter who passed as builders, some of whom occasionally appeared at 42 Walsall Place and did some so-called maintenance and sometimes they appeared and threatened a tenant who owed rent and on at least one occasion since Morris's arrival they had physically removed a tenant and all his belongings and left them in a pile in the children's playground on the corner of Walsall Place and Smethwick Avenue. You didn't play around with Carol Crapovic.

The rest of Morris's bijou residence comprised a living room / kitchen big enough to swing a cat in as long as you sawed its legs off first, and in one corner of that, through a sliding door that didn't and therefore remained permanently jammed open, was what was called the bathroom, although a bath was conspicuous by its absence. Morris could watch his portable black and white television sitting anywhere in the flat - on the sagging sofa, on the bed or on the toilet. In fact he spent quite a lot of his leisure time, which means quite a lot of his time, sitting on the toilet, smoking a joint (which he found an ideal laxative) watching the TV. Morris's critical take on television was that any moving image was worth watching.

The one thing that seemed not to have been thought of in the design of the flat, which could only be blamed on Carol Crapovic, was somewhere to keep a dead body.

The sinking sun illuminated the flat in a warm glow that failed to soften its general squalor, and Morris's spirits sank with it. He considered escaping in a cannabis-induced haze, but the part of him that irritatingly kept him doing the right thing, sometimes, said oh no, before you do that there's the small matter of the body to sort out.

Well, there was nothing for it. He got his arms under hers and hoicked her out of the bed. She was heavier than he expected and fell with a macabre thump on the floor. He held his breath, trying to detect any sounds from below that might indicate whether old Mrs Diggle had heard it. Mrs Diggle was stone deaf, so of course she hadn't.

Having got her on the only part of the floor that wasn't covered by anything, there was, when he stood up to survey the situation, nothing more he could do. She wasn't even, to be honest, quite on the floor, because there wasn't enough floor for a full-grown person, whether dead or alive, to stretch out, so her head lolled against the wall in a way that Morris had to admit was not attractive. He got a spare blanket out of the cupboard and draped it over her, but not only did this not improve her appearance but it somehow contrived to make her look more sinister. It didn't help that it was really only half a blanket (he couldn't remember what he had done with the other half, or come to that why), so her feet stuck out of the end. He pulled it down so they were covered but then her head was exposed. He stood and pondered this conundrum and decided that on balance it was better to see her feet than her face so he pulled it up again.

Then he took the twelve thousand pounds, put it in a

plastic carrier bag from the Plentiful Goodness Food Store, and placed that in the bed. If he was going to have company at night, he felt the money would be better than a corpse.

Now, he reckoned, he had earned that joint. It had been a long day. Well, it was only half past four, but in Morris's opinion it had been long enough already and nothing was likely to happen now that was worth staying compos mentis for. The body, now safely tucked away behind the bed, was almost out of sight, and in his present intoxicated state that was good enough for Morris to put it out of mind. He went to bed, finally, in the perverse belief that when he woke in the morning, should he have the misfortune to do that, today's events would magically disappear. He even made a kind of promise to himself that if they did he would mend his ways and stop leading this ridiculous life.

Of course there was no more chance of him leading a life any less ridiculous than there was of a body vanishing of its own volition, but in Morris's unreal world wanting something was enough to believe it was going to happen. It's not practical, but hey, when it's all you've got it will have to do.

The flat was unheated on account not of Mr Crapovic's unwillingness to provide the means to heat it but of Morris's inability to put any money in the electricity meter. It hardly mattered that the fridge wasn't working because the flat was more or less like a fridge anyway at this time of the year, and in any case there was never any food in it because Morris ate mostly out of tins. There was always fresh milk to be had from one of his neighbour's doorsteps for his Frosties, Morris's one culinary indulgence, in that he tended to eat them three times a day, in between baked beans and fish fingers.

5

He slept deeply all night, which you might think was because he had a clear conscience but obviously you would be wrong on account not only of Morris very rarely having a clear conscience but such a thing at this time being especially unlikely. He had only one dream, a ridiculous one about a dead body in his bedroom, and he woke up to find it wasn't ridiculous at all. Shit, he thought, why is it only the bad dreams that come true? Why couldn't that one he had last week come true? Still, this was no time to be thinking about threesomes.

He lay there, as usual, trying to pretend it wasn't time to get up, although in fairness since he never had much reason to get up except on signing-on days that wasn't far from the truth. Still, the sun was shining and the world doesn't stop just because there's a dead woman on the floor. No, today was the day to do something about it, something better than yesterday, which he had to admit wasn't a great solution to the problem. Today he would have a brilliant idea and the problem was going to go away. Yep, he was feeling better already.

Until the mouse came out and climbed up the blanket he had so carefully draped over the body last night. OK, it was a mouse, but really, did it have no respect? It sat there apparently nibbling at the blanket, which Morris thought was strange because even he knew the nutritional value of a 100%

nylon blanket from Argos was likely to be pretty small but then there's no accounting for taste. On the other hand, at least if it was breakfasting on the bedding it was going to be leaving his Frosties alone. On the other hand, now he thought about it, only yesterday he had successfully killed the mouse with the broom and dumped it in the bin under the sink. He remembered that now because in doing so he had smashed the table lamp and that was still where it had fallen in bits, so either this was another mouse, a possibility that Morris had never considered before on account of all mice looking pretty much the same to him, and to most people probably, or it was a ghost.

In his present state he was prepared to consider the latter as a very real possibility, and he found himself rummaging in the bin under the sink, past the fish finger packet, several milk bottle tops and a used condom (when the hell had that been from?) and there it was, still dead, and come to that dead still, which meant he hadn't imagined it and whatever was nibbling the blanket it wasn't this mouse.

God, if only disposing of bodies was as easy as this, just throwing them in the bin. That's when it came to him. OK, not the bin, but the council tip. He put his coat on.

'Morris, is that you?'

'Yes, Marty, it's your old friend Morris Figg, back again.'

'Well I must say this is a pleasure, twice in three days.'

Morris thought about that. 'Two days. I was here yesterday, remember?'

'Was it yesterday, was it? Well well, doesn't time fly?'

Morris wondered about that too, and found he was unable to come up with an answer so he stopped trying.

'Anyway, boy, if it's work you're after I'm afraid there isn't any. Things is a bit quiet just now.'

'Yes, I know, you told me that yesterday.' Or was it the day before? Marty was confusing him. 'Actually, Marty, I was wondering if you could do me a favour.'

'A flavour is it you're wanting? And what flavour would that be then?'

Morris couldn't resist it. 'Chocolate'.

'What? Chocolate? Morris, what the hell are you talking about? You know, sometimes I wonder about you. Have you been on the stuff this morning?'

That was when Morris realised flavour wasn't a joke, it was Marty for favour. 'Look Marty, I need to borrow your van for a while.'

'Oh, the van. Well, I suppose that would be alright, seeing as it's you. I suppose you've got a driving licence?'

'Yep.'

'And insurance?'

'Yep.'

'Well that will be fine then. Here's the keys.'

As he drove off in a cloud of blue smoke, Morris thanked the god of halfwits for Marty.

He got the body as far as the door of the flat before the thought occurred to him that taking a corpse out of a van at the council tip might arouse some suspicion, and he put it down and rested on his haunches against the door frame while he tried to figure that one out. He went back downstairs and out to the back yard. Yes, there it was still, an old carpet Mrs Diggle had thrown out in the summer. It was sodden with the rain but it would have to do. He considered whether it was better to take a wet carpet up the stairs and wrap the body up in it there, or drag the body down the stairs and do the job in the hall, and decided that neither of them was ideal. Still, it would have to be one or the other, and something told him that dragging a corpse down three flights of stairs, even in this house where no-one cared what went on in the normal run of things, might attract the wrong sort of attention.

Upstairs again, he rolled Tinkerbelle up in the carpet without much difficulty but as he started to drag the whole thing down the stairs the carpet came with him and the body

24

slid out and came to rest on the landing. No, he would have to tie it up.

Ten minutes later he came to the conclusion that there was no string in the flat, unless he counted the length of garden twine that was holding together one of the legs on the bed which had broken during an overenthusiastic shag he had had with a fourteen stone Polish woman he had picked up over the frozen food section of the Plentiful Goodness Food Store, but he decided that ought to stay where it was.

He knocked gently on Mrs Diggle's door and when there was no reply he figured out that could be on account of her being deaf, so he banged a lot harder and when there was no reply to that either he decided that deaf, in Mrs Diggle's case, meant completely deaf, and no amount of banging was going to do the job. Upon which he instinctively tried the handle and lo and behold the door opened. Mrs Diggle was fast asleep and snoring to waken the dead in an armchair in front of the TV. The volume was turned right off and Morris stood in front of it for a moment sharing the old lady's deaf world, and then he pulled himself together and crept into the kitchen. He wondered why he was creeping when she was not only fast asleep but wouldn't be able to hear him if she were wide awake and he rode through her flat on a motorbike with a broken exhaust, but creeping came naturally to Morris.

He rummaged, quietly, in the drawer under the kitchen sink and there he found, among the detritus of years of widowed life, a roll of string, still with an ancient label on from Woolworth, price 9d. Morris wondered momentarily what 9d meant, and then he crept out again and up the stairs.

When he finished the tying and stood up to admire his handiwork, he had to admit, if it looked like anything it looked like a body tied up in a carpet. But on the other hand that was what it looked like to him because he knew it was a body tied up in a carpet. No-one at the tip would know that.

Ten minutes later he had the whole package stashed in the

back of the van and he used some more of Mrs Diggle's string to tie up the door which didn't close normally which didn't bother Marty but bothered Morris today, on account of losing Tinkerbelle's body on the ring road might cause problems.

It was only another twenty minutes later when Morris pulled up in front of the gates of the council tip. They were closed. A council youth with a fluorescent yellow jacket lounged against them in a kind of triumphant way.

'Sorry mate, we're closed.'

'Closed? What do you mean, closed?'

The youth managed to look down his nose at Morris even though he had to look up at the cab of the van.

'Look mate, which bit of closed don't you understand?'

'But you're supposed to be open till four o'clock.'

'Yeh, right. And what's the time now?'

Morris looked at the clock in the van. Ten to four. Then he remembered the clock in Marty's van always said ten to four.

'Shit.'

'My thoughts exactly Sir.'

'But couldn't you just open up for a minute? I've come a long way.'

'Yes, sir, I suppose you could say we've all come a long way.'

It was just Morris's luck to get some kid on day release from a philosophy course at the polytechnic.

'Look, I'll make it worth your while.'

The youth's palms were itching, Morris could tell from the glint in his eyes, but whatever it was they were teaching him at the Poly must have got the better of him.

'OK, sir, now look we really are closed, so if you wouldn't mind.'

Yes, Morris really would mind. He briefly considered ramming the gates with Marty's van and dragging the kid's mangled remains with him while he went on to dump

Tinkerbelle, but the thought lasted only a fleeting moment, and in any case it was disturbed by a horn sounding impatiently behind him. He looked round, ready to shout some sarcastic remark about the tip being closed, when he saw it was a council dustcart. What's more, it was a council dustcart obstructing his way out.

He shouted over the combined engine nose of the dustcart and the van.

'Excuse me, I don't suppose you could just pull back while I turn this round?' This was Morris at his most polite.

'No mate.'

What? No? Why the sodding hell not? The driver looked at him blankly. The youth on the gate managed to look sorry for him while making it quite clear that he was really rather pleased at this turn of events.

Morris seriously considered getting out and smacking the kid in the mouth, and the kid sensed this and stopped gloating, at least as long as it took him to slip behind the gate and lock it again, when he carried on gloating as before. The van's gearbox screamed in agony as Morris tried to get it in reverse, and it was after about a fifteen-point turn that he finally got it facing the other way and, as his parting gift to the obnoxious kid, the van spewed a great cloud of filthy diesel exhaust over him as it pulled away past the dustcart.

For want of any other ideas he drove back to the flat. He could just return the van to Marty and feign ignorance of the body in the back but he somehow knew this wasn't going to work, not even with Marty, so there was no choice but to drag it up three flights of stairs and put it back where it was this morning.

As he relaxed on the toilet later with a joint he began to mellow, and it came to him that he was living, for the first time in his life, with a woman. OK, a dead woman, but you've got to start somewhere.

6

When he woke up Morris was vaguely aware of a strange
smell. There were always strange smells in the flat on account
of Morris's distinct lack of hygiene but this was different. This
was decidedly unpleasant, even to his nose. He didn't know
how long it took a dead body to start going off, especially in a
cold flat, but he guessed this one was just about reaching its
sell-by date. This was a problem that wasn't going to go away.
Unless, of course, it went away.

There was nothing for it, he would have to borrow Marty's
van and start all over again, only this time he would make sure
he got to the tip in time. Yes, he could make this problem go
away.

'Well, if it isn't Morris. Again. I sincerely hope it isn't work
you're after, because ...'

'Yes, I know Marty, there isn't any.'

Marty's face brightened. 'Well, that's fine then, just fine.
Just a social visit then, is it?'

'In a way, Marty, in a way. Shall I put the kettle on?'

'Well that would be most generous of you my friend. And
then you can help me with this wardrobe. It's devilish heavy
and my hernia's playing up something rotten this morning.'

Marty's business was house clearance, and it was clearance
jobs that Morris usually helped him with. They sat and blew
on their tea to cool it, neither of them with, apparently, much
to say.

'Well, this is nice, I must say. Very conviv ... very conv ... yes, very nice.'

'Yes.'

'Yes.'

Morris blew on his tea again, trying to think how to approach the question, and in the end there was only one way.

'So, Marty, I thought I'd give the van a run again today.'

'The van?'

'Yes.'

'Really?'

'Yes. Would that be OK?'

'Oh, sure, that would be just fine.'

'Oh, good.'

'Except that you can't.'

'Can't? Why?'

'Because the van's broken down. Wouldn't start this morning. I had to come on the bus.'

Shit.

Back at the flat he decided it was time to start panicking, so he did. The mouse was on his bed now, apparently asleep in a nest it had made of his bedding, but Morris was too distracted to do anything about it. The flat was smelling even worse now, or so it seemed to him, and he went out again to get away from it, plus the belief he could never grow out of, that when he came back some problem in his life would have gone away. It was as he cut across the park that the answer came to him, in the form of a supermarket trolley abandoned in the children's playground.

By ten o'clock that night Walsall Place was deserted, but he waited another hour to make quite sure, then he crept down the road and turned into Smethwick Avenue. The park gates were locked, so he had to lift the trolley over the fence and it landed on the other side with a crash. He froze, waiting to see if any of the houses nearby would come to life, but they

29

didn't, and he wheeled the trolley off down the road.

He got the body, still wrapped in its carpet, down the stairs, past old Mrs Diggle's door, but before he could get out of the hall with it the man from the ground-floor flat came in from his shift at the bread factory, mumbling something about Tesco trolleys, and let himself in through his door. Morris and Tinkerbelle stood in the shadow of the stairwell, not breathing, which was, it has to be said, a lot easier for Tinkerbelle than for Morris. He waited another ten minutes before the lights went out under the door, and then he dragged the body out of the front door, again, and somehow got it onto rather than into the trolley.

With that weight on them the wheels didn't want to go round and it took Morris over half an hour before he had it safely in the park, what with having to lift it over the fence again, during which operation the string came undone and he had to get the body over first and then the carpet and then tie the parcel up again so by the time he had finished he was just about done in.

It was as he was climbing back over the fence that he met up with Constable Penny, the Tamworth Park community police officer, which was bad luck because normally he didn't venture out this late but only the day before he had been given a reprimand from the desk sergeant for spending too much time in the warmth of the station and not enough time out on the beat. PC Penny suffered grievously from jokes about his name, what with him being a copper, and recently he had been seeing a counsellor about it who had suggested a lot of things which hadn't been in the slightest helpful except for the one thing, that PC Penny change his name by deed poll and resolve the problem once and for all, that would mean him losing a client.

The unhappy officer had chosen this time of the night to be seen out on the streets of Tamworth Park in the hope that he could be back at the station, having done his duty, before the pubs closed and the risk of having to deal with any of the local miscreants increased. Morris, on the other hand, was easy prey.

'Oho, what's this then? Figgs, isn't it?'

'Figg, constable.'

'Yes, Figgs, that's what I said. I never forget a name you know, or a face, and I've seen yours more than I want to, haven't I?'

Morris wavered between sheer panic and his usual instinct to twit the police, especially PC Penny who, he felt, was easy prey. Luckily for him, he chose the latter, because it distracted him, and PC Penny, from the real matter.

'So, PC Penny, fancy seeing you out at this time of night. That makes a change.' He emphasised change, unnecessarily.

'Look here, Figgs ...'

'Figg.'

'That's what I said. Look here Figgs, I could take you in right now if you want, for being in the park after closing time, behaving suspiciously, yes, I daresay I could keep you at the station for the rest of the night, no trouble.'

Morris contemplated a bed in a nice warm police station and breakfast in the morning. He wondered if they had Frosties. On the other hand, the whole idea of bringing the body down to the park was to leave it somewhere it would be found easily enough without pointing the finger at him. Even PC Penny, he felt, would remember this conversation in the morning when a dead prostitute was found in a supermarket trolley in the very park he had seen Morris climbing out of in the middle of the night. Then he said something he couldn't believe, even though he heard the words coming out of his own mouth.

'OK, constable, it's a fair cop, bang to rights, you've got me. I killed this woman see, and I've just dumped her in the park. You'd better arrest me right now.'

'Look here Figgs, that's not funny. Do you really think I've got nothing better to do than listen to your jokes? Now get along with you and don't let me see you again this side of Christmas. Go on, scarper.'

And Morris did exactly that.

Of course, when he got back to the flat it didn't take him long to figure out that he had about four hours of darkness, at least before the milkman came down Smethwick Avenue, to get back into the park and retrieve the body. It was half-past two before he ventured out again.

It went pretty well, as far as the bit where he wheeled the trolley along the path to the fence, and even the bit where he got the body and the trolley, separately, over the fence, but he hadn't gone far after that when the trolley got stuck in a broken paving stone and a wheel came off. It tipped over and Tinkerbelle fell out and rolled into the middle of the road. Even that wouldn't have been an insuperable problem but just at that moment Morris heard the sound of an engine approaching from Walsall Place. The headlights turned into Smethwick Avenue and he froze. Tinkerbelle, bless her, helped him out in his moment of need, and very obligingly she rolled, slowly at first, and then with more life, down the camber of the road into the gutter. The car drove past the body, and past Morris's frozen figure on the pavement, and off down the road. It was as he looked out of the corner of his eye that Morris spotted who it was. Chalky White. Chalky, he knew, would be blind drunk. Chalky couldn't drive in a straight line unless he was, and he only drove late at night because that was when the Tamworth Park police were all safely tucked up in their station, and then he drove round and round in his 1976 Ford Zephyr in pointless circles enjoying the freedom of the road. One thing Chalky didn't have that particular night, apart of course from a current driving licence or valid insurance, was any interest in whatever Morris was up to. He wouldn't, in truth, have noticed if Morris had been standing by the side of the road stark naked having it off with an inflatable doll.

By the time Morris got Tinkerbelle back to the flat it was a toss up who was more exhausted. He was too tired to do anything but dump her on the bed, still wrapped in the carpet. It was, although he didn't plan it that way, to be the second night, in a very short space of time, that Morris was to spend the night sleeping with a dead woman, although actually at about six o'clock he was woken by the smell and he moved to the sofa with the broken springs rather than put up with it any longer.

7

And that was where he was at almost eleven the next morning when there was a loud knock on the door. Only one person he knew knocked like that.

'Angie.'

'Yes Morris. You know the routine. You pretend to be surprised, I say something sarcastic, to which you reply with some gormless joke and then you finally let me in and make me a cup of contraband tea. So can we, just for once, on account of me being dead tired, skip the preamble and get the kettle on? And by the way, you still haven't had that bannister fixed, have you? Good God, Morris, what the hell is that smell?'

'Smell?'

'Yes Morris, smell, as in ... oh for God's sake, don't tell me you don't know what I'm talking about because even you couldn't fail to notice it. It smells like a dead body, not that I know what a dead body smells like but if I ever saw one I'm pretty sure this is what it would smell like.'

'Oh that.'

'What?'

Morris thought as fast as he could, but he couldn't think fast so early in the morning, or what passed for early in the morning for him. Well, honesty had worked last night with PC Penny so he gave it another outing.

'It's a dead body.'

'Yeh, sure. No really, what is it?'

'I'm telling you, it's a dead body.'

'OK, very funny. And who exactly has died?'

'A mouse.'

'A mouse? Are you joking? That's never just a mouse.'

'Did I say mouse? No, not a mouse, I mean a rat.'

'I can smell a rat all right, but even a rat couldn't smell like that.'

Morris thought about this and decided to leave it. 'Really, I'm not kidding. Mr Crapovic came round the other day and put some rat poison down and bingo, dead rat. Only apparently they go under the floorboards to die and they decompose and you can't find them and it just smells terrible for days and days if not weeks and then eventually it goes when they've finished. Decomposing.'

'Well I don't know about you but I think I'll open the window. I don't know how you put up with it. Mind you, if anyone's used to it you are.'

She opened both of the windows, so now it was freezing cold but didn't smell much better.

'Anyway Sis, why have you come?'

'Charming. Because I'm your sister should be a good enough reason, but as it happens it's not the only one. I wanted to talk to you.'

'That's nice.'

'No, seriously. Even you, Morris, must sometimes talk seriously, and I'm your sister and to be honest I don't know who else to talk to.'

'Bloody hell Angie, if you're desperate enough to talk to me it must be serious. It's not that gormless husband of yours, is it?'

'What, Roger?'

'How many gormless husbands have you got? Angie, you haven't been playing bigamy have you?'

'No, don't be stupid. It's not Roger. It's, um ...'

35

'Yes, yes, don't keep me in suspense. I haven't had any Frosties this morning and until I do I'm in withdrawal, so make it easy for me. Who or what is um?'

'Peter.'

'Peter.'

'Yes.'

'OK, so far so good. I can see this is going to take time. Let's try the next bit. Peter who?'

'Potter.'

'Peter Potter? No, I don't think I know him. One of your book group friends?'

'Yes. No.'

'OK, let me see, two across member of book group but not member of book group, two words, five and six. Let me see, let me see, I know, Peter Potter. Hang on, now I think about it I do know someone ... yes, isn't he the vicar at St Whotsit?'

'Elmo's.'

'Who?'

'St Elmo's'. It's the church on the corner of Dudley Gardens. The Reverend Peter Potter is the vicar there.'

'Right.'

'So that's it.'

'Well, look, Angie, thank you for sharing that with me and I want you to remember, my door is always open so if you ever need to talk again I want you to feel, on account of me being your brother, we can always do this again.'

'Morris, we haven't done it yet.'

'We haven't?'

'No, idiot. I've just been telling you who I want to talk about. I haven't actually talked about him yet.'

'Wow, this is going to be a long one then.'

'By your standards, given that the average conversation for you is obviously a maximum of ten sentences, yes.'

'Hold on then, I'd better pour myself some Frosties. And you'll be wanting a cup of tea.'

'Spot on, kiddo, now you're talking.'

Five minutes later Morris was feeling more human. Only the smell remained as a constant reminder that today was another problem to be faced. Once he'd got rid of his sister.

'So. The Reverend Potter. What's his problem?'

'No, he hasn't got a problem. Well sort of. It's me.'

'What's you?'

'The problem.'

'Look Angie, do you want to tell me what the hell you're talking about or shall we just go on playing this game, whatever it is?'

'Look, it's Peter, and me.'

'What's Peter and you?'

'The problem.'

Morris was starting to envy Tinkerbelle. He wondered if it was too late for a suicide pact with her. Technically, on account of her already being dead, he thought it probably was.

'Look, Morris, you're not listening to what I'm saying. Peter Potter and I have got a problem.'

'Which is?'

'Morris.'

'Angie, I'm Morris.'

'What? Oh, I mean Roger.'

'Peter Potter has been rogering you?'

'For once, Morris, but without realising it, you've hit the nail on the head.'

'You? And the Reverend Potter? Oh shit.'

'That, kiddo, just about sums it up nicely.'

Morris got up and poured out some more Frosties. If he was going to hear this stuff he needed to be on good form. As much as Angie annoyed him, and as much as he wished she would go away so he could deal with a much more urgent problem than her misbehaviour with the vicar of St Elmo's, he was touched that she had come to talk to her little brother about it. He needn't have been.

'So can you help me?'

'What, you want me to explain everything to Roger and ask him to forgive you? I don't think so.'

'Neither do I, dummy. I want you to keep him occupied for me.'

'To be honest, Sis, he's not really my type.'

'You know what I mean.'

'I do?'

Angie looked at her brother and decided that no, he probably didn't. She was starting to wish she hadn't come round. The smell was making her retch and she was wondering if she should just ask him to forget about it and pretend she hadn't said anything. Still, she had. She stood up and leaned on the window sill to try and get some fresh air.

'Look, it's like this. Peter goes to the book group, like I do, every Tuesday, only there isn't one.'

'So what do you do instead? Oh, that, sorry.'

'Quite. The book group wound up three months ago, only Roger doesn't know. Anyway, the other day we had a big row and he said all sorts of things and so did I and then he went off in a huff but later on he said he was sorry, which he always does, and I let him feel bad about it ...'

'Which you always do.'

'Quite, only then instead of buying me some flowers or taking me out for an Indian he went and said we should spend more time together, you know, do more stuff together.'

'Don't tell me, like the book group.'

'You're waking up.'

'I wish I wasn't.'

'Anyway, next Tuesday is the cup final and I know he doesn't want to come.'

'Who, Peter Potter?'

'No, dummy, Roger. He's made this promise, that we'll go to the book group together, the book group, remember, that doesn't exist, but then he's remembered that it's the England Argentina match on Tuesday night and he's desperately trying to get out of coming with me so he can watch it on the telly. He doesn't want to let me down but that's exactly what I want him to do. If he doesn't come this week he'll probably forget all about it. I just need him to watch the match on Tuesday.'

'OK, I'm with you so far. But where do I come in?'

'You're going to ask if you can watch the match with him. It'll give him an excuse.'

'Me?'

'Yeh, you.'

'But I hate football.'

'It's for a good cause.'

'And I hate Roger.'

'Come on Morris, stop making silly excuses.'

'And Roger thinks I'm a prat.'

'Yes, I know.'

'But apart from me hating football, and Roger, and Roger thinking I'm a prat, you reckon this is a good plan?'

'Well, not a great plan, but listen, it's all I could think of in a hurry.'

Morris could think of any number of reasons why he should say no, but all he could think of right now was Tinkerbelle, and if he was going to deal with her he needed Angie out of the flat, so he said yes. She came over and hugged him, then she told him he needed a shave, which he knew, and then before he had a chance to ask any more questions she was gone. All that was left was a slight whiff of her perfume, and that didn't last long in competition with eau de corpse.

8

Morris went out without shaving. Angie would have to forgive him.

'Ah, my old friend Morris.'

'Yes, I know, Marty, there's no work, things is a bit slow.'

'No, there is work.'

'There is?'

'Let me think about that. What did I just say?'

'There is work.'

'Right. In that case, I would take me at my word.'

'OK, Marty, look, I'm not sure I've got time to help you today. I was just wondering if the van is fixed yet, and as it's sitting out there in the yard I guess the answer is yes.'

'No.'

'What? So how did you get it here?'

'No, I don't mean no the van's not fixed, I mean no you can't borrow it, cos we've got a job on and I need it, or should I say we need it, cos I can't lift three chest freezers on my own, not with my hernia.'

There was something about what Marty had just said that made a funny noise in his brain. Not the bit about his hernia, the bit about chest freezers. Chest freezers, yes, there was something about them that set off bells in his head but he couldn't think why. Then Marty made one of his non-jokes.

'The Albany Hotel in town is closing down, and I've bought their chest freezers. Mind you, why anyone would want to

40

freeze their chest I don't know, but there you go.'

Chests reminded him of Tinkerbelle, and that's when it came to him. Of course, why hadn't he thought of it before? What did the Albany Hotel do with chest freezers? Freeze meat. Yes, that was it. How do you stop anything going off? You freeze it.

'Excellent.'

'It is?'

'Yes. I mean I've just remembered I have got time.'

'Good. Only there's something else. I need to ask you a favour.'

'Uhuh?'

'Well, it's my Uncle Harry.'

Morris was trying to work out a plan that involved chest freezers and Tinkerbelle and was only vaguely aware of what Marty said.

'Uhuh?'

'Yes, he's getting married.'

'Your Uncle Harry?'

'Yes.'

'Your great uncle Harry, who's eighty seven?'

'Eighty eight.'

'Right. I see.'

'Well the wedding's in Sligo, because that's where Auntie Maire lives.'

'Marty, would this be the Auntie Maire Uncle Harry used to be married to?'

'That's the one. He married her first just after the war, then he ran off with Fanny Piggott but that didn't last long, and then they got married again, and then, let me see, about 1975 he ran off to Australia and no-one ever heard of him again and in the end Auntie Maire had him declared dead so she could get her hands on his bank account and the house, and now he's turned up again and they're getting married.'

'Bloody hell. Can she marry someone who's dead?'

'Well, obviously he's not dead, is he, she just thought he was.'

'I see. So anyway, what's the favour?'

'Oh that, right. Well, I was wondering if you wouldn't mind looking after the shop for me for a few days while I go to Ireland for the wedding.'

'Yes.'

'You would mind? '

'No. I mean no I wouldn't mind and yes I'll look after the shop for you. You go to Sligo, wherever that is, and have a wonderful time and give Uncle Harry my very best wishes even if he hasn't ever met me and won't know who the hell you're talking about but then he's probably got a lot on his mind anyway what with marrying Auntie Maire for the third time. And when are you going?'

'Morris, you're rambling. But thanks anyway. Tomorrow.'

'Tomorrow? Excellent. I mean, that's fine, don't you worry about a thing.'

Most people, when you tell them not to worry, are inclined to do just that, and Marty was no exception. Still, he wasn't one to look a gift horse in the mouth, so he didn't, and they drove off immediately and two hours later there were three enormous freezers sitting at the back of his shop. They took up so much space that Marty wanted to stack them end up but Morris had heard somewhere that you're not supposed to do that with freezers and Marty didn't know if that was right but seeing as how Morris was doing him a big favour he conceded the point.

The next morning Morris drove Marty to the station in the van and returned to the shop with his head brimming full of possibilities. By twelve o'clock that very night one of the freezers was humming away nicely and Tinkerbelle was freezing down a treat. For the first time since that terrible morning, he slept with a light heart.

The next morning he drove over to the shop and opened

the lid, just to make sure she was still there. In his world, anything was possible. On this occasion, though, everything was exactly as he had left it. He looked down at her face, covered now in a kind of white frost, and for the first time in several days he felt a pang of something. He didn't know what kind of pang it was exactly so he decided to ignore it and he closed the lid and went and put the kettle on. Yes, all was well in Morris's world. For a few days anyway. Marty would inevitably come back though and by then he would have to think of something else, but just now it felt good.

He was opening a tin of baked beans that evening when there was a knock on the door of the flat. It wasn't Angie's kind of knock.

'Roger.'

'Morris.'

'Come in.'

'Thanks.'

Roger not only came in but sat himself down on the sofa without being invited to do so. 'Angie tells me you want to come round to watch the match. I was going to ring you but your phone's not working.'

'No, a fault. I'm waiting for them to fix it.'

Roger didn't believe him. He knew Morris was always getting cut off for non-payment. Morris knew he knew and he didn't care. He just wanted to get out of going round tonight to watch a game of football. Morris had never seen the point of football, not only because he couldn't see why anyone would care who did what with a silly ball but because he couldn't understand why anyone would make the effort to run around a pitch, more often than not as far as he could tell in the rain, when they could be at home with their feet up. Sport wasn't Morris's kind of thing.

'Anyway, I just wanted to tell you I'm sorry, you can't.'

Morris had a momentary feeling of panic and guilt. Perhaps Roger was going to miss the match in favour of going with Angie to the book group, the book group that didn't exist, and then there would be hell to pay, not just between Roger and Angie but for Morris as well, which is what bothered him more.

'Can't I?'

'No, I'm going to watch it at the Wig and Pistle with some mates. Sorry.'

'Oh, don't you worry about that, um, I might go down myself in that case.'

He knew he wouldn't be doing that, and so did Roger, who got up to leave but as he was halfway to his feet there was a knock at the door. For a horrible moment Morris thought this time it was Angie, but it wasn't.

'Ah, Mr Figg.'

'Mr Crapovic, um, come in.'

'Mr Figg, there is complaint.'

Roger would have taken this opportunity to escape but it was a small flat and Morris's landlord was a big man so it wasn't possible, so he stood there, pushed against the kitchen door, and listened helplessly.

'Yes, Mrs Diggle, she has complaint.'

Morris could think of a number of complaints Mrs Diggle might have, including lumbago and arthritis and of course her deafness, but he couldn't think why Carol Crapovic would have come to inform him.

'She says there is terrible smell.' Upon which he ostentatiously began to sniff as he poked around the flat. He even sniffed at Roger, who shrank back against the door post. He had never met Morris's landlord before and most people, when they met Carol Crapovic for the first time, knew instinctively that he was mean.

Each room had its own peculiar odour, the kitchen of stale food, the bathroom of, well, unclean bathroom, and the bedroom of unwashed bedclothes but they all mingled in the living room in an indescribable but vaguely unpleasant atmosphere of simple nastiness.

Mr Crapovic, fortunately, was a heavy smoker and had no sense of smell whatever.

'No, smells OK to me. You OK Mr Figg, I like you.'

Morris took this as a compliment. Mr Crapovic, he suspected, didn't like a lot of people, but then a lot of people probably didn't like him. For Roger it merely confirmed that the man must be a bit dim to like his brother-in-law.

When he finally got rid of them Morris made himself some beans on toast, washed down with a bottle of very cheap Indian cider he'd bought on special offer at The Plentiful Goodness Food Store. Then he put the television on and settled down on the toilet to watch the Open University and smoke a joint.

It was while the finer points of the mating ritual of the earthworm were flashing on the screen that it suddenly occurred to Morris to wonder if Roger had really meant the Wig and Pistle.

9

Every morning Morris went and sat in Marty's shop while no-one came in and bought anything and he wondered how Marty actually made any money. There was only one potential customer, but he was looking for a chest freezer so Morris told him they didn't have any and he went away. It was the day before Marty was due back that he came out of his stupor and started to panic again. He should have been thinking of somewhere to dump the body but he had stupidly stopped worrying about it.

Most of Morris's bright ideas were, as his friends would only too readily assent, not bright ideas at all, but it was as he was sitting in the shop with his feet up watching children's television that he had one he thought was a cracker. He locked the shop up, jumped in the van, and drove to Tesco. An hour later he was back with forty-eight family-sized packs of frozen oven chips. It broke his heart to pay for them, but this was an emergency and in any case it wasn't his money he was spending, it was Tinkerbelle's, which was kind of his now but in any case there was no-one to tell him not to.

By the time he had loaded the freezer up with forty-eight packs of chips you wouldn't have known there was a body underneath. In the back of his mind he had a cock-and-bull story for Marty tomorrow that would hold water, just about, or so he thought, something to do with going into the frozen food business. He thought as long as he was seen to take some stock out and put some more in on a regular basis that he might get away with it, until he could think of a foolproof plan for disposing of the body once and for all.

The next afternoon he drove to the station to pick Marty up. A few days in Ireland had done wonders for his accent.

'So Morris me old mate, how's tings?'

'Oh, fine, fine. How was the wedding?'

'Oh the wedding was great, we had a ball.'

'And Uncle Harry?'

'He was great, just great. A laugh a minute, until he dropped down dead of a heart attack in the pub afterwards.'

'What?'

'Sure, it was terribly convenient, what with the priest being there, so we took him back to the church and buried him straight away and then we all went back to the pub and had a wake instead.'

'But what about Auntie Maire?'

'Sure she was too drunk to know what was going on. By the time she came round the next morning we told her her husband was in the graveyard and she just said oh well, easy come easy go, and that was it, much like before the old codger came back from the dead the first time.'

'What do you mean for the first time? Did he come back again?'

'No, of course not. To be sure it was his brother, Seamus.'

'What was his brother Seamus?'

'Well, you see, Seamus had been living in sin with Maire all the while Harry was missing presumed dead, and he had to move out before the wedding, of course, so after we buried Harry he just moved back again and tings just sort of carried on like before.'

Morris could only shake his head in wonder. The story quite put out of his mind his own little story about the frozen food business. Marty, though, noticed that one of the freezers was plugged in and switched on.

47

'Oh right, I meant to tell you about that. I've um, started a little business of my own. I thought you wouldn't mind.'

Marty lifted the lid up and Morris's heart sank. He was convinced Tinkerbelle would be there plain to see, but of course she wasn't.

'Chips.'

'That's right. I'm doing a bit of buying and selling, you know, surplus food stock, that sort of thing. I thought as long as the freezers were here I might as well use one of them. I'll pay you for the electricity.'

'But Morris, it says Tesco on the bags. Surely to God Tesco don't sell surplus stock?'

'Does it? Um, no, of course they don't. No no, you see, these were made for Tesco but there was something wrong, I don't know what, some misprint on the bags I think, so Tesco refused to take them from the manufacturer and I bought them cheap instead.' He had to admit, for a complete fabrication, it wasn't bad. He felt rather pleased with himself. In any case, Marty fell for it.

'So there's noting wrong wid the chips, just the bags?' He picked one up and Morris felt a cold sweat break out on his neck. He had visions of Tinkerbelle appearing through forty seven more bags of chips, but of course she didn't.

'I hope there's not a lot of saturated fat in them, is dere?'

Morris looked at him in stunned disbelief. What the bloody hell was this gormless bloke talking about now? Where did he pick up this sort of rubbish? There's a frozen prostitute under these chips and he's worried about the fat content?

'Marty, since when did you worry about fat? Anyway, you're so skinny you should be on a diet of saturated fat and nothing else. Anyway, this lot are already ordered.'

'Oh yeh, who by?'

'The Indian takeaway on Sandwell Road.'

'What, dis lot? Chips isn't very Indian, if you ask me.'

48

'Well, mine is not to reason why, business is business and all that.' And he closed the lid firmly but politely. He wasn't sure if he was being polite to Marty or Tinkerbelle.

It occurred to Morris as he stood in the bus queue in the drizzle that perhaps he really should go and see the Indian takeaway on Sandwell Road. Maybe they really would buy them, at the right price.

And that's what he did. He unloaded twenty four bags for immediate delivery, with a promise of the other twenty four, at the same price, two weeks later. He walked out of the premises feeling pretty pleased with himself. He didn't see the downside of his little deal till much later that evening. The first was that he had just sold twenty four bags of chips at half the price he had paid for them in Tesco. That, he instinctively knew, wasn't good business. And if he kept selling the chips he was buying to fill the freezer up the freezer wouldn't stay filled up and he would have to buy more stock and then he would sell that at less than he paid and pretty soon he would get through Tinkerbelle's twelve thousand pounds just keeping her fresh. On the other hand, if he didn't sell the food in the freezer Marty would start to ask questions. No, there had to be a better plan.

Before long Morris Figg Enterprises would have to be wound up and Tinkerbelle Jagger would have to be found a permanent home. In any case, he didn't have transport, and carrying large quantities of frozen chips on the bus wasn't going to be practical for long.

It got worse though when he went back to the takeaway because while he was there the owner introduced him to his cousin who also had a takeaway and he asked Morris for the same quantity which he kind of promised to supply, at the same price, naturally, and before he knew what he was doing he had a thriving business selling frozen chips to half the Indian takeaways in the town at a loss. And Tesco were running out of stock. It was driving him nuts.

He had to find a cheaper supplier, so he got a card for a local cash and carry and now he was buying in bulk and selling at a much smaller loss than before, and he was using Marty's van when Marty didn't need it, all of which was an improvement but not a lot. By now all three freezers were in use and sometimes he forgot which one contained the body. He lay awake at night wondering what the hell he was doing this for. It wasn't resolving the problem of what to do with Tinkerbelle, he was running around like crazy, and at the end of the week he was about sixty quid down.

He was lying in bed one morning wondering where it had all gone wrong when there was a knock on the door.

'Hullo?'

'Oh, hullo, would you be Morris Figg?'

'No, sorry. He's one floor down, bye.'

He listened to the footsteps going down the stairs and then the knock. On account of Mrs Diggle being stone deaf knocking her up was never going to work, which Morris had been reckoning on. What he didn't reckon on was when the bloke went down to the ground floor and knocked on the flat there. The bakery man had just gone to sleep after a night shift. He wasn't best pleased. Morris could hear that from upstairs. The footsteps came back up again.

'Hullo?'

'Hullo.'

'Um, are you sure you're not Morris?'

By now Morris had summed this bloke up and whatever he wanted he reckoned it wasn't trouble.

'You're not here about frozen chips are you?'

'I'm sorry?'

'No, well that's OK then. You can come in.'

'Oh, thank you. I'm Peter, um Peter Potter.'

Morris knew he'd heard the name somewhere but he couldn't place it.

'I'm, um, a friend of Angela.'

'Angela? Angela? No, I don't know anyone of that name.'

'Um, I'm sorry, but I think you do. If I'm not much mistaken, she's your sister.'

'No, my sister's called Angie.'

'Yes, quite.'

'Oh shit, I mean God, I mean, I mean you're that Peter Potter, the bloke she's been ...'

'Seeing, yes. I'm sorry, what is it?'

'You're not wearing a dog collar.'

'Er, no, I don't always when I'm off duty.'

Morris wondered if he wore it in bed with Angie. Knowing his sister, he thought it entirely possible. 'Right. So, your reverend, what can I do for you?'

'Oh, do call me Peter, please. Well, it's like this. Your sister and I have been, um ...'

'Seeing each other?'

'Yes, exactly. Anyway, as you are I am sure aware, Angela, is, well ...

'Married?'

'Yes, that's the one. And of course, that kind of thing is, um ...'

'Wrong?'

'Well, yes, strictly speaking.' He shifted in his seat. Morris was making him uncomfortable and he was beginning to wish he hadn't come. No, that wasn't true, because he hadn't wanted to come in the first place. It was Angela's idea. She said it would come better from him, what with him being a vicar and all that that normally meant, only Peter didn't think that was true, first because although it was true he was a vicar he was committing a cardinal sin and he didn't know how long he was going to be one of those if the church authorities found out, and secondly because even by Angela's own admission her brother was a godless good-for-nothing and was unlikely to be impressed by Peter's credentials. Which he wasn't.

'So, Peter, tell me, what exactly is it you came round here for?'

Peter looked around the flat, in a kind of measuring up way, and Morris followed his gaze, wondering what was so interesting.

'We want to start the book group off again.'

'I see. That's nice. And you want me to join?'

'No, well yes, well, um, no, not exactly.'

'So what exactly?'

'Well, we wondered, Angela and I, if we might possibly, er ...'

'Yes, yes?'

'Hold the meetings here.'

Morris looked at him in blank amazement. It didn't make any sense. Except that Peter explained the problem was that they couldn't hold the meetings at any of the houses where they used to have them because all of the people who used to come to them knew the group had folded. That, Peter had to admit, was another problem, because the reason they were starting the group again was Roger, who was now saying he really wanted to come to the meetings with Angela, only of course there weren't any meetings so the only thing for it was to start the group up again so Roger could come. If that made sense?

Morris whistled through his teeth. He knew the thing to do was to say no. He didn't much like this bloke. To his way of thinking there were people who don't know any better, like him, and people who should, like vicars. What Angie did was her business and on account of him not much liking Roger either her little affair with this man didn't much bother him.

He said yes, though, for Angie. His little sister was the only person who could do this to him, make him feel responsible. So he said yes, and for a moment he thought Peter Potter was going to hug him he was so happy, but he shook his hand, several times, and after he had gone Morris thought what a prat. If Angie was going to risk her marriage for a bit of fun, why Peter Potter? Still, there's no accounting for taste. After all, she must have loved Roger once.

10

Peter Potter nearly made him late for the Jobcentre.

'Have you done any work in the last two weeks?'

Well, let me see, I've shifted a dead body, started a frozen chip business, sorted out my sister's affair with the vicar, but no, I don't think you could call any of that work. 'No.'

'Sign here.'

'Thank you, see you in two weeks then.'

'Not so fast Mr Figg. I see from your records that you've been claiming Jobseekers Allowance for, let me see, good grief, a long time. Haven't you had a job search review?'

'Um, let me think. Um, no, I don't think so.'

'Well you should have. I can't think what's gone wrong. Hold on a moment while I sort out an appointment for you.'

Morris wondered why, if computers were supposed to make everything happen so quickly, everything at the Jobcentre happened so slowly. He drummed his fingers on the arm of the chair but she looked at him over her glasses and he took that to mean don't do that, so he didn't. He looked around. There were two other staff sitting at desks busily playing with their computers, and a queue of at least seven people waiting to sign on, but the staff just carried on oblivious to them.

'Four o'clock this afternoon, come back here and an advisor will see you, OK?'

No, it's not OK. Excuse me, I've got a consignment of

chips to deliver to the Golden Sunset Curry House by three. Couldn't we make it a bit later?

'Yes, that will be fine, thank you.' He couldn't afford to upset these people. He had a feeling that if he put a foot wrong they would have the greatest of pleasure in stopping his benefit, and his benefit was subsidising the frozen food business and that was keeping Tinkerbelle happy. Well, not exactly happy.

He was there at five to four. The sooner he went in, he reckoned, the sooner he came out. At half past four someone came, apologised for keeping him waiting, probably busy playing on their computer Morris thought, and took him into an interview room. There, they alternated between playing on yet another computer and ploughing through a file on the desk, interspersing whatever it was he was doing with oh, I see and well, mm, right.

'So, Mr Figg, just run me through, if you would, what efforts you have been making to find work.'

You would have thought, in the intervening hours, Morris would have given at least some thought to what story he was going to give these people, but like an idiot he hadn't. He would have to rely on his native cunning. He looked his opponent in the eye, but the man just looked straight back at him. He was used to this, more used to it than Morris.

'OK, well, there's the dairy to start with.'

'Yes, what about the dairy?'

'Well I did an aptitude test with them.' Otherwise known as following the milkman round and removing the bottles of milk he had just delivered.

'And?'

'You mean what else?'

'Well, that too, but did you have the aptitude? For the dairy.'

'No.'

'I see, and what else?'

'Well, um', and here he had one of those moments of mental clarity that happen only rarely unless you're exceptionally lucky, 'I've been talking to the vicar at St Elmo's.'

'I see. What about?'

'Well, of course, becoming a vicar.'

The advisor looked up from his computer screen and put his pen down. This was a new one. This one he was completely unprepared for. He was on shaky ground here, because in all his years in the service no-one had ever taken holy orders. Mostly they went on to be bricklayers or they went to work in Tesco or the bakery, but no-one had ever gone into the priesthood. Still, there was a first time for everything. He looked at Morris and then he looked again at his screen.

'Um, how old are you exactly, Mr Figg?

'Thirty-seven.'

'Isn't that a little old for training for the clergy?'

'The what? Oh yes, I mean no. Late entry. They're short of people.'

The advisor had read something of the kind only recently in the national papers. He didn't want to believe Morris, but only that morning there had been another reminder about showing respect to clients. Respect be buggered he thought, a bunch of layabouts, but that was the old Jobcentre, they had said on his recent customer service course, and this is the new Jobcentre, centred on customer satisfaction. A load of crap, but still, it paid the mortgage. For now he was tired and he wanted to go home. It was almost five o'clock. Get the interview over with, tick the boxes, let someone else sort it out. And Morris almost got away with it.

'Hold on, not so fast. It says here that back in February you were applying for the Roman Catholic seminary to train as a priest with them. Either you've had a sudden conversion to the Anglican faith or there's something fishy here. Look, I tell you what, we'll forget all about this nonsense, shall we, less said the better.'

It was five to five. Time to play Russian roulette.

'Let's see what we've got for you. Yes, aha, excellent, this will suit you down to the ground, yes, definitely, down to the ground I should think. I'll just make a quick call, I'm sure they will still be open. Hullo? Yes, is that Widdlecombe and Tite? Oh hullo, Jobcentre here. It's about your vacancy. Yes, I think we've got just the man for you. He's mature, and I would say of a religious bent. Yes, that's what I thought. Shall I send him along then? Ten o'clock on Wednesday? Just a moment.' He put his hand over the mouthpiece and looked at Morris. 'Ten o'clock on Wednesday?' Morris shrugged. 'Yes, he says that will be fine. Excellent, thank you. Goodbye.'

'Well it's all arranged. Widdlecombe and Tite, in the High Street. They're looking for a trainee. You're lucky, vacancies like this don't come up very often. Mr Widdlecombe is expecting you at ten, so don't be late. No, don't be late.' And then he chuckled to himself. Morris wondered what the joke was and then he decided he couldn't know and didn't care, he just wanted to bugger off out of there.

The advisor printed it all out from the computer and carefully folded it up and put it in an envelope. After Morris had gone he leaned back in his seat and thought, yes, an excellent end to the day. That will serve the little tyke right. And with that thought, he went home to wherever it is that Jobcentre people live, to spend the evening doing whatever it is that Jobcentre people do, before doing the whole thing again tomorrow.

Morris, meanwhile, ran all the way to the cash and carry, and from there he got the bus to the Golden Sunset Curry House where he delivered half of the chips and then he got on another bus to get to Marty's place before he closed so he could unload the rest into one of the freezers.

There were two police cars outside Marty's warehouse. All his instincts told Morris to turn round and go home, but he had the chips. Something said run, run like hell and don't stop, never mind the chips, in fact bugger the chips, just dump them and run. But he knew that wherever he ran to they would find him, so what was the point? No, brazen it out. Walk in, innocent, and just see what transpired. Maybe they weren't looking for Tinkerbelle. After all, he had heard nothing locally about a missing prostitute. No, this was probably something else.

It was.

'Ah Morris, it's good to see you. The gentlemen of the constabulary have got it into their heads that someone is keeping drugs in my place. You wouldn't know anything about that, would you?'

For once in his life Morris was able to deny an accusation with complete truth. All his stash was at the flat.

'Sergeant Crump, sir. And you would be?'

Morris considered momentarily using a fictitious name, on account of this being nothing to do with him and on account also of there being a dead body in one of the freezers, but then he spotted PC Penny and he knew he wouldn't get away with it.

'Morris Figg, Sergeant. How can I help you?'

'Well, sir, I was just telling Mr Finnigan here that we've had a tip-off about a large quantity of cannabis in these premises, and I have here for your inspection a warrant to search the warehouse, which we are just about to commence. Unless, of course, you can make any suggestions as to where we should look first, you know, to save time.'

Anywhere except the freezers. 'No, Sergeant, sorry, but really, I have no idea about any of this. I just come sometimes to help Marty, um, Mr Finnigan out.'

'I see, sir. And would you mind me asking what it is you've got in the bags?

'No, of course not. Chips.'

'Chips. I see, sir. In both bags?'

58

'Yes, Sergeant.'

'Well, I'm sorry sir, but I shall have to ask you if we can have those bags open so we can see for ourselves.'

Morris had a feeling that what he meant by ask was not what other people mean by ask, which is a question that can have a yes or no answer.

'Yes, of course, I mean, I suppose so.' And he handed both bags over to PC Penny who spread them out on a table and, taking out his penknife, proceeded, with relish, to waste several pounds-worth of Morris's stock. And what he found, naturally, was a lot of chips.

'Well, sir, that all seems in order.'

No it didn't. Five catering-size packs of chips were by now spread out over a large table, gradually going soggy. No, this was most definitely not in order. On the other hand, chips were not Morris's biggest worry right now. He didn't know why the hell the police thought there were drugs on Marty's premises, something to do with Marty he imagined, but what he did know for sure was that it wouldn't take them long to investigate the freezers. And then the shit really was going to hit the fan.

There were six of them, and they went through the warehouse with a fine-tooth comb. For some reason the freezers were left till last, and that was PC Penny's job. Morris was desperately trying to remember which one had the body in. It looked like Marty had moved them. Why the hell had he done that?

He tried not to look worried but failed miserably while PC Penny took the entire stock out of the first one.

'Well, that's a lot of chips. Are these something to do with you, Mr Figgs?'

For once, Morris didn't bother to correct him. 'Um, yes, Constable, a little bit of business you know, all perfectly kosher and paid for.'

He shovelled the bags back into the cabinet while

59

Constable Penny opened the next lid and started, with more relish, to empty the contents. One more freezer to go. Morris could see the rest of his life flashing before his eyes, and it was spent in a small confined space.

As he threw his stock back, the constable opened the third lid. One bag after another hit the floor. Morris was sweating profusely now. Any second, Tinkerbelle was going to rise from the dead. He came closer, looking on in morbid fascination, waiting for the first telltale sign, a lock of hair or a piece of her dress, the red dress that was going to stick out like a sore thumb among the frozen food.

It was a bit of her blond hair, nestling, with frost on it, between two bags.

'Here Sarge, come and look at this.'

It came from the other side of the warehouse. Constable Penny looked up, missed the hair completely, and followed the sergeant. His hands shaking, Morris grabbed the bags off the floor and threw them in as fast as he could and slammed the lid down. The police weren't looking. They were more interested in a find elsewhere. And what they had found was an attaché case stuffed full of cannabis. Morris had no idea Marty was dealing. He was, though, eternally grateful that he had been caught.

The last thing Marty said as they were shoving him into one of the police cars, was look after the business. Morris locked up the doors after the last officer left, sank back in Marty's old leather office chair, and gave up a prayer of thanks to Saint Elmo for his deliverance from the fire.

11

There was nothing for it, the body would have to be disposed of, and this time no messing about. With Marty out of the way for a day or two, or maybe a year or two, Morris could think more clearly. He had free run of the warehouse, and the use of the van. All he had to do was find a last resting place for Tinkerbelle.

And attend an interview at Widdlecombe and Tite, whoever they were, put them off completely, and get on with his life without the inconvenience either of having to go to work or get rid of corpses. Yes, if he could just sort out those two items life would be hunky dory.

182 was at the end of the High Street that Morris never had occasion to visit. Come to that, on account of having what you might call a very small disposable income and therefore not much interest in shops, the whole of the High Street was fairly unfamiliar ground to him.

There had to be some mistake though, because he found 182, sandwiched just where you would expect it, between 180 and 184, but the sign over the top said Widdlecombe and Tite, Funeral Directors. There must be another 182, occupied by a Widdlecombe and Tite that weren't funeral directors, only as hard as he looked Morris couldn't find one. He stood back on the pavement and surveyed the window, tastefully decorated with a grey velvet curtain and a gravestone and a tastefully-printed card that said open 24 hours for private and caring consultations.

He tried to think whose idea it was to send him on this fool's errand, and of course it was that bastard at the Jobcentre. Some kind of joke. On the other hand, if he didn't go in and have an interview, no matter how perfunctory, they would take great delight in stopping his benefit, so what choice did he have? The door was locked. It said please ring for attention, so he rang for attention and waited.

He was just about to leave and go straight back and tell the Jobcentre he had been and there was no-one in, it wasn't his fault, when there appeared behind the net curtain a woman, by Morris's estimate approaching 120, who smiled a toothless grin at him and opened the door. She said nothing but turned and shuffled back inside, leaving Morris to assume he was intended to follow, which he did, and when he got to a room at the end of a gloomy corridor he found she had disappeared and it was empty. This was, he reckoned all part of the joke. Well, he would see it through. They didn't get him that easily.

In the middle of the room there were two trestles, on which rested a casket of some dark wood, with brass handles, all very tasteful he thought. He wondered if this was a showroom or the coffin was the real thing and there was a body inside. On the walls hung sepia photographs of men in tailcoats and wing collars, standing in front of horse-drawn hearses. In each corner was a large vase of flowers, all, in keeping with the general tone of the establishment, dead. The room was airless. Morris started to imagine what it would feel like to be buried alive. He was wondering if he had stayed the required length of time and he could escape, when a door he hadn't noticed clicked quietly and there was a man in black tailcoat and wing collar, only he wasn't in sepia, smiling in that way undertakers have that makes them look like they're discreetly measuring you up for your coffin.

'Yes, can I be of assistance?'

'I'm expected. Morris Figg.'

'Figg you say?'

'Yes, Morris.'

'I see. And why, may I ask, are you expected?'

'The Jobcentre sent me. Are you Mr Widdlecombe?'

'I'm Mr Tite. Mr Widdlecombe is no longer with us, I'm afraid. I'm very sorry to say he departed rather suddenly, the day before yesterday. That's him behind you.'

Morris turned abruptly, but all there was behind him was the coffin. He twigged now what departed meant. It meant dead, like Tinkerbelle. He felt he ought to say something but didn't know the appropriate words.

'Yes, we're just about to bury him. You must be the trainee he was due to see. Well, you might as well come since we're short handed.'

He looked Morris up and down. Most people would have dressed for a job interview, but Morris looked the same as he always did because he only had one look, and he didn't have much experience of interviews and he certainly hadn't been expecting to be interviewed by an undertaker, and he sure as hell hadn't been expecting to attend a funeral, not that he would have dressed any differently if he had because all his clothes were the same.

'But you certainly can't come in fancy dress. Wait here, I'll find something for you. What size are you?'

'I don't know.'

And quick as a flash Mr Tite whipped out a tape measure from the pocket of his coat where presumably he kept it on the off-chance of needing to measure up a client, and held it up to Morris.

'Uhuh, right, wait here young man.'

There seemed to be no escape now. Morris was starting to panic again.

'Shit.' He looked at the coffin and wondered if he ought to be a bit more respectful, but frankly he was getting a bit tired of dead people. He had one of his own at home.

Mr Tite returned with a suit of clothes identical to his own. He had to show Morris how to do the tie and then he topped him off with a black top hat. Now, he thought, I'm in fancy dress. Mr Tite stood back and admired his handiwork, or not.

'Mm, you could do with a shave, but there's no time.'

He looked down at Morris's trainers. They were scruffy, of course, and trainers were not the thing with a tailcoat, but the whole effect was exacerbated by the fact that they didn't even have matching laces. He tutted, unnecessarily loudly, Morris thought. He disappeared again and when he returned he had in his hand a shiny pair of black shoes, made of real leather. Morris thought they looked very smart.

'Try these on. They look about your size. They were Frank's. He won't be needing them now.'

Morris squeezed his feet into them. They were only about a size and a half too small. So this was what dead men's shoes felt like.

'Excellent, a perfect fit. Are you strong?'

'Um, well.'

'Well come on boy, answer the question, are you strong enough?'

Strong enough for what? The honest answer would, in Morris's case, whatever Mr Tite was referring to, probably have to be no.

'Yes.'

'Good, you can fill in for Jock. He's in the hospital.'

'Oh, OK.'

Jock, he forgot to mention, was a pallbearer, and he also forgot to mention that the hospital he was in was St Joseph's Psychiatric Unit.

'Have you had any experience?'

Of dead bodies? Yes. 'Um, no.'

'Young man, you say um a lot.'

'Um, yes, I suppose so.'

'Well don't.'

'Um, no, OK.'

'It's not in keeping with our profession, and neither by the way is OK, and if you are going to learn that profession you will have to make some serious changes to your personal demeanour.'

Hold on, who said anything about learning the profession?

'Like shaving. Every day.'

Every day? Don't be ridiculous, no-one shaves every day. Hold on, excuse me, who said anything about learning the profession?

'Right, go to the toilet.'

'Excuse me?'

'Come on, come on, if you don't go now you'll be bound to want to half way through the service, and who ever heard of a pallbearer disappearing for a wee half way through a funeral? It's one of the rules, always go to the bathroom before a job.'

Morris was too confused to argue and went off dutifully to do what he was told. It was like being a little boy again. He tried to think, as he stood there with his zip undone, willing something to happen so he could truthfully tell Mr Tite he had been, how he had got himself into this. It was that bastard at the Jobcentre. Well, there would be retribution. Except of, course, there wouldn't. It was just one of his usual puerile fantasies.

'Been? Good, now hold my arm, like this.' And Mr Tite stretched out his arm and grasped Morris's sleeve. Morris did likewise.

'No tighter, tighter. We don't want to drop it, do we?'

'Drop what?'

Mr Tite looked at him as if he was stupid, which just shows how perceptive he was.

'The coffin, boy, the coffin. Now come along, there's no more time. Just remember to hold on like that and you will be fine.'

The funeral was at St Elmo's, and who should be conducting the service but Peter Potter. As the coffin passed the altar he looked at Morris in disbelief. Morris wasn't at all sure he could believe it himself. The pallbearers went behind the church for a smoke during the service, and Morris levered the shoes off with a pen he found in the jacket pocket, while he got to meet the man whose sleeve he had been gripping in fear and trepidation.

'Wally.'

'What?'

'Wally 'Obbs. So you're the new man?'

'Um, no, I don't think so. I'm just kind of filling in.'

'No mate, we don't do the filling in, that's the gravedigger's job.'

Wally laughed uproariously and the others joined in. Morris wondered why that was funny.

'No, I mean I'm only temporary, I mean actually I didn't come for this, I came for an interview with, um, Mr Widdlecombe.'

'I came to talk to Widdlecombe, not to bury him. Sorry about that. Anyway, bit late, weren't you mate?'

'Well I didn't know that when I turned up this morning. And then Mr Tite just put me in this stuff and said are you strong enough and here I am.'

'Oh him, Tite by name, tight by nature. You're not thinking of taking a permanent job with this lot, are you?'

'No, but the Jobcentre people think I am.'

'Well you take my advice, don't. Once you start, that's it. No-one who's ever worked for the firm has ever left it, alive I mean. There's only one way out, and that's in a coffin, bit like the KGB. That Doris in the office, do you know how old she is?'

'Um, eighty?'

'Nah, eighty! Ninety-two is old Doris, so they say.'

'Bloody hell, ninety two.' Morris hadn't realised that was

possible.

'Yeh, she's trying to outlive old Mr Tite, refuses to retire until she's seen him six foot under. Myself, I don't think she's going to make it. Old Tite's certain he's going to bury her. I happen to know he's got her measurements already, took them once when she fell asleep on the job, didn't think she was going to wake up again but the old bird wouldn't give him the satisfaction.'

'Well, like I said, I'm not planning a future with the firm. Anyway, this gear looks stupid.'

'Yeh, but you get used to it.' Wally had loosened his tie and now he took a hip flask out of his pocket and took a swig. Then he offered it to Morris.

'Go on then, what the hell.'

He was just putting the top back on when they heard the organ strike up.

'That's it mate, time to do the old tie up, put a long face on and take the stiff to the graveyard. Come on lads, let's be having you.'

They grumbled, as if this was an unexpected intrusion on their smoke break, but Morris grumbled most of all. He was desperately trying to get Frank's shoes back on. He shuffled painfully into the church behind the others.

At the graveyard Morris found he was roped into lowering the coffin as well. And it was as the box disappeared into the darkening depths of the grave that it came to him. How could have been so stupid? Of course, there's a reason for everything. Why, if you believe that kind of thing, was he here? What did he have lying in a chest freezer in Marty's warehouse? A body. What do you do with bodies? You bury them. And who do you get to do that for you? That's right, an undertaker. The man at the Jobcentre wasn't such a prat after all. He had, unwittingly, given Morris the answer to his problem.

Widdlecombe and Tite.

When they drove the hearse back to the yard Mr Tite was out first and Morris wondered what to do about changing into his own clothes. The old man walked past him and Morris was just about to ask, when he stopped, turned, glared at Morris in a way that reminded the latter of something unpleasant he had once seen in a horror film, and said,

'Have you been drinking?'

He was about to deny it when he remembered he had.

'Well, my lad, you can take this as a first and last warning. I do not tolerate drink. It's the work of the devil and I will not have one of my staff walking down that perilous road to perdition. Learn this lesson now or forget about becoming a funeral director. Have I made myself understood?'

Become a funeral director? What was the old git on about now? Who said anything about becoming a funeral director? On the other hand, how was he going to resolve the Tinkerbelle problem if he didn't work for Widdlecombe and Tite? It was time to swallow his pride. It hurt, but it was surely worth it. Well, it had bloody well better be.

'Yes Mr Tite, sorry.'

'That's a good boy. Well, I'll have old Doris write up a contract of employment, if she hasn't gone and snuffed it while we've been burying Frank, and you can start on Monday.'

12

It was one of those rare occasions in Morris's life when he wasn't in receipt of benefits. It felt strange. Hanging on a hook on the back of the door was the black tailcoat and wing-collar shirt Mr Tite had said he should take home with him and in the bin under the kitchen sink were Mr Widdlecombe's shoes. He would use some of Tinkerbelle's money to buy a new pair.

Being in full-time employment felt even stranger, and it had the immediate effect of curbing his business activities. He told Marty the chips would have to stay in the freezers until he could dispose of them, which might take a little while, what with him so busy now. Marty took one pack home with him one evening for his tea, and Morris made him promise never, never, to do that again. He wondered what all the fuss was about. They were only bloody chips, for Christ's sake.

Morris wasn't at all clear on how his new job was going to resolve the Tinkerbelle problem. In fact he had no idea. On the other hand, working for an undertaker, he just somehow knew, had to be a good thing.

Mr Tite was surprised how well Morris took to being around dead people. He said for someone with no experience of death it came very easily to him. He didn't much like Morris but he had to admit he was a natural. Fair enough, they couldn't let him talk to customers, the relatives, that is, not the bodies. Morris could talk to them as much as he liked.

Old Doris took him under her wing because he reminded her of someone, only she couldn't remember who. She had a feeling he had gone away to war and not come back but she couldn't recall which war that was. She called him Maurice because something from the dim and distant past said this man, whoever he had been, had been French. He was. His name was Jacques, and he had come to England when the British Expeditionary Force was evacuated from Dunkirk in 1940 and hadn't, in the ensuing chaos, had anywhere to stay, and her mother had taken him in when she had found him wandering on the beach at Eastbourne. Or possibly Hastings, it was all very hazy in Doris's mind. He had stayed for some months and the inevitable happened when a young woman and a lonely man are cooped up in the same small house and they had fallen in love and one thing had led to another and she had become pregnant with Jacques' baby and then he had joined the Free French forces and been shipped off to North Africa, from where he never returned. She lost the baby in the sixth month of the pregnancy during an air raid on Southampton. Or it might have been Portsmouth. Something about Morris, anyway, reminded her of all this. It might have been his French name.

Doris told Morris all about how she came to work at Widdlecombe and Tite, only it hadn't been called that in those days, it was Widdlecombe and Son, young Mr Frank being the son. Old Mr Widdlecombe had died somewhat tragically when Mrs Fanshaw-Bligh had fallen on him and on account of her being in a sold oak coffin at the time it broke his back and he lay in a bed at the Royal Infirmary for three months before his son could find a solicitor who would agree to witness him signing a will leaving the business to him and then he agreed that the hospital could switch off his life-support machine.

Frank was very entrepreneurial and the business thrived.

Two years later he took over Tite and Son and formed Widdlecombe and Tite. Young Mr Tite was the son and when old Mr Tite ran off to South Africa, or it might have been South America, with Mavis Peabody at the age of seventy two he became an equal partner with Frank Widdlecombe.

Doris herself had been employed by Tite and Son and had joined the present firm with Mr Tite's father. A look of sadness in her eye when she said this made Morris wonder if there had been something between her and Mr Tite's father. Doris herself wondered that sometimes, only she couldn't remember for sure.

Mr Tite took Morris with him to the hospital to collect the bodies in an unmarked black van they kept for the purpose. He told Morris to do just as he was told and on no account to open his mouth. He had a feeling that should Morris ever do such a thing in public he was likely to put his foot in it. He was probably right.

'There are two things you will have to learn in this profession, young Morris. The first is to look like a funeral director, and the second is to talk like a funeral director. The rest will come from books.'

To get Morris to look like an undertaker he took him to Jones's Men's Outfitters on the High Street, an old-fashioned establishment with dusty shelves of shirts in boxes and a glass topped display counter with sliding trays underneath that contained a range of regimental ties and all the other paraphernalia of middle-class life as it must have been lived in 1955. He bought him a black suit and several white shirts and a black tie, which Morris struggled with for at least ten minutes every morning.

On the first day at the office in his new outfit Mr Tite made him stand in front of a mirror.

'Now, boy, take a good look. What do you see?'

Morris had a feeling there was a right and a wrong answer

to this question, but since he was ignorant of both he said the first thing that came into his head.

'Um, me?'

'Yes, exactly.' It was, apparently, the right answer. 'And that's the problem. Clothes maketh the man, only in this case they don't. There's a right way and a wrong way to wear clothes, and I want you to tell me which you are doing.'

'Um, the wrong way?'

'Excellent, excellent. At least you can see what the problem is. That's a start.'

The problem was, as far as Morris was concerned, that the old git had made him put on a suit of clothes that made him look daft, and that made him feel daft, and that might be what the old git was picking up on.

'Now, take them off.'

'What, here?'

'Yes of course. Come along, I haven't got all day.'

Morris slipped the jacket off and threw it on a chair. Mr Tite tutted, loudly, and put it over the back. Never treat a jacket like that, he said. Morris made a mental note about that. He stood there in his shirt sleeves, wondering what to do next.

'Now look, can you see what the problem is here? He was pulling at Morris's trousers, which Morris wished he wouldn't. He looked in the mirror. No, he couldn't see what the problem was. Well, apart from the ridiculous get-up.

'The belt. Take it off. Never wear a belt, the trousers don't hang properly'

'But they'll fall down.'

'No they won't. Where are the braces I bought you at Jones's?'

So that's what they were. Morris had wondered about them. He had them in his coat pocket to ask Mr Tite what to do with them.

'Look, take the trousers off and I'll show you how to put

the braces on.'

'What, here?'

'No boy, out in the High Street. Of course here.'

'But, um.'

'But what? Come along, we're all men here.'

'But Doris might come in.'

Mr Tite laughed so much Morris thought his teeth were going to fall out.

'Don't you worry about old Doris. I don't think there's much chance of your underpants driving her into an access of passion.'

Morris didn't know what that meant but he could tell it was sarcastic. Whether he was laughing at him or Doris he couldn't tell. Probably both, on account of Mr Tite having a propensity for laughing at people generally.

By the time Mr Tite had fitted the braces, and redone the tie and put the jacket back on, Morris looked, in some way he couldn't define, like an undertaker. He didn't know if that was a good thing or a bad thing but Mr Tite looked satisfied. Except for one item.

'Now, shaving.'

Aha, he couldn't catch him out there, Morris had started a new regime of shaving every other day.

'In the funeral directing business we are clean shaven. That means shaving every day, and if we're doing an afternoon job it means twice a day.'

What? Now Morris knew he was nuts. Who ever heard of shaving twice a day? Mr Tite came up close and examined his face. This close, Morris could smell something on him he had never smelled before, at least on anyone living. He wondered if Mr Tite used embalming fluid on his hair.

'Mm, if that's this morning's effort it won't do.'

'No?'

'No. You used one of those electric contraptions, didn't you?'

If he meant a shaver, he was dead right. What else did people use?

'Wet shave, it's the only thing. Wait here.'

He was back a minute later with a bag which he emptied out on the desk.

'Badger's hair brush, soap stick, and just in case you imagine we are at all old fashioned in this establishment, the very latest, a safety razor. You will be issued with a new blade once a month on return of the old one. This was Frank's, and I am sure he would like to know it is going to be put to good use. Take it home and I don't want to see you looking like a hedgehog with alopecia again.'

He tried, it has to be said time and again, to correct Morris's posture. Given that most of his life was spent slouched on one or another item of furniture at the flat, this was not good. It was even worse when he put on his undertaker's outfit because then it made him look positively lugubrious and Mr Tite thought you can go too far trying to look the part.

'No come on, boy, stand up straight. What did they teach you in the army?'

'But Mr Tite, I've never been in the army.'

'What, of course you have. Didn't you do your National Service?'

He was either under the delusion that this was nineteen fifty something, or that Morris was a hell of a lot older than he looked, say about seventy, in which case why did he persist in calling him boy? Still, Morris decided to humour him.

'No, rejected, bad posture you see.'

'I'm not surprised. Well in this job you have to be fit and strong, this is not a vocation for layabouts, you know.'

Which made Morris, who was in little doubt that this described him to a T, wonder what the hell he was doing here. Oh yes, finding a way to bury Tinkerbelle. And, perversely, quite enjoying himself. This wasn't like a real job, because it wasn't like the real world. Mr Tite and Doris occupied some place that was quite separate from the rest of humanity and they had invited Morris to join them for reasons best known to themselves and actually it was quite fun. Well, no, fun would be the wrong word.

Still, apart from the business of getting up every morning, and shaving, and having to press his suit and iron his shirts and polish his shoes, and the smell of Mr Tite's hair, and the dust in the office which made him cough, and listening to Doris's ramblings and about twenty-five other irritations, he could quite get to like his new life.

There were even days when he forgot about the corpse in the freezer in Marty's warehouse.

13

At the end of Morris's first week at Widdlecombe and Tite Angie came round to arrange the inaugural meeting of the book group, not of course that it was inaugural as far as Roger was concerned.

Morris was standing in the bathroom trying to figure out how to use Frank's shaving gear.

'Help me out, Sis. What do you do with all this?'

'Morris, it might have escaped your attention but I'm a woman. Women, in case you haven't noticed, don't shave.'

'Oh yeh, what about your legs?'

'Yes well, we certainly don't use all this stuff. Let's have a look. Come on, it's not that difficult. You need a soapy face, so you put the brush under the hot tap, like this, and then you get a nice lather with the soap stick, uhuh, and now, face up, you swish all over and get to look like Father Christmas. So far so good.'

She was enjoying this. Morris could tell.

'Now, you take a nice sharp blade, yep, like this ...'

He flinched as Angie came close with the razor.

'Oh come on, don't be a scaredy-cat. What do you think I'm going to do, cut your throat?'

'You might.'

'Don't tempt me kiddo, and stop shaking, or I really will.'

The end result of her work, even on Morris's dissipated face, was not unimpressive.

'There, you look almost human.'

'Thanks.'

'If you carry on like this I'll start to think you've become like the rest of us.'

'Nah, not much chance of that. Don't be fooled by any of this. I've got to do it otherwise it's back to the Jobcentre and they'll cut me off without any dosh if I don't keep a job.'

'Well, my favourite little brother, I hate to say it but you're becoming almost respectable. Here you are with a suit, and polished shoes. It'll be a pension plan next.'

'Anyway, this is really nice and all that but why exactly did you come round?'

'Oh yes, the book group.'

'Oh, that. I thought maybe you'd changed your mind.'

'Sorry kiddo, can't do that. If we don't have at least one meeting Roger will start getting suspicious. I can't say the group's packed up just the week he decides to come.'

'Well anyway, what does a book group do?'

'Look, this is going to come as a bit of a surprise, but it well, reads books.'

'Yeh? And why do you need a group to do that?'

'Well, it's not all you do. First you read a book, and then you talk about it.'

'Why?'

'Well, it's interesting.'

'Is it?'

'Look, Morris, never mind all that. You don't think Roger really wants to talk about books, do you? He just wants to be with me.'

'Can't he be with you at home? '

'He is. Oh, look, just do it for me will you? '

'Why? '

'Because if you don't I really will cut your throat. Is that a good enough reason? '

'Um, yeh, OK.'

'Good boy.'

'Don't you start.'

'What? '

'That's what Mr Tite says. Look, what do I need to do? '

'Well, tidy this room up, for a start.'

'Why? '

'Morris, do I have to explain everything? Look, you've got a nice suit, shiny shoes, don't you want a clean and tidy home?'

'Um, no.'

'I give up. OK, I'll come round on Monday night and do it. Now, what about chairs?'

'What about chairs? '

'Morris, if I'm going to have to explain everything in words of one syllable this is going to take a long time. Give me a piece of paper.'

He tore off the back cover from an old paperback book he found lying under the sofa and gave that to her. She wrote out a list of actions for Tuesday, plus a shopping list which included tea, coffee, sugar, milk, and a selection of biscuits.

'And you're to buy the milk, because Peter doesn't want stolen milk in his tea. It wouldn't be right.'

'Whereas having it off with a married woman is?'

'If you're going to put it like that, don't. I don't think you're in any position to tell other people how they should live their lives.'

'Anyway, how many chairs?'

'Well, let's see. There's Me and Peter, and Roger, and you of course, plus Marjorie, Ella, Sue and Jane. That's eight.'

'Hold on, hold on, how am I supposed to fit all those people in here?'

'Don't worry, Marjorie, Ella, Sue and Jane won't be coming.'

'How do you know?'

'Because I won't be telling them there's a meeting.'

'Why the hell not?'

'Because the book group folded months ago. We don't want to start it up again. We just want Roger to get the idea that it's always been here, and that this is where I've been coming every Tuesday.'

'But won't he notice that all those people aren't here? '

'Of course he will, he's not stupid. I'll just say they rang to say they couldn't make it.'

'What, all of them?'

'Well, not all of them. Not Peter.'

'No, of course not Peter. Natch.'

'And you.'

'Yeh, let's not forget good ole Morris. Look, Angie, do you really think this is going to work? And, let's be honest, I've met Peter Potter. Is he worth it?'

Angie had that look on her face that Morris was used to from childhood, the look that said he had come close to the truth. Angie wasn't sure if Peter was worth it, in fact she wasn't at all sure why she had got involved with him or why she was carrying on, let alone if it was going to cause all these problems. It certainly wasn't for the sex. Roger wasn't up to much in that department but Peter was about the same. No, there must have been a reason. As far as she could remember it was because she was angry with Roger, for being a useless husband generally, and the only way she could could take it out on him, without actually leaving him which she didn't want to do because, well, she couldn't think of a good reason for that but there always seemed to be one, which was probably as much to do with having a husband was better than not having one, was to have an affair, and Peter had been available, what with him coming to the book group every few weeks and looking lonely. She more or less had to push him into it because he was after all a vicar and vicars don't, after all, normally do that kind of thing but she caught him at a bad time, just after his mother had died and he was vulnerable. Yes, that was it, she was probably a surrogate mother for him.

Well, she had had years of that with Roger and now here she was with two men who needed mothering. It was getting tiresome. On the other hand, she was still angry with Roger and Peter was still the only way she knew to get her own back, and on top of that she had once hinted to Peter that they might end it and he had looked like he was going to cry so she didn't have the heart to take it any further. And now here was Morris making a fuss, when what she needed was just a man who would for once do what he was told.

'Look, Morris, don't worry, it'll work, and if it doesn't, oh I don't know, it'll work, let's leave it at that. Anyway, it's not your problem.'

Morris had that look on his face that she was used to from childhood, the look that said he slightly resented her bossiness but he actually did love her and he was a bit of a soft touch as far as his sister was concerned and if she pushed him he would give way and do what she wanted. He always had.

Angie looked like she wanted to put a sisterly arm round him and he looked like he wanted her to do that too, only he didn't know if he was supposed to want that so he didn't show any signs that it really would be alright and she didn't know if she was supposed to feel like she wanted to so she didn't.

'So, can you get the extra chairs, you know, just to make it look right?'

'Yeh, Marty's got loads, though how I'm going to squeeze them in ...'

'Well, as soon as we're all here and I say the girls aren't coming after all, we can put them in the bedroom.'

'OK, I'll get folding ones. So, what happens once you and Roger and Peter Potter and I are sitting comfortably?'

'Well, we'll talk about the last book.'

'Which was?'

'Well, of course, there wasn't actually a book, because there

80

wasn't actually a book group.'

'So it's going to be a short meeting.'

'No, dummy, of course we'll have to talk about a book, I mean as if there was one we'd all read.'

'Angie, this is getting ridiculous.'

'No it isn't, it got ridiculous a long time ago, but we've got to see it through.'

'If you say so.'

'I do. Now, let's decide what the last book was.'

She turned over the paperback cover Morris had torn off for her to write the shopping list on. It featured a semi-clad woman and a lot of blood.

'No, well, not this one, for a start. Any ideas? What was the last book you read?'

'That one.'

'OK, well, before this one.'

'That one.'

'What? Morris, have you read this book twice?'

'No.'

'So why did you say you have?'

'I didn't. I said it was the last book I read, and it was the last one before that. I've read it lots of times. I like it. It's the only book I read.'

'Morris, you're barmy.'

'Uhuh, tell me something I don't already know.'

Angie sighed. 'OK, I'll come up with something, and then you can get it out of the library and read it before the meeting.'

'No, I don't think so.'

'Why not?'

'Look, Angie, I'm OK with the book group thing, just to get Roger off your back, but I'm not reading a book for you. Anyway, I'm a slow reader. That one takes me about a month.'

'But you've read it lots of times already. How can it take a month to read it when you know what happens?'

'OK, look, I admit it, I'm a very slow reader.'

'Very.'

'Yes, whatever, but it does mean I could never read a new book, I mean one where I don't already know what happens, before next Tuesday, even if I wanted to which I don't, not even for you, as much as I love you and want to help.'

'Morris, did you mean that?'

'What, about not wanting to read a book for you?'

'No, that you love me.'

'I didn't say that.'

'Yes you did.'

'No I didn't.'

'Did.'

'Didn't.'

Angie stood up and put an arm round her brother and gave him a kiss on top of his head.

'No, Morris, you're probably right. But thank you all the same. Don't worry about the book, you won't have to say anything.'

And with that, in the way Angie had always had, she was gone. Morris rubbed the top of his head where he had kissed her. She was getting soft in her old age.

14

Morris had Fridays off. He decided to pay Marty a visit.

'Oh, well if it isn't my old friend Morris. Long time no see. How's the body business?'

'Oh, you know, it has its ups and downs.'

'More downs than ups, I shouldn't wonder.'

It was, Morris presumed, another one of Marty's jokes. 'So how was prison?'

'Fine.'

'Really?'

'No, they gave me a fine.'

It was while he was wondering whether to enquire further that he noticed it was darker than usual in the warehouse.

'Marty, are you saving money or something? Why are the lights off?'

'Oh that. Power cut, they say it'll be another couple of hours.'

'Oh, right. Oh shit, the freezers. Marty, how long has the power been off?'

'Oh, well let me think, um, when was it?'

'I don't know, you tell me. When was it? Come on man, think.'

'I am, I am.'

'Well think faster.'

'I am.'

'No you're not. What time was it when the lights went out?'

'Well, let me see ...'

'Yes, yes.'

'You know that programme on Radio 4 with whatshisname, you know the one I always listen to.'

'Marty, for God's sake what the hell are you talking about?'

'Well, I was just saying.'

'Well just say it faster so we can get past Radio 4 and on to the more interesting bit, like what time the power cut started.'

'Well, if you'll let me get a word in edgeways that's what I was coming to. The programme had just finished, and the news was coming on, I think. Or was it? You know, now you've got me all flustered I can't remember.'

'OK, OK, I'm sorry. Look, what time does this programme start?'

'Eleven o'clock.'

'Right, good, and what time does it finish?'

'Oh, probably about twelve I should think.'

'Right, and was the electricity still on when it finished?'

'Oh, I should think so. It's a mains radio, you see.'

'Right, good, so the freezers were going at twelve. That's, let me see, three and a half hours. How long does it take for them to warm up without power?'

'As long as you don't open the lid, longer than that. I think.'

'You think? Don't you know?'

'No, why should I?'

'Well come on, you sell the things, you should know.'

'No, I don't think so. No-one's ever asked me before. Anyway, how many freezers do I sell? The only three I've got in stock you've got full of chips, so I can't. And this geezer came in only yesterday and was looking for one and I had to say I didn't have any for sale. You ought to be paying me rent on them, you know.'

'OK, OK, I'll pay you rent.'

'Really?'

'Yeh, look you only have to ask, you know. I'm not an

unreasonable man. It's only fair.'

'Well that's very good of you, Morris. Just for that I'll put the kettle on and make you a nice cup of tea.'

'You can't. There's no electricity.'

'Oh no, sorry.'

So they sat there in the gloom, not saying much. Marty asked him questions about his new job and Morris tried to answer them while all the time what he really wanted to do was go and check on Tinkerbelle, only he knew if he opened the lid that would only make things worse. As it was, he sat there working out which defrosted first, people or chips, and decided it was chips on account of them being thinner, so even if Tinkerbelle came to no harm, as long as the power came back on soon, he was likely to have about a hundred bags of unsaleable crinkle-cut chips. Still, the frozen food business was, he decided, now a thing of the past. He wouldn't be paying rent for long. All he had to do was figure out a way to get Tinkerbelle buried through the good offices of Widdlecombe and Tite.

Marty wittered and eventually the power came back on and Morris wanted to go and check on Tinkerbelle but instead he sat there and pretended to listen. While he did that he had a momentary notion that even now he would just tell the police the truth, only he realised that the truth as it stood now was a lot worse than it was a few weeks ago when he might just have had a chance of getting away with it. Waking up next to a corpse is bad enough, but keeping her in a freezer in a second-hand furniture warehouse struck him, in some way he was unable to define, as almost certainly worse. No, there was nothing for it, she was going to get a decent burial. Somehow.

Anyway, things were going well in the job. Old Horace, as Doris called Mr Tite despite the unarguable fact that he was at least twenty years younger than her, had, for some reason Morris was unable to figure out, taken a liking to him. True, he treated him like a child, but maybe that was part of liking him. And Morris was learning a lot about the dying business, rather more, in fact, than he ever thought he would want to know, but still in for a penny in for a pound, there was no getting round it, this was his best chance of sorting Tinkerbelle out once and for all.

The next day, being Saturday, was a normal working one. In fact Widdlecombe and Tite, like all funeral directors, was available, if not actually open for business, twenty-four hours a day, seven days a week. Mr Tite answered the phone at home at any time of the night, and he insisted that Morris had his phone reconnected so he could be on call as well, in case they needed to fetch a body out of hours. That somewhat curtailed Morris's alcohol and cannabis intake, because he knew that even if Horace didn't obviously smell his breath he was on the watch out for the demon drink at all times. Anyway, after a day at work, Morris was too tired to be bothered. He had never done so much hard work in his life. There were endless jobs, specially if you were the junior member of staff, and if he ever found him sitting taking a break Horace sent him out to polish the hearse, even in the rain. Widdlecombe and Tite was not just a business, it was a vocation, and that meant being ready to spring into action at a moment's notice.

Even after weeks in the firm, Morris was still unable to tell what it was that old Doris did there though. She made endless cups of tea, but on the other hand she also drank endless cups of tea so Morris reckoned one cancelled the other out and if she hadn't been there there would have been no-one to make so much tea but on the other hand there would have been no-one to drink it either. So she kind of justified her existence by her very existence. Morris came to find it hard to imagine how the firm would run properly without her, even though she really only made cups of tea and then drank them.

Morris meanwhile got the flat ready for the book group, or the not book group, as he was calling it. He borrowed Mrs Diggle's vacuum cleaner, moved everything out onto the landing while he sucked up several years of dust from under the bed, and then he wondered why the hell he was cleaning the bedroom when the book group people, as few as they were, would only be using the living room, but still, why not? He opened the windows to let some fresh air in while he scrubbed the kitchen with something he bought from the The Plentiful Goodness Food Store with instructions entirely in some script he was unable to decipher but he had a feeling it was surplus stock normally used to clean the inside of railway engines. It burned through a pair of industrial rubber gloves he got from work and seared the membranes in his nostrils. It had the desired effect in that it removed years of cooking grime but the undesired effect in that it also removed the enamel. He hesitated over his prized 1988 Pirelli calendar but out of deference to the Rev. Peter Potter he rolled it up and put it in a drawer.

An hour before they were due to arrive he had the tea and coffee all ready, with full-cream milk and skimmed for those who preferred, plain and milk chocolate digestives laid out on a plate with a crack in it but as long as no-one actually ate any of the plain ones it wouldn't show. Angie was the first to arrive, as promised.

'Roger's got a teachers' meeting, thank God, he's coming on a bit later. OK, here's the book you've read, or haven't read. Actually, it's not bad.'

'Mm, The Case of the Missing Millionaire, an Inspector Bumbridge Mystery. Doesn't sound very promising. You'd better give me the low-down.'

'Well, it's pretty straightforward. I thought you'd prefer that.'

'Thanks.'

'In case you haven't read any of the Inspector Bumbridge books ...'

'Which of course I haven't.'

'No, quite, well they're all the same really. He lives in this imaginary place somewhere up north, and it starts off with them finding a body and he's got a whole load of suspects, and then one by one each suspect is bumped off.'

'Making his shortlist of suspects shorter all the time.'

'You've got the idea. And he always thinks he knows who the villain is but he's always wrong because one morning he's having breakfast with his wife and she says something completely innocent and he says hang on that's it and she says hang on what's it, but by that time he's got his coat on and he's out of the door, having stopped only briefly to phone his sergeant to tell him to meet him at the real culprit's house in ten minutes, and his wife is left staring at a cold cup of tea. In the last chapter he confronts the baddy, who pulls a gun and takes a pot shot at him but only grazes his shoulder while his sergeant manfully wrestles the villain to the floor. And that's it.'

'And what about the millionaire?'

'Oh, he's the villain. He hadn't really vanished at all, of course. He's been blackmailing his nephew to murder all the victims because he's made some disastrous investments and his money has all gone so he needs to inherit his great aunt someone or other's fortune but he's only about sixth in line because she thought he didn't need the money.'

'Oh, right. And why was he blackmailing his nephew?'

'Do you really want to know?'

'Um, no, not really.'

'Good. Anyway, think you can remember all that?'

'No.'

'Morris!'

'Only kidding. Anyway, did I enjoy it?'

'Yes, except you thought it was a bit like all his other novels and you wonder how long he can get away with the same plot.'

'Do I? Does that mean I've read the other ones?'

'Well I suppose so.'

'And what are they called?'

'Oh I don't know. Look inside. Does it say anything about his other books?'

'Hold on, let's have a look. Um, oh here we are. Yeh. The Case of the Missing Professor, The Opera Singer goes Missing, The Case of the Vanishing Scientist. Yeh, I see what you mean now. If he goes on much longer there won't be anyone left to write about.'

Angie was looking round the room.

'Well, I must say I'm impressed. I've never seen it this clean.'

'It's a bit crowded though, with all these chairs.'

'Well, the girls will be ringing you here to say they're not coming and then we can clear some of them away.'

'But if they don't actually know there's a meeting who's going to ring?'

'Peter, from the phone box down the road just before he turns up.'

'Hopefully after Roger turns up, otherwise it might look a bit suspicious.'

'Yes.'

Only it didn't work out like that. Peter rang, all right, but Roger hadn't arrived.

'Hullo, is that Morris?'

'Yes.'

'Morris, it's Peter Potter.'

'Yes, I know. And Peter, you can stop whispering.'

'Right, well I'm ringing to say that er, Marjorie isn't coming.'

'Oh, really?'

'No. And neither is er, oh, gosh, I've forgotten the other names.'

'Well look, Peter, I wouldn't worry about it if I were you because Roger's not here. He's late. So there's not much point in you phoning, is there? Why don't you just come round? '

'Oh, right, will do then, see you soon.'

'OK.'

'Oh, Morris, are you still there?'

'Yes.'

'Well, I just wanted to say how much ....' Beep beep beep.

'And the same to you. That was Peter.'

'Yes, so I gathered.'

'He says Marjorie and some other women whose names he couldn't remember aren't coming.'

'No, really? Well, that's a shame.'

'It's an even bigger shame that Roger isn't here so we can stop playing silly buggers. Or do I mean start playing silly buggers? I'm confused already.'

Then Peter came panting up the stairs, and they all sat down and waited for Roger, and then ten minutes later Angie said well let's put the kettle on, he'll be here soon, and then Roger rang to say he was held up in the meeting, they should carry on without him, sorry to mess them about, and they all sat and drank their tea and ate biscuits, digestives with and without milk chocolate, and then Angie and Peter pushed off.

So, Morris thought as he surveyed his nice clean flat, that's the case of the missing book group.

15

Marty rang.

'Morris, is that you?'

'No, Marty, it's someone else.'

'Oh, sorry.'

'Hold on, Marty, of course it's me you silly sod. What is it?'

'Oh, Morris, I'm glad of that.'

'What?'

'That it's you.'

Morris realised, too late, that however Marty's sense of humour worked it was dangerous to make any assumptions.

'Marty, why did you ring? Could you spit it out, only I've got a funeral to go to.'

'Really, oh I'm sorry, anyone I know?'

Morris banged his head on the desk.

'Marty, if you don't get on with it, yes, it's going to be someone you know, intimately. You. Now, let's take this one stage at a time. You rang. You want to say something to me. What?

'I need two of the freezers.'

'What? Why?'

'Well, this is going to come a shock, I know, but I sell second hand stuff here and this geezer wants two freezers and I don't want to lose a customer.'

'Two? Why does he want two? Bloody hell, that's just greedy.'

'I don't know. It's none of my business, or yours. Look, can you get rid of a load of those chips?'

'I don't suppose this bloke would take them as well?'

'Er, no I don't think dogs eat chips.'

Morris gave this a split-second thought and decided it wasn't worth the effort. 'I didn't think so. OK, OK, I'll come round tonight. Hang on till I get there, will you?'

'Sure mate.'

'Thanks. Bye.'

'Oh, and Morris?'

'Oh God, not you too.'

Shit. Now he had a body and about fifty bags of frozen chips to dispose of. He would have to borrow Marty's van and flog them off cheap to some of his old customers. The chips, not Tinkerbelle.

The funeral was, as more often than not, at St Elmo's. Peter Potter tried to avoid Morris's eye during the proceedings, and Horace noticed. He took Morris into his office afterwards.

'Morris, how do you think that went?'

'Oh fine, fine, didn't it?' He was waiting for the catch.

'Oh yes, pretty fair. I needn't remind you, here at Widdlecombe and Tite we set high standards.'

Meaning?

'Hair, boy, hair, it's time you got it cut.'

Oh, right, of course, find something to complain about, as always, and if there isn't anything just find something anyway.

'Sit down, boy, sit down.'

Horace was smiling now, which most people would think was a good sign. Morris had already learned that that wasn't necessarily so. He was, as Morris said, a sly old bugger.

'So, Morris, what did you think of the minister today?'

'Peter?'

'I beg your pardon?'

'I mean the Reverend Potter. Oh I thought he was his usual

self.' A bit boring, pedantic and pompous, as usual. 'Yes, about average I would say.'

'You didn't think he was a little odd? '

Well now you come to mention it I did, but then I think he's an odd sort of bloke anyway, so no change there. 'Odd, no Mr Tite, I didn't notice that. In what way? '

'Well, Morris, I couldn't help but notice that he looked at you a little strangely.'

'Me? Why would he do that?'

'That's what I was wondering. You haven't had words with him, have you?'

No meaningful ones, no. 'Words? No, I don't think so Mr Tite. What sort of words?'

Horace didn't know what sort of words. He just smelled something fishy. He liked Morris, it was true, more than he had expected to when he joined the firm, but still there was something, something he couldn't put his finger on. He was torn between hoping he would make a mistake and his suspicions would be vindicated and hoping that he would come good and that one day, one distant day perhaps, there might be someone he could trust to run Widdlecombe and Tite. He looked at Morris sometimes and wondered if that was just being fanciful.

'Well, Morris, I must say you have made fair progress since you started with us, yes very fair progress. Doris agrees with me therefore that it's time you started studying for your Certificate.'

Certificate? What certificate would that be? No-one mentioned certificates at the Jobcentre.

'As you know, Morris, being a funeral director is a public service that must be taken very seriously. There is, as you have already discovered, a lot to learn, and Doris and I feel, in the absence of poor dear Frank, that we must make a decision about your career with the firm, and that you should therefore start studying for your Certificate.'

Er no, I don't think so. 'Yes, Mr Tite, that would be most interesting.'

'Excellent, Morris, I'm so glad you see it that way. Well, I shall make the arrangements. Leave it with me.'

Oh I shall, don't you worry, well and truly.

Morris treated himself, as soon as he got home, to a joint. He needed to think. This was going too far. Tinkerbelle was still in her freezer ... shit, he was supposed to be round at Marty's.

'Morris, well well, a bit late but better late than never. Are you alright?'

No he wasn't. Whether it was the cannabis or the rushing around or one after the other, but Morris was feeling distinctly queasy.

'OK Marty, let's sort these chips out.'

It was then that it hit him like a cold shower. How was he going to empty the chips out of two freezers if he didn't know which one the body was in, at least without Marty watching?

'Look Marty, I'm really sorry. I suppose you've got to be going somewhere?'

'No, no, that's all right.'

'Really, look, why don't you go off and I'll sort this out. I've got a key, I can lock up.'

'Oh, OK then.'

Thank God for that.

'Hold on though, how are you going to carry all those chips over to the other side of town?'

Shit.

'I know, you can use the van.'

Great.

'Oh no, hang on, I'll need it later, got a house to go and see tonight. Sorry.'

Shit.

'OK Marty, I tell you what, don't you worry about it. I'll get a taxi.'

'A taxi?' Marty obviously found the idea of Morris carrying half a ton of chips across town in a taxi a challenging one, which so did Morris, but he was getting desperate.

'Sure, just for once. Now, which freezer can I keep?'

Marty showed him the two he was selling, and then he let himself out with Morris's assurances about the taxi ringing in his ears. Morris got to work emptying the chips into black bin bags he had brought for the purpose. When he got down to Tinkerbelle, he stopped in surprise. All this time he had known she was there but there she was face to face, and suddenly it didn't feel right, any of it. He had got used to dead people by now, but they were fresh, they weren't deep frozen. He had to admit, Tinkerbelle didn't look good.

Anyway, as it turned out she was in the wrong freezer, so she would have to be moved. He got her as far as over his shoulder.

'Bloody hell, Morris, what the fucking hell is that?'

Marty. Shit. Oh, shit, oh, shit, oh, shit. He couldn't figure out whether he should try to explain with Tinkerbelle in his arms, or put her down, and if he did that whether he should place her back where she came from or lay her out on the floor. He didn't want to make any decisions. He didn't want to be here at all. He wanted it all to go away, for ever. His wishes, as always, failed to come true.

Anyway, the ice coating the body was starting to melt from his own body heat and trickle down his neck. It felt very, very unpleasant. Tinkerbelle started to slip through his hands and she landed, on her feet, kind of standing next to him. In different circumstances he would have said Marty, this is Tinkerbelle, Tinkerbelle, Marty, but that was different circumstances.

'Marty, I can explain.'

Marty stared at Tinkerbelle in disbelief. 'Morris, tell me this isn't a stiff.'

'Marty, this isn't a stiff.'

'You're lying aren't you?'

'Yes.'

'OK, OK, now let's calm down here. Look, put it back in the freezer and then you can tell me what the bloody hell you're doing with a corpse in my warehouse.'

Morris told him the whole story, about how since he'd gone to work at Widdlecombe and Tite he had started to do a little freelance work of his own, helping people who couldn't afford proper funerals, and this girl came from a poor family of Irish immigrants and had been worked to death by an evil sweatshop owner and he had told the family he would do what he could but he was waiting for a plot at the Catholic church up the road. He wondered if he had gone too far with the Irish thing but as it turned out it was the clincher.

'Irish, eh.'

'Yes Marty.'

'What was her name?'

'Um, Marie, Marie O'Shaunessy.'

'Well, that's a good Irish name and no mistaking.'

'That's what I thought.' Morris wondered if it would be safe to stuff a hanky down his neck to soak up the meltwater. It felt really, really bad.

'And you've promised to do the family a good turn?'

'Yes, Marty.'

'Well, I can't say I like it, no. In fact I don't like it one little bit, but well, what can I say?'

Quite a lot. 'Look, it'll only be for another couple of days, then I'll find somewhere to bury her and that will be the end of it. And the family will be really grateful.'

Marty, Morris could tell, was hesitating. Who wouldn't in his position? 'I suppose it's all legal?'

'Oh yes.'

'Good, good. A couple of days, you reckon?'

'A week at the most.'

'Well .... well OK then, a week.'

'Two at the very outside.'

'And I want her out of here by then, and listen, it's absolutely nothing to do with me if anyone comes looking.'

'Yes, definitely, only one thing?'

'What's that?'

'Can I suggest you don't keep any cannabis here until we get rid of her, I mean arrange the funeral?'

'Oh that, listen, it was just for a friend.'

'Sure Marty. And Marty?'

'What?'

'Thanks.'

He slammed the freezer door shut. Morris one, Marty nil. Marty left and Morris dragged several black bin bags of frozen chips out of the door, locked up, considered briefly trying to find a taxi in a quiet back street at this time of night, gave up on the idea, and dragged them over the road and dumped the whole lot in a skip.

16

'Come in Morris, come in. Do sit down.'

He was smiling. Morris was trying to figure out if it was a friendly smile or the kind of smile he had on because he was going to get you. He gave up.

'Well, here is the starter pack you will need for your studies.'

Oh yes, the bloody certificate. Fat chance.

'I think you will enjoy it, I know I did, and I was rather younger than you.'

Morris tried to picture Horace being younger than him and gave up on that too.

'Oh, and Morris, before you go ...'

Oh yes, here it comes.

'I believe you don't have a driving licence?'

'No Mr Tite, that's right.'

'Well I must say I find that very odd, a chap of your age. Still. Well Doris and I think you should learn.'

Hold on, hold on, who said anything about not learning? Learning was the easy bit. Passing the test was another easy bit. And the next easy bit was losing his licence when he was caught over the limit. For the third time. Going through a red light at twice the speed limit. Yes, that wasn't hard at all. Still, only another three months, and he would have his licence back.

'Yes, we need an extra driver, so you will have to have lessons. The firm will pay for them.'

That's uncharacteristically generous.

'And you can pay it back out of your wages when you've passed your test.'

Yes, how did I fall for that one?

'Give Quickpass a ring and get started as soon as possible, will you? They're only at the other end of the High Street.'

Morris rang Quickpass. Norman was out on a lesson but Mrs Quick promised to have him ring back as soon as he returned. Three days later he found himself behind the wheel of a learner car. It felt strange. He wasn't at all sure how he was going to handle this.

'So Morris, isn't it?'

'Yes.'

'Not Morris Minor I suppose?'

'What?'

'Just my little joke, we can't be serious all the time, can we? Well, Morris, most people learn to drive younger than you but look, a lot of mature people do too, so there's nothing to worry about.'

Are we talking mature as in years here, or mature as in grown up?

'You've got a provisional licence, I suppose?'

No, will a full one do? 'Yes.'

'Er, could I see it, do you think?'

No you can't. 'Um let me see, now where did I put it? Oh foolish me, do you know I think I've gone and left it at home. What a silly I am. Shall we cancel the lesson and I'll bring it next time?'

Norman thought about this for three seconds and decided, on account of him not wanting to lose twenty quid, that it would do when they had the next lesson.

'Now, I'm sure you've been a passenger in lots of cars, so you'll be pretty familiar with the position of the controls and the pedals.'

'Yes, I think so. Let me see. That one's the clutch and that's the brake, so I guess this one's the accelerator?'

'Well done, that's great. Now when you're ready turn the key in the ignition, just apply a little pressure to the clutch as you do, and she'll start up.'

She? One of those, huh? Morris did as instructed and, as predicted, she started up nicely.

'Now, first gear is here, try that .. good, good, and this is second ... yes, good .. now let's try third up here ... fine, fine, and finally, fourth, down like this, have a go, yes, that's it, you've got it. Well Morris, I think you are going to be a quick learner, or as we say at Quickpass, a quick passer.'

We say that, do we? Well, this is going to be fun.

'Now, how do you feel about moving off gently and trying it out on this nice quiet road?'

Morris slipped it into first, moved out gently so as not to scare Norman, quickly went through second and third and before Norman knew what was happening they were on the High Street. From there Morris hung a left in third through a rat run he knew and they were on the bypass in fifth while Norman clutched his seat in fear. Morris took them about four or five miles as far as the gyratory system, which he negotiated without let or hindrance, then back on the bypass, down the High Street and into the quiet little back street where they had started half an hour earlier. Norman hadn't said a word. He had wanted to, but at no point could he find the right ones. Morris, he knew, was some kind of prodigy.

'Well, you seem to have got the hang of the controls all right. Um, you weren't nervous, were you?'

Norman, on the other hand, had been terrified.

'So, next week we'll do three point turns, reversing round a corner, that sort of thing, and we'll get to grips with the Highway Code.'

Yes, Morris had heard of the Highway Code, although he

wasn't entirely sure what it was about. He shook Norman's hand, which was still sweating, and promised to study the code before the next lesson. Right, that was two things he had promised to study that he didn't need, the Highway Code and the Funeral Directors' Certificate coursebook. He only ever read one book, and it wasn't either of these.

He had a lesson every week and soon learned to make mistakes. As long as he didn't take his test he wouldn't have to pay back the money for the lessons. Anyway, there was a bigger problem, just to add to his ever-growing catalogue of problems he couldn't solve. How, he wondered, do you take a driving test when you've already got a driving licence, even, or perhaps especially, when as in his case you've got a licence with don't whatever you do let this bloke drive for the next nine months scribbled all over it in red ink, or whatever it is they do at the department of making motorists' lives difficult? He felt sure a computer somewhere was keeping an eye on him and he felt equally sure it would notice if he put in an application for a driving test, let alone when he passed and applied for a licence.

Norman forgot about the provisional licence. He reckoned as long as Morris had it when he went for his test that would do. Morris, of course, had no intention of ever taking such a thing and therefore the problem would not arise, although it must be said that the not taking the test bit was of itself a problem, but still, in Morris's world a problem that can be put off to tomorrow was a problem solved.

And just to make his life a little bit more troublesome Marty had taken to phoning about once a day to ask about Tinkerbelle's burial. Morris took the calls in the front office and he took to whispering loudly at Marty in the hope of getting him off the line before Horace wondered what was going on. Doris, who had decided in some remote part of her brain that Morris was the reincarnation of her long-lost lover, got it into another part of her brain that these calls were from

101

another woman and the reason he was whispering was so she wouldn't find out about her. She started hanging around when a call came for Morris and this made him whisper even more and that made her even more suspicious, although of course she wasn't suspicious about what Morris assumed she was suspicious about.

Norman Quick, meanwhile, was beginning to wonder what was wrong with Morris. He had had difficult students before but no-one like Morris. He complained to Mrs Quick about him. Mrs Quick was used to him complaining. He complained a lot, mostly about his work but to be honest about anything and everything. Norman was not especially a happy man. Oh, he had a jolly demeanour, but it was a front. He made jokes all the time but like a circus clown under the jovial exterior was a man in pain. Mrs Quick knew this, although she couldn't have said just what it was that was causing this pain. Life she supposed, and she hoped while she supposed that that it wasn't her part of his life. Mrs Quick was a woman of a nervous disposition. Mr Quick had met her many years before when she came to him for driving lessons. She was the first and only student ever to crash his car. He had banned her strictly from having any more lessons after that, from him or anyone else, especially anyone else. Norman didn't want his colleagues in the business to know he was married to a woman who couldn't learn to drive. Everyone can learn to drive was his motto, or at least it was one of his mottoes because Norman rather liked making them up.

In fact that was the main reason he had married Mrs Quick. He reckoned that a woman can't testify against her own husband. And now she had to lie in bed last thing at night and whereas Norman used, occasionally, to engage in amorous pursuits once, long ago, now he lay there and complained, especially about Morris. Mrs Quick was actually quite pleased that the amorous pursuits bit of their marriage had come to an end, but given a choice of that and her husband's moaning about Morris she did sometimes think she would be prepared, in desperation, to lie there and let him have his wicked way.

Norman, sadly, no longer had a wicked way, but he did have Morris, and Morris troubled him, deeply, which of course Mrs Quick could tell by the way he wouldn't stop going on about him. Morris could drive, he could in fact drive reasonably competently, certainly well enough, in Norman's judgment, to pass a test. A lot better in fact than a lot of the seventeen-year-old youths who whizzed through the test and who wouldn't, if he had anything to do with it, be allowed to sit behind the wheel of a car until they were at least fifty and even then only after they had had their testosterone surgically removed.

No, Morris wasn't a bad sort. He was mature, he was actually a good driver. It was almost, he told Mrs Quick, as if he didn't want to pass the test. Who, he asked her, would take lessons if he didn't want to pass the driving test?

Mrs Quick couldn't answer that. In fact the long-suffering woman had finally been granted the blessing of sleep, and was blissfully unaware of what her husband was going on about.

Well, Norman thought, tomorrow is another day. Tomorrow, come what may, Morris is going to get it right.

Or not.

17

Morris's driving lessons were in the afternoon, usually at three o'clock. In the morning Horace was visiting a family out of town and Morris was sitting idly in the chapel of rest wondering how he was going to screw it up satisfactorily today when Doris came to inform him there was a customer. Morris, he had been told in no uncertain terms, was not allowed to talk to customers. Either Doris dealt with them in Horace's absence, or they were asked to come back, but Morris, who was not trained for that delicate task, was not permitted to discuss funerals with the bereaved. Which is why he was surprised when Doris insisted he see this one.

'Who are you?'

'I'm Morris Figg. Can I help you?'

'Dunno. Where's the other one?'

'You mean Mr Tite?'

'Yeh, that's the one. Tite.'

'I'm sorry but Mr Tite has been called away. Can I help?'

Morris was feeling pleased with his performance so far. It was a bit hammy, but for a first attempt not bad.

'It's my Wilf.'

'Wilf? I'm so sorry. May I ask, Madam, when the gentleman passed away?'

'You what?'

'Um, when did your husband, you know, die?'

'Oh, 'im. 1964.'

'I see, and um, you want us to arrange a funeral now?'

'I shouldn't think so dearie. Not unless you want to dig 'im up first.'

'I see.'

Which he didn't, at all. He was trying not to say um, which he knew Horace strongly disapproved of, but he couldn't help himself. 'Um, Mrs ...?'

'Yes, that's right dearie, married forty seven years, though the last thirty I've been a widow. Never remarried, you know. Could've, for sure, with my looks, but well, out of respect for my dear departed 'Enry, you know 'ow it is I expect.'

No, whatever this woman was on about it was a complete mystery to Morris. And if her looks had once qualified her to find a second husband he could only think they had faded somewhat dramatically over the years. In any case, he didn't care. He didn't know what she wanted but he was beginning to think it had more to with wasting his time than arranging a burial.

On the other hand, if he didn't handle her carefully and it got back to Horace, there would be repercussions, and repercussions were something he could do without, at least until he had arranged the burial he had come to this godforsaken place to sort out. He wondered sometimes if he was ever going to do that, or in years to come someone would uncover Tinkerbelle's mummified body in the long-since packed-up freezer in a derelict warehouse and there would be one of those cold-case police investigations he had watched on the TV and when he was old and doddery they would come and arrest him and drag him away on a zimmer frame to face trial.

On the other hand, while the old woman droned on and on apparently oblivious to the fact that he wasn't listening he started to wonder about the whole thing. Maybe it was a set-up. Yes, the way Doris had come and insisted he see her. Yes, now he came to think about it, how convenient that

Horace was out of town and this crazy old woman should appear and he was asked to deal with her. Yes, now he knew, it was a test, cooked up between Horace and Doris to see how he coped.

'And my Cyril said I should so that's what I did and well, I mean, you would, wouldn't you?'

Would you? And who the hell was Cyril? He must have been asleep when she introduced him.

'Yes, I should think you would.'

She seemed pleased with that answer. Yes, she was warming to him, which now he came to think about it he didn't want her to do, he wanted her to bugger off. He had enough to worry about today, and at the top of his list of things to worry about was how he was going to screw up his driving lesson this afternoon. He was finding it a bit of a strain finding something to do wrong, and get Norman Quick to put off applying for the test for another week. It was reaching crunch time. What he needed was a miracle, only in Morris's thirty seven years miracles had been in short supply, which means non-existent. He was an eternal optimist, though, and he never stopped believing, against all the available evidence so far that it was a forlorn hope. Miracles may or may not happen, but if they do Morris was permanently off the list of potential and deserving recipients.

'And Cyril said I shouldn't have done that, and you know Cyril, well, you don't of course, why should you, but I mean if you did, well, you wouldn't 'ave been at all surprised, would you?'

Bloody Cyril again. 'No, madam, no I don't think I would.'

He was starting to wonder if, given the choice, he would opt to bludgeon this woman to death or kill himself, and then he remembered why she was here, and he smiled sweetly and even though his eyes were glazed he managed to sound like he had some notion of what she was going on about. And then, suddenly and without any apparent reason, it was over.

106

'Well, dearie, I can't stop here all day talking to you, some of us have got busy lives you know.'

And she gathered up two large shopping bags stuffed full of what looked to Morris like dirty washing and shuffled out of the door. Doris came in and offered him a cup of tea. She was giving nothing away, but just smiled in that way she had that showed her missing front teeth and Morris decided he was now so tired he wouldn't have any difficulty fluffing his driving lesson.

But he didn't. He was too tired to think of a way of doing it wrong. He just drove, and while he drove Norman looked on and smiled. Morris, he felt, had cracked it. Yes, whatever it was that was blocking him before had removed itself and now, bless him, he was ready for the test. Norman smiled in evident self-satisfaction. OK, it wasn't a quick pass but it would undoubtedly be a pass. Morris watched him smiling and he knew he had done it wrong, or right, depending on whose side you were on.

Shit.

Now there was no getting away from it. That last three point turn had been perfect, textbook, Norman wished he could have filmed it for the promotional video he had always dreamed of producing but never would. One more reversing round a corner and that would be it. He took Morris to the junction of Aspen Avenue and Gardenia Walk, the corner all the driving schools used to teach this manoeuvre because it was a quiet residential area. Morris had done it many times. All Norman needed was for him to get it right this time. Would he? The tension rose in the car as Morris approached and slowed down by the kerb. Norman said nothing as Morris put it into reverse, smoothly and quietly. He put his right foot gently on the throttle and lifted his left gently from the clutch. Norman was clutching the sides of his seat. It was becoming unbearable. He was mouthing a silent prayer to the god of driving schools. His eyes, he realised, were closed.

And then it happened. The car came to a stop, Norman opened his eyes and ... it was over. A perfect manoeuvre. Morris put the handbrake on and he knew he was defeated. It showed on his face. Norman was too happy to notice though.

He was also too happy to notice another car reversing round the corner, a car belonging to Lizzie Pink, the ladies-only driving teacher, a car reversing round at precipitate speed. It jerked to a halt about two feet in front of Norman's front bumper, and all would have been well, but then for reasons best known to the god of driving schools, who must have been having a bad day, either that or he was exacting a price for Morris's success, the car took another leap backwards and, covering those two feet in a split second, hit Norman's car with a resounding crash and tinkle of breaking plastic.

Norman and Morris got out to survey the damage. Lizzie Pink got out to survey the damage. The only person who didn't want to see the damage was her student. The bumper was badly broken and half of it was lying at an awkward angle on the road. One headlamp was shattered, and the number plate hung from a single fixing.

And the person who sat frozen in the driving seat of Lizzie's car had good reason to hide her head in shame and fear. It was Mrs Quick.

Morris returned to the office in high spirits. It would, he knew, be some time before Norman would concern himself with his driving test. Norman had other things on his mind right now. In fact Morris never saw him again. It was rumoured, some time later, that he was living, without Mrs Quick, somewhere in New Zealand.

Yes, Morris was in a good mood. A miracle had happened, the first one ever. OK, Horace was going to want to know when he was taking his test, but what with Norman Quick's current mental state it wouldn't be difficult to put that off for some time.

'Ah, Morris, how did the lesson go?'

'Oh, very well, Mr Tite. Mr Quick thinks I'll be ready to take my test very soon.'

'Excellent, excellent.'

'As soon as the car's fixed.'

'What, you didn't ...'

'Oh no, not me, um, someone else.'

'I see, I see. Well, changing the subject, I understand you had old Mrs Goggins in this afternoon?'

'Mrs Goggins? No I don't think so. Oh, was she the old lady who, um ...'

'Yes, that's her.'

'Well what a charming lady, I must say, most interesting to talk to. Now I know, Mr Tite, that you don't normally like me to talk to customers but, well, Doris felt it was important that someone talk to her and I was the only one available, and, if I say so myself, it all went very well. Yes, very well.'

'Excellent Morris. I'm really very pleased about that. Old Mrs Goggins is something of, shall we say, a nuisance. She goes round all the funeral directors in the town and wastes their time. She comes in here at least once a month. In future, my boy, you can deal with her yourself.'

'What? You mean she wasn't, um ...'

'Wasn't what?'

'Oh, well, I mean never mind.'

By the time Morris got home that evening he reckoned he had earned his national minimum wage. He stopped off at The Plentiful Goodness Food Store and stocked up on fish fingers, baked beans and a twenty-five gram pouch of Old Holborn. An hour later his stomach was comfortably full and he was sitting on the toilet, smoking a joint and watching a bizarre programme about Japanese gameshow contestants doing unspeakable things to themselves with a variety of sharp instruments.

Yes, it was the end of a very satisfactory day. All was well in

Morris's world at that moment and he felt justified in believing, no matter how bad things had been in the past, that fortune was now smiling on him and, yes, he dared to hope that she would continue, for whatever reason she had changed her mind about him, to do so. The day's events, combined with the effects of the cannabis, were making him feel really rather mellow.

A knock on the door eventually found its way into his fuddled brain. It took him a moment to gather his wits, and his trousers. When he opened the door there stood a man, somewhere, at a rough guess, between six foot ten and seven feet, with one hairy hand leaning on the frame. From his neck hung a loud assortment of gold jewellery, and both of his massive hands were similarly adorned. Morris, in his stupor, took all of this in without concerning himself with their possible meaning.

'Are you Morris Figg?'

Now on any other day the answer would have been no, try one floor down, in the certain knowledge that Mrs Diggle wouldn't hear him knocking and this person would then go, but he caught Morris off guard.

'Yes, that's me.'

'My name's Mick.'

'Hullo Mick. What can I do for you?' He was still thinking like an undertaker.

Mick pointedly put his foot in the doorway. Morris looked up into his face and for the first time saw what he should have seen before.

'Where's Tinkerbelle?'

18

Morris was sweating. It was cold in the flat but he was still sweating. Mick, on the other hand, wasn't, he was cool. He was wrapping a gold chain round his fist and then letting it go and then wrapping it round again, which had the effect of drawing the viewer's attention to the size of his fist.

'Look, Morris, it's like this. Tinkerbelle is like a sister to me, and well, you know how it is, don't you.'

Morris was getting tired of people assuming he knew how it was. No, he knew absolutely bugger all about anything.

'I promised her dear departed ma and pa I would look after her an' I been doin' that ever since.'

'But Mick ...'

'Yeh, what is it Morris?'

'Um, I mean, what makes you think I know anything about your sister?'

'Nah look, Morris, I didn' say she is my sister, jus' that she's like my sister. Don' go putting words in my mouf now.'

No, definitely not. Morris had no intention of putting anything in his mouf, mouth, whatever, other possibly than the cricket bat from the back of his wardrobe, should the opportunity arise, which he had to concede was unlikely. He had a feeling that any miracles he was due had by now been used up. He just wished he had been given the option to save them up for an emergency. 'Any'ow, as I were sayin' about Tinkerbelle.'

Oh yes, her.

'Well she went back to Wigan see ... '

Warrington actually. Get your story straight.

'To visit 'er little boy.'

Little boy? Oh no, not a little boy, please.

'Only I 'eard she didn' go there at all. She stayed 'ere.'

What, here, in this flat?

'In town.'

Phew.

'Any'ow, I gets this call, see, to ask after her, and I says well I thought she were up there wiv you, and they say nah, she's down there in't she, and I says nah, I put her on the coach like, but any'ow, she never got there. Well, then I starts to wonder, I mean like, if she got off the coach at the next stop, you know.'

No, I can't imagine. Why would a nice girl like that want to do such a thing as not be scrupulously straight with a nice chap like you?

'Any'ow, it turns out she did, cos a friend of mine was on the same coach an' he saw her. Any'ow, 'e reckoned she came back 'ere because my mate Terry says he saw her at the Pink Flamingo. Talkin' to a bloke 'e sold some gear to. You. So 'ere I am.'

Shit. This wasn't looking good. It was at precisely this moment that, had the god of unlikely coincidences been on his toes, there would have been another knock on the door and someone would come and rescue him, but sadly it was not, on this occasion, to be.

'The Pink Flamingo? Isn't that the club behind the old wharf?'

'Yeh, that's it, you're beginning to remember, see?'

'No, I've never been there. Your friend must have been mistaken.'

It was, apparently, the wrong gambit. Mick, he could tell, didn't like it.

'Morris, nah look, don' mess wiv me, cos I'm not in a good mood today, and I fink you know what that means. You was the last person what saw her, so you jus' tell me what 'appened.'

Morris decided, in a moment of clarity, to try the old telling the truth ploy.

'Oh, hold on now, yes, I do remember, now you mention it, the Pink Flamingo.'

Mick, he could tell, approved.

'Yes, I bought some stuff from this bloke and then I asked someone the way to the gents, a very nice young lady, let me see short, blond hair, would that be your friend?'

'Yeh.' Mick was beaming now.

'Yes, it's coming back to me. I went to the gents and smoked some of the stuff I'd just bought and then I went outside and, oh, do you know, I don't think I can remember what happened next. All I can remember is waking up in the hospital.'

'The 'ospital?'

'Yes, the Infirmary. There must have been something in the stuff I bought, something funny. You wouldn't know anything about that, would you?'

'What, Terry sold you some rough dope? That's not right. An' you ended up in the Infirm'ry?'

'Yes, I'm afraid I did. And the police were called because the doctors realised what had happened.'

Mick's demeanour changed. 'An' did you tell them anythin'?'

'What, me, no absolutely not. Even though I could have done, I mean, selling rough dope, well, that's not right, is it?'

'No it ain't mate. Look here, don't' you worry about anythin'. I'll sort Terry out.'

Morris wondered what exactly that meant, but on balance he decided that if being sorted out by Mick was in the offing he would be happy for Terry to have that experience instead

113

of him.

And before he knew it Mick was filling the doorframe on his way out. And no sooner had he gone than there was a knock. He briefly considered grabbing the cricket bat but decided that would be grossly insufficient if he had changed his mind and come back.

But it was Angie.

'Oh, God, Angie. A bit bloody late.'

'Charming. Anyway, who's your friend? I squeezed past him on the stairs.'

'Oh him. That's Mick.'

'Mm, Morris, you do, as I think I've told you before, have some very strange acquaintances. Good God, kiddo, you're shaking. Been having words, have you? Here, let Angie make you a nice soothing cup of tea.'

Morris let her. There are times when a sister is just what you need. He told her what had happened, well, a version of it on account of if he had refused to tell her what she wanted to know she would have been upset, and Angie upset, whilst not in the same league as, say, Mick upset, was exactly what he didn't need right now. While she made the tea he went through to the bedroom to check on Tinkerbelle's money, in case Mick had by some bizarre sleight of hand removed it whilst at the same time threatening him with some GBH. He would have to find somewhere else to hide it. Mick, his instincts told him, like Arnold Schwarzenegger and General Douglas MacArthur, but more like the former, would be back.

'There, get that down you. Now, my deviant little brother, what have you been up to?'

'Really Angie, look, I hope you don't mind but it's been kind of a long day, so could we skip the next bit and get to why you came round?'

'Whatever. Well, it's about Roger.'

'Yeh, I had a kind of feeling it might be. No, not another

book group meeting, please.'

'No, it's alright, he's over that now. Reckons football is more his thing and what with me sharing your complete hate for the game rather than his love of it, that's one thing we don't have to do together.'

'OK, what is it then?'

'I think he suspects.'

'What, that you hate football?'

'Morris, you're not taking this seriously.'

'Sorry. How do you know?'

'Well, on Monday he came home early.'

'And? Oh no, not you and Peter Potter in the kitchen?'

'Yes.'

'Shit. Angie, what the hell were you thinking of?'

'Morris, did you just think what I think you thought?'

'Huh? Could you run that past me again, with different words preferably.'

'Are you saying you think Peter and I were engaged in, um, things, in the kitchen of Roger's home?'

'Yes, weren't you?'

'Morris, don't be so bloody stupid. Of course we weren't. We were talking and drinking coffee.'

'Oh, right. And Roger caught you? Wow, coffee, and Roger never suspected before.'

'Morris, I don't know what's happened to your brain today, but I can see that talking about anything serious to you is a waste of time. Thanks for the tea, I'm going.'

And she did. Morris felt sorry. He had, he knew, been less than sympathetic. On the other hand, what the hell was his sister doing with that useless oik anyway? Peter, not Roger. Actually, come to think of it, him too. It was late, he was dog tired, and now he had Mick to worry about on top of everything else. He needed some sleep. Tomorrow, he knew, the problems would still be there, but tomorrow at least he wouldn't be so tired and he might be able to think straight.

At two o'clock Mrs Diggle's cat woke him, crying at her window pathetically and as it happens pointlessly on account of his mistress being deaf, to be let in. He couldn't get back to sleep after that and finally at half-past three, after another joint and a repeat from the Open University about the mating ritual of the earthworm, he went back to bed and tried counting sheep. That didn't work so he counted money instead, and in the morning he woke, late for work, with great wads of cash scattered over the bedding and spilling onto the floor.

He was, as it turned out, only five minutes late. He might have got away with it but Horace was in the front with a client and ignored him as he walked through to the office but ten minutes later he had finished with the client and stopped ignoring him.

'You're late, Morris.'

'Yes Mr Tite, the number 47 broke down and they had to send out a replacement bus.'

It tripped off the tongue so easily it never occurred to Morris that Horace would even consider believing it.

'You should have left earlier.'

'I did.'

Horace wasn't sure about that. He hid his confusion by going to talk to Doris, leaving Morris to wonder what on Earth Horace thought he meant by you should have left earlier. He sometimes wondered about Horace. Not often, on account of him preferring not to think about him most of the time, but sometimes. Anyway, he had other things on his mind today, like Mick, and Tinkerbelle's money. Or was it Mick's money? Was Mick looking for Tinkerbelle so he could recover the cash, or to kill her himself for reasons best known to himself, or, and Morris thought this was pretty unlikely, out of love?

In any case there was now an urgent requirement for a home for both Tinkerbelle and the money. Well, the second was easy. He would pay it into a bank. On the other hand, he had a feeling that banks might have scruples about accepting that kind of cash from complete strangers. What about the Post Office then? Ditto, especially since they all knew him in the Post Office because he went once a fortnight to cash his Girocheque, and they were pretty likely to wonder why a bloke who cashed one of those every other week was also in possession of a very large quantity of the folding stuff. No, definitely not the Post Office.

There were just too many problems right now vying for his attention. Horace was about to dump another one on him.

'Now, Morris, I want to go through the course work with you this afternoon, see how you're getting on. Can you find some time for that, do you think?'

'Yes of course. Oh, just a minute, no, I've got it all at home. I was working on it last night. Couldn't sleep, so I thought I'd not waste my time on idle thoughts or the TV, you know, get on with something useful.'

'Excellent, Morris, that's most impressive. Well, shall we say tomorrow, after the Biggs job? You won't forget to bring it, will you?'

No, he wouldn't forget. He'd stay up all night reading up on the dos and don'ts of client interviews, preparation of the remains, floral arrangements etcetera etcetera, inbetween finding a final resting place for Tinkerbelle and her money and worrying about what he was going to do if, no, when, Mick paid him another visit. Possibly with a friend. No, skip the friend, because Mick on his own was more than sufficient for the job. Yes, it was a good job Morris was staying in tonight.

Things, however, went better than expected that evening. He got home in good spirits on account of nothing else going wrong for the whole of the rest of the day. Sometimes, he thought, it doesn't take a lot to make you think life is almost worth living.

He opened the Funeral Directors' Course Book and put some fish fingers under the grill. then he dealt with the money. He had read about hiding cash somewhere. He took out the roll of aluminium foil he had bought at The Plentiful Goodness Food Store, tore off two sheets about a foot square, and wrapped a thousand pounds in each one. He put the packages in the fish finger box and stuffed these in the freezer compartment of the fridge. He had to put the entire contents of a family-sized fish finger box under the grill to make room. The fish fingers were his own innovation and he felt quite pleased with himself. Then he opened two baked bean tins, emptied the contents into a saucepan, washed and dried them, and rolled a thousand into each one. He carefully placed them, upside down on account of not thinking to open them at the bottom but still you can't think of everything, at the back of the food cupboard. He carefully lifted the bin liner and placed another two thousand underneath, and in the bathroom he put three bundles, carefully wrapped in plastic bags, in the toilet cistern. Two thousand went under the bedroom lino, spread out like a paper underlay and finally, in desperation, he unscrewed the back of the television and stuffed the last thousand beside the tube.

He stood back and admired his handiwork. Yes, brains beat brawn every time. Mick could take the place apart and he wouldn't find a penny. He hoped.

Which just left twenty-four fish fingers and two tins of baked beans to be consumed.

An hour later Morris was trying to digest that lot whilst struggling with the legal requirements pertaining to the cremation of human remains, when there was a knock at the door. It was gone eleven o'clock. Too late for Angie or Carol Crapovic, his landlord. About the right time for someone bent on mischief. He was looking out of the bedroom window weighing up the chances of survival from two floors up against surviving the attentions of an angry seven foot gangster, when the knocking started again, and this time it didn't stop. But this time it was accompanied by a stage whisper.

'Morris. Morris, are you there? Open up.'

He didn't recognise the voice but even so he somehow didn't see Mick asking politely like that.

'Roger.'

'OK Morris, where is she?'

Shit. Now Roger wanted to find Tinkerbelle. This didn't make any sense at all.

'Roger, where's who?'

'Come on Morris, don't pretend you don't know who I'm talking about.'

'Well mate, I'm sorry to disappoint you but I'm not pretending. Now tell me what the hell is going on or piss off, preferably the second one.'

'Angie.'

Morris let him in. He was confused.

'Angie?'

'Yes, Angie, you know, about five foot five, brown hair with streaks, got a bit of a mouth on her, you came to the wedding, you must remember.'

'Hold on, hold on, you want to know where Angie is?'

'Well well, you seem to have grasped the idea.'

'But Roger, I seem to remember she lives with you.'

'Not any more she doesn't. She's gone.'

'Gone? Where?'

'If I knew that I wouldn't be wasting my time here passing the time of day with you, would I? I was hoping you could shed some light on the matter.'

'Me? Why? I mean, how?'

'Because Morris, you are her brother, and I happen to know she comes round here pretty often and I wouldn't be at all surprised if she tells you some of her sordid little secrets.'

Yes, that's true. 'No, she doesn't talk to me about that kind of thing.'

'What kind of thing?'

'Um, you know, what you're talking about. She probably tells her girlfriends, yes, I expect that's the sort of thing women talk about, I mean, if there is anything to talk about, which I don't think there is. In Angie's case.'

'Well look, she's gone, so there is.'

'But how do you know? Maybe she's had an accident, or got lost and can't find her way home.' Morris was, he realised, struggling.

'Oh, that's what you think, is it? I don't think so. I mean, people who have accidents and end up in hospital don't usually leave a note beforehand saying Roger I'm leaving you goodbye.'

'She did that?' Bloody hell. Angie. 'Where do you think she's gone?'

'Well it's obvious, isn't it?'

Yes. 'No, where?'

'She's with some other man.'

'Angie? No, surely not. Angie? I mean, look, Roger, tell me straight, have you and her been having, you know, marital problems?'

'No, everything's been fine. That's what I can't understand.'

Lying toerag. 'Well why would she leave you then?' He was going to add and who do you think the man is but he felt on safer ground not talking about men at all.

'Well, it's obvious.'

'Uhuh?'

'Yes, she's come under the spell of some unscrupulous manipulator. She's gone off with him thinking it's going to be better with him than me and she's going to be used and end up being thrown away. You wait. Then she'll come running back to me to beg me to take her back again. You'll see.'

Roger was sounding more and more hysterical. Morris would like to have put him right. Anyone less likely to manipulate Angie than the Reverend Potter would be hard to imagine. He wasn't at all sure why his sister had done it, but done it she undoubtedly had. She must have been having some kind of brainstorm. He wondered if it was her idea or Peter's, and knowing Angie very well and Peter a little came down strongly in favour of this being all her own doing. He imagined Peter Potter at home in the vicarage, trying to get rid of Angie before her husband, and the Church authorities, descended on him like several tons of bricks, before he lost his job, his home and his front teeth, not necessarily in that order.

Well, there was only one thing Morris could do for Angie right now, and that was not to tell her husband anything. Not telling people things was, fortunately, something that came quite naturally to him.

'Look, Roger, I promise you if I knew anything I would tell you. You believe me, don't you? '

He wanted to but he knew Morris too well. On the other hand, what Morris said might be true, probably Angie hadn't confided in him.

'Yes.'

Fool.

'Now look, it's late. There's not much we can do now.'

Roger liked the sound of we. It made him feel Morris was on his side. Fool.

'Anyway, I've got a big day tomorrow at work, so if you don't mind I would like to get some kip. I tell you what, I'll come round to the house after work tomorrow and we'll go through the possibilities. Anyway, look, she'll probably have seen reason by then and come back.'

'I might not want her back.'

'Well in that case what are we talking about? Why are you here looking for her if you don't?'

Roger was surprised at the logic of that. So was Morris. It rounded off the conversation nicely and Morris was finally able to shut the door behind his brother-in-law and crash out on the bed. His gargantuan evening meal was beginning to make him feel queasy and he needed some serious quiet if he was going to have any chance of digesting it.

He slept moderately peacefully until three o'clock in the morning, when Mrs Diggle's cat started up again. In a state of nervous exhaustion and nausea, Morris opened the window, leaned out in the cold night air and threw up, copiously, all over it.

20

In the morning he woke up with the wind blowing straight through the window he had omitted to close. He had a quick shower, decided to skip breakfast under the circumstances of last night, pressed his suit and polished his shoes for the Biggs funeral, gathered up his study materials, carried out his routine check of the money in the fridge, the water cistern and under one corner of the lino in case a sprite had come in during the night, possibly through the open window, and purloined it, which it hadn't, and left the flat on time with a sore head and a sorer stomach, but at least on time.

While Doris made tea, Morris went through the order of service with the pallbearers in the usual briefing place which was the alley behind the office on account of Wally not being allowed to smoke anywhere else.

'Dear oh dear Morris, you don't look too bright this morning, if I might be so bold. Rough night?'

'Wally, why would you think such a thing? I was, as planned, tucked up by eleven o'clock, with my copy of Embalming for Beginners for bedtime reading. And give me a light.'

'D'you know, I'm beginning to worry about you. You're taking this all a bit seriously, aren't you?'

OK, the bit about Embalming for Beginners wasn't true, but Wally had a point. Morris realised he was looking forward to the funeral. Yes, try as he might not to, he was actually starting to like the funeral business.

While he gave the cars a last-minute inspection he tried to put today's list of problems to be dealt with out of his mind, and if that wasn't possible then at least in a section of his mind that wasn't needed for the job in hand. There were so many problems now that he was forgetting the one that had brought him here, Tinkerbelle. He sometimes wondered if she couldn't just stay where she was. Except of course for Marty. And Mick. And possibly the police. No, on second thoughts, perhaps she couldn't just stay where she was.

Before they set off though, Horace called him into his office. He looked serious, more serious than was usual even for him, even before a funeral.

'Morris, come in, sit down please.' He wasn't smiling, not even the way he usually did when he wanted to put Morris off his guard. This really was serious.

'Morris, before we leave, there is something I must talk to you about, something, I'm afraid, of a rather serious nature.'

Morris could think of a lot of things going on in his life right now of a pretty serious nature, but he couldn't think that any of those would concern Horace or even come to his attention.

'Something has been brought to my attention by, well, let's say by a client.'

'Yes?'

'Yes Morris. I believe you were heard to make a comment at the Rumbelow job last week.'

Well get on with, for God's sake, whatever it is.

'Yes, a comment, that if it turns out to be supported by further evidence or, should you be honest enough to confess you yourself would admit to it, would, I am afraid, have serious repercussions.'

'Repercussions?'

'Yes, of the P45 kind.'

Morris racked his brains over the Rumbelow funeral, but

nothing would come. What the hell had he said?

'Mr Rumbelow, you may recall, died of lung cancer.'

Shit. Now he remembered.

'And you were heard to say, in a whisper that was unfortunately heard by one of his relatives, that the last time Mr Rumbelow would ever smoke would be at the crematorium.'

Yes, that was it. Wally thought it was hilarious. It was a brilliant joke, only the timing was perhaps unfortunate.

'Do you admit to making this comment?'

If he said no, Horace wouldn't believe him, so he went for the honesty card and said yes.

'I see. Well, that leaves little to be said. Morris, I shall be sorry to lose you, but if you have been planning a future in funeral direction you may want to think again. I shall discuss the matter with Doris when we get back and let you know of our decision. That is all. Go and do your job.'

They transferred the coffin from the chapel of rest to the hearse, climbed into the cars and waited for Horace to start the engine up. There was a momentary pause of anticipation, like there was before every job, and then the Daimler's engine purred into life, and nothing happened. What was supposed to happen was that Horace put the automatic transmission into drive and slowly moved off, but he didn't. What actually happened was that he slowly slumped forward onto the steering wheel and remained there, quite still, while Morris, sitting next to him, watched in fascination. He sat there for several seconds while Horace continued to do nothing slumped over the wheel, before it dawned in him that this wasn't what normally happened. No, there was something wrong, he could tell.

He put his hand on Horace's shoulder, gingerly, and shook it gently at first and then more vigorously.

'Mr Tite? Mr Tite, are you alright?'

The answer to that was a resounding no, he was not alright.

Morris, goaded into action now, leapt out of the car and ran for the office. The others in the car behind looked on in confusion, unable to see what was happening.

They were still there, sitting gormlessly, making jokes about Horace dying at the wheel, when the ambulance pulled up with its blue light flashing. It was, the paramedics later commented, the first time they had been called to resuscitate someone at a funeral parlour.

While the ambulance took Horace to the hospital there still was, Morris reminded them, a funeral to attend to. Wally said if they hang on a while they could deal with two together but Morris said first of all that wasn't funny and second of all the Biggs family were waiting at St Elmo's Church and the funeral was going ahead as planned, now, because service is service and a well-run funeral was what Horace would have wanted, would want, since let's not assume he's actually dead shall we. They said something like ooh, what's got into him, and then Morris took over the wheel of the Daimler and they did exactly what he had said.

While he drove, Morris pondered on what was happening to Horace, and while he was doing that he wondered if his disappointment in him was in some way implicated, or perhaps that was being fanciful. The paramedics had said he was still alive, but that was when they put him in the ambulance. He felt something, but he couldn't figure out what it was and it finally came to him as they pulled up at the church, and normally he would have seen Horace get out and take charge, the job he now had to take over himself. It was about his relationship with Horace. Angie had said something a few weeks ago about it, even though she had never actually met the old man, but just from the way, she said, Morris was always going on about him. Horace had become, over the months since Morris joined the firm, a replacement for the person Morris never admitted to missing, since he left his mother when Morris was six. Yes, he could see it now,

127

Horace Tite had taken on the role of father figure to Morris Figg. He sat there a few seconds more while the others busied themselves, pondering on this idea, realising it was true, and the last thing he thought before he put on his funeral director's face and buried Mrs Biggs, was that he hoped he wouldn't be doing the same next week for Horace.

The Biggs family thanked Morris afterwards for a smoothly-run funeral and enquired where Mr Tite was, to which he replied, tactfully, that he was rather poorly and was sorry not to be able to look after them personally. He got away as soon as possible and drove over to the hospital in the limousine while Wally took the hearse back to the office.

He found a nurse to ask directions of and then he found Doris waiting anxiously for news herself. He comforted her as best he could but he wasn't exactly sure if it was comfort she wanted or congratulations. Yes, he thought, you'd love it if he dies and you can win your little bet by outliving him. Well, the old bastard's made of stronger stuff than that, you'll see. He wasn't at all sure that was true, and when a doctor came to advise them that Mr Tite had had a stroke, and was now in ITU, Morris found himself worrying as if he really were his father. He tried to hate Horace and resent all his petty meannesses, but he found he couldn't. He found that he didn't want to lose him like he lost his real father, except that his real father didn't have the grace to die but just walked out on them.

They sat waiting, not talking much. Morris didn't know what to say, and anyway he suspected Doris of disloyalty and he wasn't sure if he liked her now. In fact, now he came to think about it he didn't think he had ever liked her. Of course, he knew, he might be overreacting. And then, out of the blue, she started talking. He wasn't sure at first if she was talking to him or herself, or perhaps some unseen third party, but he listened and as he did that she faced him and spoke directly to him, even if he couldn't be sure if she knew it was him she was talking to.

'I've seen a lot of dead people in my time. It's funny, well not funny at all but you know what I mean. In the hospital, like us, the friends and relatives gather round the dying man and they don't want him to die, of course, unless they hated him or they want his money but no, most of them don't want him to die.'

In the bright lights of the waiting area Morris sat and listened, not daring to interrupt. Anyway, what was there to comment on, to agree or disagree with?

'Yes, I've seen thousands, too many. And they don't realise till it's too late.'

Morris wondered what they didn't realise, whoever they were.

'It changes, everything changes, in a flash, in that moment between life and death. A dead person isn't just someone who isn't alive. They're someone who isn't anything. They lie here in this place, dying, like old Horace, but as long as they hold on they exist, they're a person, with all that means, then after they die, in that split second it takes, they move from being to not being. From a person to a body. From someone to worry about to someone to bury. Except even the word someone isn't appropriate, is it? We don't bury people, we bury bodies, and bodies aren't someone, they're just lumps of something that used to be people.'

He wondered now if she was going to start on religion. He'd never heard her talk about any kind of faith before, just responding to the particular ritual requested for any particular funeral. He realised then how very little he knew about Doris at all.

Then she no longer stared into nothingness and looked intently into his eyes.

'Young Morris, do you have any idea what I've just been saying?'

What he thought was that Doris had, perhaps for the first

time, been looking at her own mortality, but he didn't want to say that. He put his hand on her arm. The skin was wafer-thin, like onion-skin he thought, only soft, surprisingly soft, and immediately beneath it, it seemed to him, was her bone. Doris was not made of flesh, it seemed to him, and it seemed to him too that she was nearer to death herself than anyone he had ever known. Except, perhaps, for poor old Horace Tite.

They sat for a while, saying nothing, and it got late and finally he sent her home in a taxi and said he would wait for news and phone her if there was any.

There was, about one in the morning.

'Mr Figg, isn't it?'

'Yes doctor.'

'Are you a relative of Mr Tite?'

'Yes, I mean no, I'm um, a colleague, well I work for him actually.'

'I see. Are there any family here?'

'No, not yet. They're on their way from Nottingham. Look, can you tell me?'

'Oh yes, he'll be fine.'

Well why the hell couldn't you say that before? 'Thank you doctor.'

'If I were you I should go home and get some rest. I promise you he'll still be alive when you come back in the morning.'

Morris sat in the car park of the hospital oblivious to the bustle of ambulances and people and lights, and tried to feel whatever it was he needed to feel. The old man was threatening to fire him. Did he care about that? He wasn't sure. Yes, there was Tinkerbelle, who was the reason for all of this in the first place, but now there was more, something else. Maybe Doris had started him thinking. He didn't know what to think though, and he was still there, fast asleep, when the sun came up in the morning and the doctor knocked on the car window.

'Mr Figg? Good morning. Look, I'm just going off shift, but why don't you go up and see him. I think you'll find him as well as can be expected.'

Whatever that meant. Well, of course it meant alive, because not even the most inept doctor would call a dead man as well as can be expected. Mind you.

But he really was. OK, he wasn't talking, or moving, but the machines by his bed said he was definitely alive. The nurse reassured him.

'You see this one here, watch the line. You see how it goes up and down, well that means his vital functions are pretty normal. This one's his brain and that's not quite normal I'm afraid, but don't worry, he's strong. He'll do pretty well the doctor reckons. He may not be able to return to work for a while though. What sort of work does he do? '

'Funeral director.'

'Oh, I see.'

And with that she suddenly remembered she had another patient to see to. Morris stayed a little longer, realised he was starving and drove home for a shower and some breakfast. An hour after that he opened up the office, only when he tried the lock he found it was already open. Doris must have come in early and forgotten to lock the door behind her. Well, she would be waiting by the phone. He should, he thought too late, have called her at home to give her the good news.

She wasn't in the front, so he checked the kitchen and she wasn't there either. It was quiet, and he wondered if she had got a taxi straight back to the office last night and fallen asleep somewhere. He tried the chapel of rest, which was where she usually slept, but no, that was empty. Which only left Horace's office. The door was shut and it creaked a little as he opened it. He had been meaning to oil the hinges. It was gloomy inside. The curtains were closed and only a chink of early morning sunlight found its way in.

He saw her through the gloom at Horace's desk, sitting in her straight-backed way in the half-light, an odd way, he thought, to fall asleep. Except that when he came closer he could see that her eyes weren't closed, they were open and staring blankly ahead. Doris was doing a very good imitation of dead.

The old bastard had won the bet.

21

Morris sat down in the other chair and looked at her. He tried to understand what all this meant. Everyone around him kept dying. Well, no, that wasn't strictly true, because they usually only died once. Maybe it was something about working at an undertaker's. Or maybe something had brought him to Widdlecombe and Tite because death was somehow part of his life now. Well, at least Horace wasn't dead, at least he wasn't the last time he saw him but you never know, two hours was beginning to look like a long time in Morris's life.

He was used to dealing with bodies by now, what with Tinkerbelle and then death becoming his profession, but he had never had to deal with someone who had died unofficially. Everyone else, apart from Tinkerbelle obviously, came with a nice certificate which said they were allowed to be dead and Widdlecombe and Tite were allowed to bury them. Now, he had a real live corpse on his hands that had died without the right paperwork. He panicked for a moment and then when he had finished panicking it came to him that what you do when someone dies, as long as the circumstances aren't suspicious in which case you might want to think about it before you do anything precipitous, is to phone someone.

But do you phone the police or the ambulance? Well, it was a bit bloody late for an ambulance, on account of Doris being obviously way beyond the possibility of resuscitation, but on the the other hand what did it have to do with the fuzz?

Oh yes, sir, I see, she's a bit dead, isn't she, have you phoned the ambulance? No, I thought you might know what to do. Oh no, sir, we only deal with suspicious deaths. This isn't suspicious, is it sir, I mean you don't know something else that you ought to tell us, do you?

No, perhaps not the police. He keyed 999, then before it rang he slammed the receiver down. Hold on, this wasn't an emergency. It was a bit bloody pointless an ambulance screaming round here with its lights flashing to pick up a stiff. On the other hand, how do you get an ambulance any other way? On the other hand, maybe he shouldn't call them at all, maybe he should call a doctor, but on the other hand how was he supposed to know who Doris's GP was? He didn't even know where she lived.

'Hullo, emergency service, which service do you require?'

'Um, ambulance, I think.'

'Is someone ill or injured sir?'

'No.'

'Then why are you calling the ambulance service?'

'Because, um, I've got a body.'

'I think, sir, we should send the police round. What's your address?'

'No, no, don't do that. Look, it's Doris.'

'What's Doris sir?'

'Doris is dead.'

'Are you certain about that sir?'

'Look, I've seen enough dead people in my time to know one when I see one.'

'Um, look, we're tracing your call now, so don't you worry about anything, because we'll have someone with you in no time at all. I'm Jenny. Do you want to tell me your name?'

Shit. Now they were trying to trace some psychopathic killer and when they did that he had a horrible feeling they were going to send an armed response unit to Widdlecombe and Tite to rescue Doris's body. This wasn't going well. He was about to slam the phone down but it occurred to him that if he did that they had probably already traced the number and in about ten minutes the premises were going to be surrounded by men in balaclavas with orders to shoot on sight.

'Look, Jenny, are you still there?'

'Yes, don't worry, I'm not going away. How are things there?'

'Look Jenny, I think I should explain.'

'Yes, why don't you?'

And he did. He told Jenny everything, for once exactly how it happened. She didn't sound totally convinced but she said she would get an ambulance there and, just for his own reassurance, the local police would check in on things as well. How did that sound? Well, it wasn't exactly what he meant but it was at least better than the Flying Squad.

Then he sat down for a last quiet few minutes with Doris. He found her staring eyes unnerving but he didn't want to touch her. He tried to figure out what the events of the last twenty four hours meant, for him anyway. He knew what they meant for Doris on account of her being out of things now, and he thought he knew what they meant for Horace because whatever happened it was going to be some time before he came back to work, if at all. He looked round at Horace's office, the pictures of him and Frank Widdlecombe and sundry other men whom he took to be their predecessors in tail coats in front of a variety of hearses over the years. He felt he should tell someone, but he didn't know who. Well, of course there were Horace's relatives, they would be down from Nottingham today, they would know what to do.

That was when he remembered they had a funeral to do today, the Forbes-Smythe cremation. It would have to go ahead, the show must go on, he didn't know how but he knew it was somehow his responsibility. Once he had dealt with

Doris. He was woken from his reverie by the ambulance, which thankfully arrived without its blue light going.

They took her away quickly and efficiently, which just left the police.

'Good morning sir, I'm Sergeant Crump. You found the body, did you?'

'Yes Sergeant.'

'Um, just a minute. Do I know you?'

I hope not. 'I don't think so, Sergeant. Have you ever used our services before, for a relative perhaps?'

This satisfactorily threw him off the scent.

'Well, name?'

'Morris Figg.'

'No sir, the deceased.'

'Oh, right. Doris.'

'OK, Doris. And did the lady have a surname?'

'I expect so.'

Sergeant Crump had been on shift all night dealing with a fracas at the Pink Flamingo. He had been getting ready to go off when this call came in. His patience was at a low ebb.

'Look Mr Figgs ...'

'Figg.'

'Yes sir that's what I said. Well look sir, it would assist me greatly if you could just answer my questions and then we could go to bed.'

'What?'

'Me, I mean me, I could go home, if you wouldn't mind.'

'Oh, no.'

'So, Doris's name?'

'Oh, um, Fosdyke.'

'That's better, Doris Fosdyke. Occupation?'

'No, I wouldn't say so. She was ninety-two.'

'Blimey. I mean, well, that's a good age isn't it? Was she your grandmother then?'

'Oh no, she was, well she was Doris. She made the tea.'

'I see. Well, if you could just give me a name of a relative, we can do the rest.'

Morris realised he knew just about nothing about Doris. 'I don't think she's got any, I mean had any. The only person who would know is Horace, um, Mr Tite, the owner of the business.'

'I see, and where can I contact him? Will he be at work later perhaps?'

'Oh no, he's at the Infirmary. He had a stroke yesterday you see.'

'Yes, I'm beginning to. Things aren't going well here, are they? A run of bad luck, you might say.'

'Mm. Well, Sergeant, if that's all, to be honest I've got a lot to sort out.'

And so Morris found himself in sole charge of Widdlecombe and Tite, with a cremation to do and God knows what else. He had a stiff neck from sleeping in the car, and in any case it had hardly been enough sleep to see him through a busy day's work. He lay down in the chapel of rest for half an hour. Two hours later Wally came in and woke him up.

'Oi Morris, come on man, wake up.'

'Oh, it's you Wally, God, what's the time?'

'Ten o'clock, well just gone.'

'Oh shit.'

'Yeh, probably. Anyhow, what's happened?'

'Oh, she's dead.'

'What? Who's dead?'

'Doris.'

'No, mate, you mean Horace.'

'What? No, not Horace, Doris.'

'Look, Morris, wake up, come on. Horace took ill yesterday, remember? They took him to the hospital. And he died, yes?'

'No Wally, he didn't, Doris did.'

Wally whistled softly. He couldn't compute this. 'Look, Morris, I distinctly remember Horace collapsing and going off in an ambulance.'

'Yes, that's right.'

'So?'

'So he had a stroke, but he's OK, well he's not OK like you or me but he's alive. But Doris isn't.'

'Bloody hell! Why not?'

'Dunno. I came in this morning and she was sitting in Horace's chair, dead.'

'Bloody hell.'

'Yes, that's what I've been thinking.'

'Shit.'

'That too, and more. Anyhow, we've got the Forbes-Smythe job at two o'clock. We've got to get ready. Can you find another pallbearer? I'll have to do Horace's job.'

'Yeh, I'll see what I can do.'

Morris sat with his head in his hands. What he needed was a nice cup of tea. Now he knew what it was Doris did.

There was, of course, an inquest, but after the post-mortem report there was little doubt about how Doris had died. Her heart had simply stopped beating. Morris wondered if it was because she thought she had won the bet and outlived Horace, or it just gave up with the excitement. Anyway, the coroner released the body and that just left the funeral. Wally thought they should give the job to the Co-op but Morris insisted they do it themselves.

It was when her bird-like body was in the casket that Morris's brain had one of those moments of clarity, only it was helped along the way by something Wally said.

'Blimey, I never realised she was so small.'

'Yes, they shrink somehow, don't they?'

'Yeh, you could get two in here and save some money.'

Morris looked at Doris, and then he looked at the coffin. It was true, there was a lot of space. He waited for Wally to leave and then he got out Horace's measure and calculated how much room was available. Doris took up less than half the depth with her frail little body. Yes, he could see it now. There was, indeed, room for two.

Doris and Tinkerbelle.

22

Morris rang Marty.

'Marty, are you busy?'

'Well well, if it isn't my old friend Morris, the man who calls when he wants something. What is it?'

'I want something.'

'Aha, told you. What? Well, that's the first question and the second one is will there be any money in it for me this time? Oh and the third one is when are you going to arrange a decent burial for that poor girl in the freezer?'

'I want you to help me get her to Widdlecombe and Tite for her funeral, which nicely covers questions one and three and the answer to number two is yes, there's a hundred quid in it for you.'

Marty was trying to remember what the questions were so he could work out what the answers meant. He gave up and focused on the hundred pounds instead.

'OK, I'm your man. When?'

'Friday afternoon. The funeral's on Saturday. I've got another job on at two, so I'll be round about six. Is the van working?'

'Sure, but aren't you going to take her in a hearse?'

'I don't think so. That might look a bit odd, loading up at a second-hand furniture warehouse, don't you think?'

'Yeh, maybe. Shame though.'

The Forbes-Smythe cremation went pretty smoothly apart

from the spare pallbearer Wally found who turned out to be only five foot two and the coffin sloped so much while they were carrying it from the car the flowers kept sliding off. Morris made a mental note not to ask Wally to help again. Assuming of course that there was an again after the last job on Friday. Well, there was Doris of course.

On the Friday he dashed home afterwards and got changed into something less like a funeral director and ran all the way round to Marty's warehouse. They got Tinkerbelle out of the freezer and wrapped her in a large heavy-duty plastic bag Marty had saved from a roll of carpet. Once she was safely in the back of the van Morris was about to close the doors when Marty stopped him.

'Morris, Morris, have you no sense of dignity? And you an undertaker and all. Wait a mo.'

A mo turned into twenty minutes. Morris paced up and down anxiously. Hanging around with a corpse in the back of a van wasn't exactly his first choice of activities at half past six on an autumn evening. Marty finally came panting back with a bunch of assorted flowers in his hand.

'Couldn't find anywhere open, only the park, so these will have to do.'

He climbed up and placed them reverently on Tinkerbelle. And then, to Morris's further amazement, he made the sign of the cross.

'For God's sake, Marty, get a bloody move on. This is no time for that stuff. You can come to the funeral.'

That was a mistake. There wasn't, of course, going to be one of those, not an official one anyway, and certainly not a Catholic one. He slammed the door shut once again, tied the handles together for good measure, and they climbed into the cab, and Marty put the key in the ignition and turned it and nothing happened.

Shit.

They got out again and opened up the bonnet. It was too

dark to see anything, not that either of them had the kind of mechanical expertise that would have made being able to see under the bonnet a good thing, but still, it's a man thing, staring blankly at an engine that won't start as if staring at it is part of what makes it go again.

'Morris, get in and turn the key again.'

That's another man thing. If the engine won't start, one person stares at it while the other turns the key, on account perhaps of engines like to be watched while they work. Or in this case, surprise surprise, don't work.

'It's not starting.'

No, well, something to do with the bleeding obvious comes to mind.

'OK, look, there's no time to hang around, call the AA.'

'Morris, I don't think Alcoholics Anominous are going to be much use.'

Morris banged his head on the side of the van. It made a hollow, mocking kind of sound.

'Look, don't you have breakdown cover?'

'What, you mean medical insurance?'

'What? Marty, what the hell are you talking about?'

'You know, in case I have a mental breakdown?'

Morris banged his head on the side of the van again. Tears were starting in his eyes. He didn't know how much longer he could carry on before he himself had one of those. Or killed Marty. Only then there would be two bodies, and he didn't think Doris's coffin had quite that much room to spare. All of these thoughts passed through his mind while he tore at his hair. And it was while he was doing this that he thought he heard a voice.

'Hullo hullo, what's all this here then?'

He looked up. Marty looked up. No, they hadn't imagined it.

'Sergeant, um Sergeant ....'

'Crump, Sir. I do believe we've met before. Having a

problem are you?'

Yes, well, it's like this, we've got a dead prostitute in the back and we're going to bury her illegally tomorrow in someone else's coffin, and if we don't get a move on ...

'Yes, Sergeant, it's the engine.' Morris hoped that Marty would stay in the shadows. Fat chance.

'I see. Aha, Mr Finnigan, I think. Yes, how interesting. And what, may I ask, are we up to this evening?'

Look, it's the body, I told you.

'Well, I sometimes help Mr Finnigan here out with a job, on account of his accident, and he's got a house job to do this evening in Telford Road and well, we're trying to get there but we can't.'

'Accident?'

'What? Oh yes, well, he doesn't like to talk about it, but I believe it happened at the police station. He broke his arm. Accidentally, I expect.'

'But Morris ...'

'No Marty, this is no time for niceties. you know what happened better than anyone.'

'But Morris ...'

'Yes, yes, of course. This is not the time to have this discussion, which I'm sure your solicitor will be writing to the police authority about very soon, so if you don't mind Sergeant?'

'Well, sir, if it's like that, I'll be off. Oh, just one minute though.'

Yes, what the bloody hell is it now? Fancy a bit of a chat do we? No-one else to bother at this time of night?

Sergeant Crump stuck his hands under the bonnet of the van and did something that neither of them could see.

'Uhuh, yes, that's the problem, now if I can just ... uhuh ... got it, right, get in and try starting her up sir.'

Oh yeh, very impressive. As if.

'Right, go on Marty.'

143

Morris's driving licence still had ten days before it sprang back into life, and he had a horrible feeling Sergeant Crump might know that and that sitting in a vehicle with the engine running might constitute driving. No, he wasn't going to fall for that. On the other hand, the engine wasn't going to run anyway. Except that it did. It coughed, it spluttered, it started and then it stopped, but Marty kept his foot on the throttle and turned the key again and it coughed into life. A cloud of blue smoke belched out of the exhaust and the engine settled into an irregular beat.

'Well sir, I think you'll find that will get you to your appointment. Well drive safely now.'

Morris and Marty leapt into the cab and were about to drive off. The Sergeant leant through the window though.

'Oh, actually, you can do me a small service, if you would. I've got to get back to the station now, so if you wouldn't mind, you've got to go right past it pretty well on the way to Telford Road.'

'Telford Road?'

'Yes, your appointment.'

'Oh, yes, of course. Well, um, hop in.'

And he did. It was a bit of a squeeze, and conversation was a bit awkward, but Marty set off for the police station. There was hardly a choice. And they almost made it, but no more than two minutes from their destination the sergeant's radio crackled into life.

'Sergeant Crump. Yes? Yes. I see. Yes, I've got transport, I can be there in ten minutes.'

Got transport? Got bloody transport?

'OK lads, sorry about this, but important police business. There's been an accident up at Tamworth Park. I'm going to have to ask you to take me there, won't take long.'

Did they have an option? Marty took the next left and Morris closed his eyes in prayer. The accident turned out to be a cyclist who had hit a lamppost. A bit bloody careless,

Morris thought, but then he wasn't feeling charitable. Sergeant Crump got on his radio. It seemed an ambulance had been sent but had since been diverted to a priority job, a major RTA on the bypass. Could he get the cyclist to the hospital himself?

Oh yes, why not, we'll put him in the back with the stiff.

PC Penny was in attendance. He looked more than a bit surprised to see his sergeant get out of a rusty white van, and surprised again when Morris jumped out too. He was trying to work this one out when Sergeant Crump instructed him to help him get the injured party into the van.

'Open up the back sir and Constable Penny can sit with him.'

'Er, actually, that would be a problem.'

'Yes sir, why is that?'

'The fish.'

'Fish?'

'Yes, you see Mr Finnigan and I have been fishing, and we caught about half a ton of mackerel and well, we've got to take it to my, um, sister's place and freeze it so we can pick up the job we're going to. Later. Only the fish has come out and it's all over the floor and, well, it's a horrible mess, so I don't think Constable Penny would want to sit with all that, would he?'

PC Penny looked like he wouldn't.

So they put the cyclist in the front, spread carefully over Sergeant Crump and Morris, while Marty threw his bike, or what was left of it, in the back with the fish, AKA Tinkerbelle, and PC Penny continued on his foot patrol. Then Marty climbed back into the cab, again, and set off for the hospital while the cyclist groaned and bled slowly onto Morris's trousers.

'Well lads, this is most public spirited of you I'm sure. Yes, especially you Mr Finnigan. This will go a long way to mending relations with the service.'

145

Excellent.

Twenty minutes later Marty screeched to a halt outside A and E at the Infirmary. A nurse helped the sergeant get the cyclist out and they were about to drive off when there was a bang on the side of the van.

'Oh, one more thing, lads. If you wouldn't mind dropping the bicycle off at the station sometime. At your convenience of course. Well, thanks a lot and, as if you need me to say it, be careful out there.'

Oh we will, we will. If we see any of your colleagues, we'll be careful and drive off in the opposite direction.

When they got to Widdlecombe and Tite they found the plastic bag had come adrift and they had to spend ten minutes untangling the remains of the bike from the body, which they didn't completely succeed at so Tinkerbelle, when she finally got buried, was laid to rest with half a mudguard inextricably attached to the hem of her dress but Morris thought that was better than tearing the material any more than was absolutely necessary.

They put the coffin on the floor and Marty let Morris get Doris out. He had a thing about bodies. He'd helped move Uncle Harry when he died in the pub after the wedding, and now Morris was making him do it again. They got Tinkerbelle in the coffin but Doris was light enough that Morris could manage on his own. He laid her gently on top of Tinkerbelle, silently apologised for the indignity, and placed Marty's flowers on top. Then, with considerable relief, he screwed the lid down.

'Catholic, was she?'

'Who, Tink, um, Mary?'

'Marie, you said. And anyway, I mean the other one?'

'Oh, Doris, dunno.'

'If you don't know if she's Catholic, how can you give her a Catholic burial?'

Really, any other gormless questions while we're at it?

'Look, Marty, I think you can see that what we've got here is, shall we say, an unusual situation. I mean burying two people in the same coffin is, I would be the first to suggest, economical, but I would also have to admit it's not exactly what you would call, well, totally in accordance with the regulations.'

'But you said it was all legal and above board.'

'Well, strictly speaking, yes. Sort of. But look, I couldn't find any other way, and you wouldn't want Marie here hanging around for ever, would you? Now come on, help me out here Marty, for God's sake let's just get this over with can we because frankly I'm pretty bloody knackered and I don't think I can do this much longer.'

Marty looked shocked. He had never seen his friend this emotional before, not and sober at the same time. He felt guilty now. He put his hand on Morris's shoulder.

'There there old pal, don't you worry about it. I'm sure your reward will come at the appointed time and all that. It's a grand thing you're doing. And by the way, can you give me that hundred quid you promised?'

And with that he gave Morris a last manlike hug, stuffed a wad of tenners into his pocket, and drove off into the night.

And for once, Morris really was too tired to think anything bad of Marty. No, just at that moment, he thought his old friend was really not such a bad bloke. Which just goes to show how far gone he was.

When he got home there was a message on his answering machine. Would he ring Roger?

No.

23

Morris recruited another couple of pall bearers in time for Doris's funeral on the Saturday. They would need all the help they could get. Tinkerbelle had defrosted overnight, which Morris hadn't thought of, and he had to mop up a large pool of water on the floor before he let the others in.

Wally was his usual complaining self.

'Bloody hell, Morris, she was only a little old lady. This coffin weighs a ton. What have you put in here, a second body, you know, bury one, get one free?'

'No, no, it's, um, the sand.' How he did it he didn't know.

'What the hell are you talking about mate?'

'It's the sand, in the coffin.'

They put it back down again so Wally could argue.

'Morris, why the bloody hell are we burying a load of sand with Doris?'

'It was in her will.'

'Nah, you're not making sense mate.'

'Look it turns out Doris was a Copt.' Thank God for the Open University.

'What, you mean she was a retired policewoman?'

'What? No, not a cop, a Copt.'

'Oh yeh, and what's one of those when it's at home?'

'Wally, this is why you are a pallbearer and I'm a management trainee. It's the education. The Copts are the descendants of the ancient Egyptians.'

Wally weighed this one up. 'Look mate, are you tying to tell me we're going to mummify Queen Nefer... , Neferthingy here?'

'No, of course not. It was in her will, see, she wanted to be buried with Egyptian sand. On account of her being a Copt. It's some kind of Copt thing, apparently.'

'So did you get the sand all the way from Egypt then?'

'No, B and Q.'

'Right. Aha, but if she's one of these Copt things, how come she's being buried at St Elmo's?'

'Because, my dear Wally, the Copts, unlike you, are Christians.'

'Really?'

'Cross my heart and hope to die.'

'I wouldn't go saying things like that round here mate. A bit bloody risky if you ask me. Actually, now you come to mention it, it's like that bloke we did last year, now what was his name? Herbie, what was that bloke's name, you know, the one we did last year from the nut house?'

'Napoleon.'

'No, his real name.'

'Dunno mate.'

'Well anyway Morris, there was this bloke up at the asylum, reckoned he was Napoleon Bona ... , Bonathingy, and anyway one day he died and we got the job, only it turned out he had a will too.'

'You don't say.'

'Yeh, he said on account of him being the Emperor of France he wanted to be buried on French soil.'

'So did you take him to France and bury him there?'

'Oh no, the family wouldn't pay. They had a vanload of earth carted over from Dieppe and they put that in the grave before the coffin. Technically, you see, he was then buried on French soil, so they'd complied with the will and got their hands on his money.'

Morris whistled through his teeth. He was impressed. He didn't feel quite so bad now about Tinkerbelle and Doris together.

By the time they got the coffin in the church they were badly in need of a cup of tea and a smoke. Morris could have done with something stronger, on account of the particular stress he was under but that, he felt, would have been risky.

Horace was wheeled into the church by one of his relatives down from Nottingham. He didn't recognise Morris and Morris was pretty sure he didn't know why he was there. Well at least it meant he wouldn't remember what happened before the stroke as far as firing Morris was concerned, or the driving test he was supposed to take, but that might be pretty unimportant now because Morris knew that without Horace there was no Widdlecombe and Tite. So it was back to the Jobcentre on Monday.

The funeral went off with only one small hitch. They were carrying the coffin from the hearse to the grave when one of Wally's stand-in pallbearers started twitching. Then his spare hand went down the back of his collar and he had a look of extreme disgust on his face which he tried unsuccessfully to hide from the congregation. Morris could see what the problem was, Tinkerbelle was dripping down his neck. Yes, he sympathised with the man, but there was nothing he could do. Well, he would have to remember to ask Wally to find a stand-in for the stand-in for next time, if there was a next time.

And then, thankfully, it was over, and Tinkerbelle was safely under six feet of Barton clay.

'Hullo there, you're Morris I think?'

'Yes?'

'Rachel da Souza. How do you do. I understand you have been running the firm since my father's stroke.'

'Your father?'

'Yes, Horace Tite, remember? Your boss. Da Souza is my married name.'

'Well, I wouldn't call it running. Just minding the shop, kind of.'

'Well, Morris, I think you've been doing very well, by the look of today's funeral. Doris, wasn't it?'

Yes, and Tinkerbelle.

So, the old bugger had a daughter then. And, although he was trying not to be too obvious about it, not bad, either. No wedding ring. Morris assumed that meant even if she did have a married name she no longer had the husband who gave it to her. Mind you, these days, who could tell? Most people weren't married. It didn't mean they weren't shacked up.

'On your own are you? I mean, for the funeral. Mr da Souza not with you then?'

'Not very subtle, I'm afraid. No, Freddie da Souza is in Florida with Ellie Colbeck, my erstwhile best friend.'

'Oh, why's that?'

'You mean why is he with her or why is she erstwhile? Well, the answer's the same. Because she's younger than me, she's got bigger tits, and her father's rich.'

She had such a nice smile when she said it he smiled too, then he suddenly stopped smiling in case she thought he was smiling because he was pleased she wasn't married, or something like that. Morris was a bit confused.

'Morris, actually, I wanted to talk to you. Could we arrange that for later? Strictly business, I'm afraid.'

Shame. Still, that's what she says now.

When all the funeral directing had been finished Rachel took her father back to the nursing home, and Morris walked back to the cemetery, which was empty now, of living people anyway, and stood by the fresh graveside. He tried to imagine what it was like to be in a coffin, under six feet of earth, the way Doris had talked about it so recently at the hospital. One minute she was alive, sitting in the office, and the next she no longer existed. He was trying to get his head round that one at the same time as trying to understand what it meant now, for

151

Doris. Was she there, with Tinkerbelle, or wasn't she? He wasn't at all sure why he wanted to know that, but he thought it might be something to do with his feeling of guilt for putting them together.

Rachel came back and picked him up in her car.

'Let's eat, shall we? No disrespect, but I don't do funeral food. Fancy a Chinese?'

Anything, as long as it's with you. Morris realised he was suffering not only from the stress of the last few weeks but from serious woman deprivation. He just hoped he wouldn't do anything rash. He didn't want to spoil his chances out of desperation. The last time he did that ... well, they had just buried the result.

He ate like it was the last supper. He felt like he hadn't eaten for weeks. He enjoyed it so much he forgot to lust after Rachel.

'Well, you can pack it away, can't you?'

'Um, sorry, I've been under a lot of stress lately, haven't been eating properly.'

'No, that's what I wanted to talk to you about.'

'What, my not eating properly?'

That lovely smile again. 'No, the stress of running the business.'

Well, running the business and one or two other things we won't go into here.

'Yes, as far as I can see you've done pretty well. We wondered if you would consider carrying on for a while, just until Pops is better.'

Pops? 'We?'

'Yes, the family. My brother James wants to sell up but well, I think we should wait a little while, you know, see if he gets well enough to take over the reins again.'

Or dies.

'James is an accountant. His thing is money, not what it means to Pops.'

'Could you sell? I mean, is it worth much?'

'Not a lot. The premises are on a lease which expires in two years anyway. Pops was going to retire then, but well, things have taken a different turn, haven't they? James has put some feelers out already and the Co-op are interested, just in the goodwill really. To be honest, if they bought that I think they'd just close it down to eliminate a competitor. Makes sense.'

Morris considered this. What did he have to lose? It was better than the Jobcentre, and anyway he thought that although it went against the grain to work, actually he was quite enjoying the whole thing. Well, he might if he didn't have a lot of extramural activities getting in the way.

He looked at Rachel's beautiful smile while she talked to him about her father, and her mother dying when she was at school and how James and she didn't get on very well, and a whole load of things he only half listened to while he sat there and enjoyed the sound of her voice. When she asked him if he would carry on at the firm for a while he found it easy to say yes. He would have said yes to anything she asked. Morris was falling in love.

'So, don't you want to ask me any questions, like how much we can pay you for example?'

'Um, OK, how much can you pay me?'

'Not a lot, I'm afraid.'

'That's fine.'

Morris, she knew, was thinking about her, not business. Well, she was used to it. She also knew how to put a stop to it.

'OK, any more questions then?'

'Um, no, I can't think of any.'

'You haven't asked me about myself. I mean, you're taking me rather on trust aren't you? You don't know anything about me, like what I do for example.'

'OK, what do you do?'

'I'm not telling you.'

'Oh. So what's the point of asking you?'

'Because you've got to guess.'

Morris's mind had one of its clarity moments. Why was this woman doing this? To put him off. OK, what job could she have that would put him off?

Shit.

'You're not a policeman are you?'

She laughed. She had lovely teeth. No, he didn't think she was a policeman.

'I give up then.'

'Good God man, you give up easily don't you? OK, look, I'll make it worth your while.'

'Yes?' He was sipping at his beer, not taking her seriously. She leaned in to him and said something she had absolutely no intention of saying.

'If you can guess what I do I'll take you home and give you the shag of your life.'

Morris spilled beer down his funeral shirt. Rachel blushed, which thankfully he didn't see in the half light of the restaurant. It would be hard to say who was the more confused.

He pulled himself up in his seat and looked into her eyes to see if she was serious. She had regained her composure, decided there must have been a reason why she said it, and now she held his gaze.

'OK, here goes. Not the police?'

'No, I promise you.'

'Uhuh. Nurse?'

'No.'

'Um, doctor?'

'No.'

'Osteopath, homeopath, radiographer, physiotherapist, chiropodist, surgeon?'

'No. You're a linear thinker, aren't you? You need to get

over your obsession with medicine.'

'OK, solicitor?'

'And the law.'

'Hold on, hold on, you're not an undertaker, are you?'

'That's right.'

'You are?'

'No, I said that's right, I'm not an undertaker.'

'Oh. Um, you're not one of those women vicars?'

'Good God man, what the hell made you think that?'

'Dunno.' Your angelic smile. 'Um, hairdresser?'

'No.'

Twenty minutes later he was running out of ideas. He had covered just about every job he had heard of and some he hadn't, from pole dancer, which made her laugh, to accountant, which didn't, and he was beginning to wonder if he cared about having the shag of his life. He was slumped in his seat and it was getting late. The restaurant was empty apart from the staff, who were sitting at the back eating their own dinner and laughing about something they couldn't hear and wouldn't have been able to understand anyway on account of it being in Chinese.

'OK, look, you win, I give up.'

'Sure?'

'Yeh, sure.'

Rachel reached into her handbag, took out a leather wallet and flashed it in front of him. He couldn't see it clearly and took it from her to peer more closely.

'WO2 da Souza, R. Huh?'

'Warrant Officer Second Class.'

'Oh yes. And that means what?'

'Sergeant Major to you.'

'Bloody hell! You're a soldier?'

'Yep. Well, PT Instructor, Second Battalion, the Devonshire Regiment.'

Morris sat up and handed the wallet back. He was trying to

compute this and found he couldn't. Rachel knew exactly how he was feeling. Every man she had got close to since her divorce had reacted in the same way. It was a shame. She was rather getting to like this one.

24

Rachel took Morris home and went back to her father's house, where she was staying while she was on compassionate leave.

At the flat there was a message from Roger written on a scrap of paper and pushed under the door. It said Morris, you promised to come round.

Shit. Angie.

He wandered round the flat, trying to figure Rachel out. He felt something about this woman, and it wasn't what he usually felt. He didn't really even mind missing out on having sex with her, and it worried him that he didn't mind. On the other hand, he had to admit to himself that he was just a bit put off by what she'd told him, without being about to figure out why it made any difference. Maybe it didn't, then.

He looked around the place and for the first time he saw what a dump it was. The thought of bringing Rachel back here worried him. On the other hand, the thought of having it off with her in Horace Tite's house didn't bear thinking about. Anyway, was it even going to go that far or was he getting carried away? He was tired by now and he went to bed without a joint, and when he woke up in the morning he realised he had had the best night's sleep he'd had in a long time. Was that something to do with Rachel? More likely, he thought, it was something to do with Tinkerbelle. He sat and ate a huge bowl of Frosties and pondered the fact that it was over. He did something he had stopped doing since getting used to being an undertaker. He imagined her in her coffin in the ground, and then he thought of Doris on top of her, and he wondered what he thought about what he'd done. Well, one thing he knew was that he would never be able to tell anyone.

He got to work and opened up for business. Since Doris had died it had been different. OK, she hadn't actually done anything, but she had been there, and now she wasn't he wasn't quite so sure he could do this. A couple of people had been in and he'd done the best he could which presumably wasn't good enough because they hadn't come back and booked, for which he was grateful. Now, though, there was Rachel. She wanted him to do this, and he wanted to do it for her. Right, well the next person who came in was going to be sold a funeral.

It was Mrs Goggins.

'Mr Morris.' She had decided that was his name and he had decided it wasn't worth trying to disabuse her.

'Hullo Mrs Goggins, and what can we do for you today?'

'It's my Cyril.'

'Oh yes?' Now the normal response would be oh yes and what's Cyril, but Morris knew it was a pointless question, nothing was Cyril, Cyril probably didn't even exist.

'Yes. My Cyril says I should have a funeral plan, and he's going to pay for it. I want you to arrange it, Mr Morris.'

He looked at Mrs Goggins and wondered how old she was. The answer, he was as certain as it's possible to be, was over the age limit for funeral plans, on account of you having to pay something in to them before you die and he suspected Mrs Goggins might not have long enough for that. How to put it to her tactfully?

'Well, Mrs Goggins, let me see if I can find some forms for you. Mr Tite isn't well, you know, so I'm all on my own at the moment.'

'What about that other one, Doris?'

'Oh, well, you see Mrs Goggins, I'm afraid Doris died recently.'

'Really? That was silly.'

Morris pondered that. As barmy as it was, he wondered if it was as barmy as all that. Yes, what a silly thing dying was. On the other hand, Doris, bless her, had solved his Tinkerbelle problem, so maybe it wasn't silly after all. He found the forms.

'There you are then. You come back and see me when you've read through that.' Which with any luck will be never. 'Will that be all, Mrs Goggins?'

'No.'

Oh, come on, help me out here. Go away. 'Oh?'

'No, it's my 'enry.'

Half an hour later Morris found himself on a desert island with someone who resembled Rachel but had bigger tits, so it might have been Ellie Colbeck, but whoever it was she had boxing gloves on and was giving him a good going over. Then she changed into Mick and that's when he woke up. Mrs Goggins had gone.

He went and sat at Horace's desk and rifled through the drawers. Nothing much of interest in them, except in the bottom one, hidden under a 1973 calendar from Aldridge and Humbert, hearse fitters, was half a bottle of scotch.

The sly old bastard.

The filing cabinet was full, unsurprisingly, of paper. Morris didn't do paper. In the intray on the desk was a VAT return, several unpaid invoices and something from the Inland Revenue. Well, Rachel's brother James could come in and sort that lot out. He would enjoy that.

There were no more burials booked, but one item in the diary caught his eye. The Reverend Peter Potter was due to come in at two o'clock for his monthly meeting with Horace.

Morris wondered if he would turn up, because he knew

Peter knew about Horace being in the nursing home because he had visited him there as part of his pastoral care responsibilities.

At two o'clock sharp. Peter Potter was knocking on the door.

'Oh, I see, um, Morris.'

'Yep, it's me alright.'

'Oh, I thought ...'

'Well, there's no-one else, is there? They keep dying, which is pretty handy what with this being a funeral director's, but it does leave us somewhat short-staffed. Apart from Mr Tite, of course, who is making good progress, so I'm told. Anyway, never mind business, I want to talk to you.'

'Oh yes, what about?'

'Not what, who, and don't come the innocent with me, you know who.'

'If you mean Angela, it wasn't my idea.'

'No, I didn't think it was. Look, it's your business what goes on between you and my sister, but I've got her husband on my back and he wants to know where she is.'

Morris saw the sweat break out on Peter's forehead.

'You haven't told him?'

'Well if I had you wouldn't be standing here, you'd be on crutches. And I can tell you you're not the reason I haven't told him, Angie is. Well, what are you going to do about it?'

'Me?'

'Well sunshine, as I look around I don't see anyone else who is shacking up with my married sister.'

Peter visibly winced. Morris, he sometimes felt, could be unnecessarily cruel. Not to mention crude.

'Look, Morris, you know your sister. I've tried telling her, I've tried reasoning with her. To be honest I don't think I'm the reason she's at the vicarage anyway.'

'No, well who is?'

'Her husband. I think the vicarage is a kind of refuge from

him. Yes, she's claiming sanctuary from her marriage.' Peter thought he was doing quite well.

Morris thought it was crap, although from what Angie had told him about Peter, and from his own observations of the vicar, he tended to believe there might after all be some other reason. Yes, now he thought about it, it wasn't such crap after all.

'Well anyway old fruit, just send her back will you, because Roger's making my life a misery and I've got enough of that without his help, and to be honest I don't see why I'm involved in this mess. Now, about funerals. There aren't any.'

'Oh, is business not so good then?'

'No, it's not that, it's that I don't know what I'm doing here. I expect people are still dying, it's just that they're going to the Co-op instead. Probably for the dividend.'

'If there's any way I can help?'

'Well, if you're doing any of that last rites stuff you could always bung in a card.'

'Sorry, the Anglican Church is a bit like the BBC. We don't do advertising.'

Morris saw him out with a last word of admonition about Angie. Poor sod, he thought, he doesn't know what's hit him. He should find some good woman and settle down.

As he was closing the door Rachel appeared.

'Customer?'

'The vicar of St Elmo's. He comes round to liaise on funerals, they all do, or we go to them, or rather your father does, did, how is he?'

'He's OK, but let's face it, he's not coming back to work.'

'Ever?'

'Ever.'

'Well, come and have a cup of tea and let's talk business.'

'Yes. Look, Morris ...'

'Yes?'

'About last night.'

'Look, Rachel ...'

'Yes?'

'About last night.'

'Well, that's covered that then.'

'Yeh.'

Then he took her face in his hands and gently kissed her lips.

'That's what I really wanted to say.'

'Uhuh, me too.' And she kissed him back.

And they spent that day sitting in Horace Tite's office talking, like you do when you've just fallen in love, about this and that, getting to know the person you've just fallen in love with, and then they locked up the office and went home to Morris's flat.

'You're going to find it a bit untidy, I'm afraid.'

'Listen, I'm a soldier, I can slum it if I have to.'

And then she saw what he meant.

'Yes I see what you mean. Come on, it's not that bad, well OK, it is, but really, why don't you just tidy up occasionally?'

'Well I did once but it just got untidy again so I sort of stopped seeing the point.'

He was already regretting being a slob. He wanted to tell her he would never be a slob again, as long as she would go on loving him, but as far gone as he was he wasn't completely gaga.

He made her some fish fingers and beans and then they settled down on the sofa with the broken spring for a bit of what people do when they feel like they did. And there was a knock on the door.

Shit.

'Angie.'

'Yes, Morris and get that bloody kettle on because I am not in a good mood and whilst something stronger would be welcome a cup of tea will have to do since I'm driving and ... oh, hullo, sorry, I didn't know you had company.'

'Yes. Angie, this is Rachel. Rachel this is Angie. My sister.'

Morris made the tea as instructed and when he came back into the sitting room the two women were chatting like old friends. He felt a bit left out. He pretended to have no milk so Angie would go but she said she would drink it black, thank, you, and are there any biscuits?

For two people who had never met they had a lot of catching up to do, and then Angie was in the doorway, whispering to Morris.

'She's very nice, your new girlfriend. Too nice for you kiddo. You watch you treat her well.'

Alone at last.

'She's great, your sister.'

'Yeh, well, I wouldn't know. She's just my sister. She's OK I guess.'

'Well look Morris, she thinks the world of you, so you should appreciate her more.'

'Does she?'

'Yes, now come here before I forget what I was going to do to you.'

And there was a knock on the door.

Shit. Shit.

'Morris.'

'Roger.' Good God, they must have passed on the stairs, Angie must be hiding in the shadows in terror.

'Um, Rachel, this is Roger. My brother-in-law.'

'Oh, you must be Angie's husband, you've just ... '

'Arrived in time for a nice cup of tea, on account of me just telling Rachel here about Angie, your wife, and how she seems to have disappeared and you think she's run off with some other bloke but I don't think so. Yes, that's what I was just telling Rachel when you arrived. Funnily enough. Tea?'

'No Morris, I don't want any bloody tea. I want to know where she is. You said you would talk to me about her. I've been trying to contact you. What do you know?'

'Look, Roger, some of us do have lives to get on with, you know, and work and that sort of thing, so to be honest your missing wife, as much as I feel for you on the matter, has not been my number one priority these past few days.'

'If you know something ...'

'Well I don't, and if you don't mind my friend and I were, um, looking forward to a quiet evening in and you come charging in here like I'm my sister's keeper or something, so if you wouldn't mind.'

It was touch and go, but Roger went in the end, after extracting a promise from Morris to contact him if he heard anything at all.

'Right, I think you need to tell me about this situation.'

'Oh God, Rachel, I wish I knew what was going on. You see it all started with the book group ...'

'Huh?'

'No, on second thoughts forget the book group and fast forward to last week. Angie has left Roger and gone to live with the Reverend Peter Potter, the vicar of St Elmo's.'

'Hang on, wasn't he the one who was at the office today?'

'Yes, that's the one.'

'Mm, well I don't think much of your sister's taste in men.'

'No, well, it's a bit of a mystery to me as well, but funnily enough she didn't ask my opinion.'

'But what's the attraction of this Peter Potter?'

'I don't think there is one really, unless it's that he's not Roger.'

'Yes, I can see what you mean.'

'Anyway, the Reverend doesn't actually want Angie living in sin with him at the vicarage.'

'No, I can see the thinking behind that one.'

'And to be honest if I know my sister I think she sees it was a bit of a mistake. I think that's why she came round here this evening but you were here and she couldn't talk to me.'

'Oh, sorry.'

'Not your fault.'

'Anyway, where were we?'

And there was a knock on the door.

'Ah, Peter, we were just talking about you, come in, come in, why not, I mean just make yourself at home, cup of tea, chocolate digestive, perhaps you'd like to watch the ten o'clock news with us because we weren't doing anything special. Oh, this is Rachel. Rachel, Peter Potter.'

'How do you do vicar. I think we met briefly earlier today. At Widdlecombe and Tite?'

'Oh yes, you're Mr Tite's daughter.'

'That's right. So ...'

'So, Peter, it's been very nice but perhaps we could do this some other time?'

'But I just wanted to talk to you about ...'

'Angie, my married sister who's living with you at the vicarage as your common-law wife and whose husband has already been round here this evening, shame you missed him, looking for her and muggins here kept his mouth firmly closed only God knows why because excuse me does anyone ever do me any favours, no, so vicar, unless there's any life and death matter you urgently need to discuss like someone's funeral ...'

'Er, no, well, thank you Morris, as you say ...'

'Yes, goodbye.'

He slumped into the sofa. He couldn't take much more of this. Then to be on the safe side, he got up and put the chain on the door. Then Rachel led him back to the sofa and, determined not to waste time on chat, got her lips planted firmly on his.

There was no knock on the door this time. Instead, it shuddered under some unstoppable force, the chain flew off and the whole thing was thrown open to reveal Mick.

Oh shit. Oh double shit.

'Morris, glad I caught you in. Push off, sister, Morris an'

I've got fings to discuss.'

'Look, Mick.'

'Shut it Morris. I don' want any more of your crap, just shut it and give me what I'm looking for.'

'Look, Tinkerbelle ...'

Mick now had one hand round Morris's throat and the other one was getting ready to hit him.

'Fuck Tinkerbelle. Where's the ... '

'Excuse me my man, I am not accustomed to being spoken to in this way. And that's my boyfriend you're mishandling, so if you want to survive the next twenty seconds ...'

'Look girlie, I told you ...'

'Girlie? Girlie? I don't think so mate.'

And before Morris could feel himself breathing again Mick had let go, on account of Rachel having one of his hands twisted behind his back while the other one was clawing frantically in mid-air trying to find some part of her to get hold of. She was too fast for him though. Her other hand was now firmly attached to the front of his trousers. It wasn't a large hand but it was like a bull terrier. Once it had a hold it wasn't going to let go. Mick was sweating profusely. It was scary, seeing such a big man in such obvious agony. Rachel's face was about two inches from his, and she was hissing.

'Now, look here, shit face. I don't know who you are or what you think you're doing here, but I can tell you this. If I ever see you again, I'm going to hurt you. And don't think I mean what I'm doing now, because I promise you this isn't pain, not by a long way. You are going to feel what real pain is, shit face, if ever you and I come up against each other again. Do I make myself understood?'

A noise came from Mick's mouth that could have been anything but was good enough for Rachel. She eased up on his crotch and his own hand went there either in a futile attempt to relieve the pain or else a futile and belated attempt to protect himself from assault. Rachel had done with him

166

though. She pushed him towards the door.

'Oh, just one more thing, shithead. There's a small matter of repairs. Wallet.'

She extracted a hundred pounds and stuffed his wallet back into his jacket, and then he hobbled down the stairs cursing under his breath. They closed the door as best they could, bolted it, and pushed the sofa up against it for good measure.

And Rachel promised not to leave Morris alone until the morning.

25

Rachel left early the next morning after giving Morris instructions about getting a new lock fitted and an extra bolt. They talked about a lot of things before she left, but what she didn't ask him was who Mick was and what he wanted. Rachel was a smart woman.

It was the end of her leave and she had to be back in Catterick. Her battalion was working up for an overseas deployment and she was working on the men's fitness in preparation. They exchanged phone numbers and after a lot of the kissy kissy stuff she drove off north.

Rachel, it seemed, was not only a PT instructor, but a martial arts instructor too, which Morris had witnessed the night before. She was a modest woman, but he managed to extract from her the information that she would be following her battalion out only after representing England in the Commonwealth Games. Morris had never met anyone like Rachel, and he was confused. She was a strong woman, not just physically but mentally too, and she could easily dominate a man, but she was canny enough to know that if she dominated Morris he would be supine for the rest of their relationship, however long that turned out to be which wouldn't be very long in that case, and strong women come in two kinds, those who want a weak man and those who don't, and Rachel didn't. Being strong was good in the Army and in competitions, but what she wanted to come home to was a man who would be her equal, and not give in to her strength.

Why on Earth she thought Morris was any kind of match for her was hard for him to imagine. Still, perhaps she saw something in him no-one else ever had, including him. Maybe, just maybe, having met his sister, and seeing what kind of personality she had, Rachel could see Morris being like her, if only he got the chance to grow up. Yes, perhaps Rachel had sussed Morris out pretty well. That probably came from her own experience of being a commander of men.

Anyway, Morris knew nothing about any of this as he surveyed the damage from Mick's visit last night and pondered on the possibility that he would almost certainly be back, possibly with backup next time. His pride would be wounded, being beaten by a woman, but it would heal, and he would be looking for vengeance. And of course the loot.

The first thing he did when he got to work was phone a locksmith. He wondered how he could defend himself next time in the absence of his guardian angel and as the day progressed his daydreams progressed too, from pepper spray, through a ready-trained Dobermann which he discounted if for no other reason than Mrs Diggle's cat, and finally, by five o'clock, to asking Marty if he knew anyone he could obtain a gun from, what with him being in the second-hand business.

Then he decided he wouldn't go back to the flat but would sleep in the chapel of rest. Then he decided that was a stupid idea on account of there being twelve thousand pounds secreted about the place and while Mick might not find it on a first pass he would simply tear the place apart until he did. Morris seriously began to wonder whether it was worth keeping the money. He hadn't thought of a use for it, possibly because he hadn't come round, finally, to the idea that it really might be OK to keep it, so why not just hand it over and get rid of the problem?

He decided to walk home to delay his arrival. When he

did finally get back there was a new lock on the door and a socking great bolt and Mrs Diggle had taken the keys in for him and unusually he accepted a cup of tea from her but what with her being deaf if wasn't a very social occasion and anyway he was worried she might say something about him being sick on Tiddles, so he went up to get some food.

It was half past nine before the first knock on the door, which from recent experience wasn't bad.

'Mr Crapovic.'

'Ah, Mr Figg.' His landlord always acted like he was surprised it was Morris who opened the door.

'Mr Figg, if you don't mind.'

'Um, no, what is it?'

'Aha, I see you have new lock. Very good.' He admired this, and the bolt, and said very good again, several times. It was, Morris thought, the first thing he learned to say when he arrived, penniless, from Croatia. Well he wasn't penniless now, was he? He owned this house and several more in and around Tamworth Park.

'Mr Figg, you are very good tenant, I like you.'

Well that's nice.

'If you don't mind.' Upon which he took out a builder's measure and started walking round the flat making mental notes.

'Uhuh, uhuh, hold please, Mr Figg,' and he placed one end in Morris's hand and walked across to the other side of the bedroom.

'Yes, all very good. Thank you. Goodbye.'

Well, as long as everything was very good, what was there to worry about? He was just about to light up a joint when there was another knock. He was beginning to wish he had thought to have a peephole installed while the locksmith was here. Still, Mick wouldn't knock like that.

Which just shows how wrong you can be.

'OK Morris, this 'ere is Mad Dave.' Even with backup he

170

looked nervous, but a quick inspection of the flat revealed no hidden danger and he puffed out his chest again.

'Yeh, Mad Dave is goin' to tie you up an' you are going to tell me where my money is.'

Morris forgot for the moment that actually he had already decided to hand it over so the tying up bit was unnecessary but he was too late because Mad Dave, who was a lot smaller than Mick but that didn't stop him looking even nastier, and anyway when he got close enough to do the tying up he smelled bad too, a mixture of sweat and alcohol Morris thought but he tried not to analyse it too much, had for some inexplicable reason put gaffer tape over Morris's mouth. It was unpleasant in the extreme, although not as unpleasant as Mad Dave's smell, and that almost certainly wasn't as unpleasant as his fist in your face, but even that wasn't the real problem because the real problem was that with gaffer tape over his mouth Morris couldn't say look Mick, OK, I'll tell you where the money is. So it was, you might say, a tactical error on the part of the baddies.

Morris said something to the effect of mmmmmm, but all Mick said to that was shut up Morris and tell me where it is, to which Morris in desperation replied mmmmm, but to no avail. Then Mick ripped the tape off, which hurt like hell, not in order that Morris might answer his question but because in Mick's world people could hear you better if their mouth wasn't taped up, and while Morris was wincing with the pain Mick was shouting at him to come clean.

'OK, OK, I'll give you the money.'

'You will?'

'Yes.'

'Oh.'

'What's the matter, you sound disappointed.'

'Yeh. We was 'oping we could 'urt you a bit and then you would give us the dosh after.'

Morris might have felt sorry for Mick's disappointment, but

he couldn't quite bring himself to do that. Mad Dave untied him, only that took a while because he couldn't undo one of the knots and in the end they had to fetch a sharp knife from the kitchen to cut the rope and for a moment Morris thought things were going to turn ugly, as if Mad Dave wasn't ugly enough already, but they didn't. Mick's anger seemed to have exhausted itself, possibly because it was more fear of Rachel than anything, and now he was in his old easygoing mood.

'Now Morris, that's my man. OK, go get.'

Morris lifted the lino up in the bedroom and gathered up a pile of banknotes. He took them out of the freezer and the toilet cistern, the bin under the sink and everywhere else he had hidden them. When they counted them up they came to eleven thousand pounds exactly.

'I don't fink so Morris. There should be another two grand 'ere.'

Two? Shit.

'Well I can honestly say, Mick, that that was all I found. She was a lovely girl, your Tinkerbelle, but I mean, perhaps she spent some of it herself.'

Mick was not an unreasonable man. He couldn't dispute the logic of that. He weighed up letting Mad Dave hit Morris anyway, just so it wouldn't have been a wasted evening for him, but instead he told him to drive round to the Pink Flamingo. He had other business to attend to. Morris did worry just a little what other business that might be but in the event it turned out to have nothing to do with him. Mick put his arm round Morris's shoulder.

'Morris my man, you're not such a bad geezer, but listen, don't get involved wiv such a bad crowd in future. You could get yourself in trouble, know what I mean? Oh, an' by the way, the next time you see that girlfriend of yours, tell her I aint scared of her, I was jus' taken by surprise like, an if she wants a rematch she knows where to come. Silly cow.'

And with that he slammed the door behind him.

172

It might have been a sudden feeling of loss over the money, but actually it was far more probably hearing his beloved called a silly cow. Morris's cool deserted him just as the door closed, and he did something totally insane. In the bedroom wardrobe he found his old cricket bat. It was only fifteen seconds after Mick left that he flung the door open with the ludicrous intention of having a go at him. If Mick hadn't stopped on the landing to stuff the money into various of his pockets he would by now have been halfway down the stairs and Morris would have stayed out of trouble, but he had, and he wasn't, and Morris didn't.

He turned in surprise just as Morris said his name in a challenging kind of way and raised the bat head height. He had a wad of notes in both hands and he instinctively put one hand up to protect himself, releasing a shower of tenners down the stairs, like confetti at a Greek wedding. The other hand went to the bannister, just a split second before he lost his balance and started to lift off from the landing. Mick was a big, heavy man. The bannister's feeble fixings into the wall were no match for his seventeen stone. They didn't even try. As the railing came away in his hand, Mick's face registered a kind of horrified recognition of his fate. His great bulk flew in an ark into space, and then gravity did its work and sent him crashing down the entire flight of stairs.

Morris ran after him as if he might have some chance of grabbing hold and breaking his fall, but it was a foolish hope. Mick fell faster than he could run. When Morris reached the landing below, Mick's body was lying in a grotesque position viz-a-viz the floor, and his head was resting against the door of Mrs Diggle's flat. Judging from the angle, and the fact that he wasn't breathing, Morris made an educated guess that his neck was broken.

This couldn't be happening. It wasn't actually, because it already had happened, past tense, and you can't turn the clock back, not even by twenty seconds, not even when it's

173

really really important. If only you could, but you can't. To add to the pathos, a twenty pound note floated down and finally came to rest on Mick's forehead.

Morris had never been more grateful for Mrs Diggle's deafness, and the man on the ground floor's shift working, than at this moment. Tiddles was in the hall and came to sniff at Mick's face, and Morris made him promise not to tell his mistress about this.

He was trying not to panic but the urge was overwhelming. And everything was going so well. He ran upstairs to call an ambulance but something rang warning bells and he put the phone down again. An ambulance would mean the police, on account of Mick being deader than is normal for your average household accident. And the police would certainly be a problem.

Well, Mr Figgs, isn't it, and the notorious Thick Mick from the Pink Flamingo. Well I wonder what on earth a well-known local villain could possibly be doing lying dead in your house. Don't know officer, I just came down the stairs and there he was so I did the proper thing and called the emergency services. No, perhaps not. Well, you see, it's like this constable, this man came to the door and threatened me and then he accidentally fell down the stairs. No. Um, I thought he was a door-to-door salesman. Worse. OK, it's a fair cop, he wanted to know about Tinkerbelle, on account of her being found dead in my bed and I buried her in someone else's coffin and he just came round to get the money I stole from the body, so if that will do perhaps I can come round to the station in the morning and make a statement?

No, no police, and so no sodding ambulance.

Well, there was no way he was going to move seventeen stone of gangster without some help and looking at Mick he could tell he wasn't going to get any assistance from that quarter.

'Marty?'

'Morris, my dear friend, and how are you?'

'Marty, I need you to do something for me.'

'Now Morris, look, we are old friends I know, but you know I would like it if one day you would just say Marty how are you and let's go for a drink because I would really enjoy your company.'

'Yes, yes, one day, but not now I'm afraid because actually I am in deep deep shit, and there's no-one else I can ask.'

'Is this deeper than the shit you were in recently, or would you say about the same?'

'Um, deeper.'

'OK, OK, I'm on my way. Give me twenty minutes.'

'You couldn't make that ten, could you?'

'No Morris, cos I haven't got any clothes on so ...'

'No, that's OK, twenty will be fine. Oh, and Marty ...'

'Yes?'

'Thank you.'

Marty arrived looking like he was ready for an evening out. He was alright until they got to the first floor landing.

'Oh Morris, what the fuck have you done?'

'Me? Why has it always got to be me?'

Marty looked around. Tiddles had gone. The hall was deserted.

'Well mate, I don't see anyone else. Just you and me and a stiff. God, he's a big bugger. Hang on, he looks kind of familiar now I look at him this way up. Oh shit, Morris, this is ....'

'Yes, Thick Mick.'

'But what the hell are you doing, I mean is he, I mean, oh bloody hell, what are you going to do?'

'What we are going to do, my old and trusted friend, is get this bastard upstairs. Now come on, before Mrs Diggle comes out looking for Tiddles, so give a hand, or preferably two.'

They struggled, they heaved, they dragged and swore and inch by inch they got him onto the top landing.

'Hold on Morris, just hold on. What are you going to do with him once we get him in the flat?'

'Oh bloody hell Marty, why couldn't you have said that before?'

'Well, excuse me, but whose problem is this anyway?'

'OK, OK, look there's nothing for it, we'll have to get him to the warehouse and stick him in the freezer.'

'Oh no.'

'Oh yes. Can you think of a better idea?'

'About a hundred, but I just know you're going to say no to all of them. Come on then, let's get on with it. I've got a date tonight.'

And they dragged Mick's body down the stairs, or it might be more accurate to say they pushed him and gravity did the rest, and they managed, with great difficulty, to get him into the van, and an hour later he was safely ensconced in the freezer, which was now switched on again and gradually chilling his not inconsiderable bulk down to the correct temperature for keeping meat, if you happen to be in the restaurant business.

It was, as it happens, no more than about two minutes after they closed the van doors and drove off that Constable Penny came round the corner of Smethwick Avenue into Walsall Place. Just two minutes earlier and Morris would have been looking at a long rest at one of Her Majesty's establishments for the criminally incontinent, but tonight the god of unbelievable coincidences was washing his hair or some such and neither Morris nor PC Penny would ever know what might have been.

The high note of the evening was that when they gathered up all the money Mick had taken off him, plus the couple of grand he had in his wallet, Morris was in profit.

26

Marty got to his date late, but with two hundred pounds in his pocket, so he didn't feel too bad about having Thick Mick's body in the freezer in his warehouse, although he didn't feel too good about it either and the last thing he said to Morris before he drove off was we're talking about days here, not weeks, and this has got absolutely nothing to do with me, although on account of it being his freezer and his warehouse that was perhaps a bit on the optimistic side. Morris didn't like involving him but what are friends for if not to look after corpses for you?

He sat in Horace's office the next morning and gave the problem his full attention. Was there any way they could arrange a funeral without the right paperwork? No. Would Peter Potter help him out? No. Would Marty help him to dig a hole in Walsall Wood and bury him? No. A lot of questions, and a lot of answers, but sadly the answers were all no, which didn't really help.

Rachel rang and they did some long-distance kissy kissy stuff, although Morris could hear someone shouting parade-ground orders in the background and it dawned on him that he was now involved with a Sergeant Major in the Army and he knew it was going to take a while to get his head round that one. Rachel was a bit distant, which you would expect what with her being more than a hundred miles away, but distant in the other way too, as if she had switched back into her other life. She asked him if Mick had been back and he lied. When he put the phone down the first thing he thought was that he hoped he would never lie to her again.

This made him think, as he sat there in an undertaker's office pretending to be someone he never thought he could be or come to that would want to be, that his life was changing, and it was doing so without asking him. It occurred to him he was getting to be like Angie. Apart, obviously, from the bit about fancying Peter Potter.

Who can say when you start to see things differently? Is it a sudden thing or does it grow in the mind over time? Either way, by the end of the day Morris knew where he had been going wrong. Well, he had been going wrong in a lot of ways, which was why his life was always such a mess, but in this case where he had been going wrong with Mick. He had been trying to think of a way to dispose of a body. Well, wrong. The problem wasn't how to dispose of a body at all. It was how to dispose of a freezer. What the freezer contained was academic. Well, almost. And where do you dispose of a freezer? You don't have to arrange a funeral for it, you just have to take it to the council tip. OK, it's true, you have to lock it first on account of not wanting anyone to know that you've accidentally left something inside, but that's all. It's that easy.

'Marty.'

'Ah, Morris, and I don't think I would be lying if I said that today I am genuinely pleased to hear from you. I expect you've got good news for me.'

'Yes.'

'Yes?'

'Yes.'

'Oh, well, blimey Morris, that's a first. You've thought of a way to get rid of Mick?'

'Yes.'

'And this is really really going to work, and no-one is going to know, and even if they do they won't know I had anything to do with it?'

'Yes, no and no.'

Marty thought about that for a moment and decided it was probably alright.

'So, tell me.'

'We're taking the freezer to the tip.'

'OK, OK, I'm with you so far, although it's a perfectly good freezer but look, you're a clever bloke Morris and I'm sure there's a reason for throwing away a perfectly good freezer which I could sell once I've got the blood off the inside away.'

'Yes, because, my trusted old friend, Mick is going to be inside it.'

The phone went silent while Marty thought about this one. There wasn't even the sound of breathing, because Marty always held his breath when he thought.

'Um, Morris, now I don't want you to think I'm being negative, but no.'

'That's negative, Marty. Look, there's no choice, is there? I mean a body is a body and trust me, they're not easy things to get rid of when you've got a bit of a surplus, but old freezers, well, that's a different matter, people throw them away all the time.'

He let Marty think again. He thought he could hear the sound of his brain working but it might have been interference on the line. He knew he was right and he knew Marty would be able to see that. Marty just needed time to come to the same conclusion himself.

'When?'

I'll take that as a yes then. 'Whenever's convenient for you.'

'Wednesday?'

'What time?'

'Three?'

'I'll be there. Bye. Oh, and Marty.'

'Don't say thank you.'

'OK.'

Morris leaned back in Horace's old leather chair and let out a long breath. It had been touch and go. One day, one day he would have to do something for Marty to say thank you properly. OK, he was a bit of a moron, but right now Morris felt truly, deeply grateful. His reverie was interrupted by the phone.

'Hullo, is that Morris Figg?'

'Yes, can I help you?'

'Yes. This is James Tite.'

The second bit was familiar, the first bit wasn't. Then it was.

'Oh, right, Rachel's brother.'

'Really?'

'What do you mean, really? Are you or aren't you?'

'I have a sister called Rachel but I wasn't aware you were familiar with her.'

Oh yes, very. 'Oh, well, she was here for Doris's funeral, she came to bring your father in the wheelchair. We chatted, you know.'

'Yes, well, it's about the firm.'

'What is?'

Morris heard what sounded like an impatient sigh. James wasn't a patient man, and he tended not to bother hiding that fact.

'The family are considering what to do about Widdlecombe and Tite, now that my father is, er, incapacitated, and is unlikely, sadly, to recover enough to return to the business.'

Yes, well you could try to sound sadder about it than that. 'Yes, your sister mentioned me continuing to run things here for a while. Actually, there's very little going on anyway, so that's not hard.'

'Exactly. It won't reach its targets this quarter for burials so profits will be down. Unless you feel you can do something to turn it round in the short term we will have to look at selling.'

How could such a wonderful woman have such a prick for a brother?

'Look, James, I don't know about the business side of things. To be honest I've had all this dumped on me and if you want to sell the firm leave me out of the equation.'

'Excellent. I'm glad you see it that way Morris. Well, I'll keep in touch and let you know what we decide. Cheerio then.'

Cheerio Rachel's brother who has turned out to be a big disappointment. Morris might have left it at that, but suddenly he had a cricket bat moment and he was angry. I'm glad you see it that way Morris. Uhuh. Well maybe I do and maybe I don't Sonny Jim. It was while he was developing an extra-strong dislike of her brother that Rachel rang.

'Morris, I've had a call from James. He says you've agreed to redundancy.'

What? I take back everything I've said so far about you James. You are in fact a fully paid-up bastard.

'Um, no I don't think so. He just said you were thinking of selling and I would be informed about developments. I didn't agree to anything.'

'I'm sorry. That's my brother the accountant, I'm afraid. Look, I haven't got a lot of time. I leave for the Games tomorrow and after that it's back here for three days and I follow the battalion out. Look, Morris, I don't know when I'm going to see you but I want to say something.'

Something nice I hope. 'Yes?'

'This isn't easy. Look, since I got back everything's been such a rush and I've thought about my life and your life and I don't see when we're ever going to see each other and make this work and it's all very new so maybe it won't. If you see what I mean. It's my fault, not yours.'

'I see.'

'Do you, really?'

181

'Yes, and now it's my turn. You're wrong. If what I feel about you is this strong there's no way I'm walking away just like that. OK, it might not work, but I'm damned well going to try, even if I have to enlist in the Army myself.'

'I don't think that will be necessary my love.'

'Oh good, because on second thoughts that wasn't a great idea.'

'But I cherish the sentiment even so.'

'You do?'

'Yes.'

'So no more talk about giving up before we've started?'

'No. Look, I've got to go, but I'll try again tomorrow. Bye.'

'Bye.'

'Oh, and Morris ...'

'Yes?'

'Thank you.'

27

On Wednesday Morris drove round to Marty's warehouse and they loaded the freezer onto the van. They had to take Mick out first because it was too heavy with him in it, and then put him back again. He had been ugly enough when he was alive but as a frozen corpse he really wasn't a pretty sight. Marty swore this was the last body he was ever going to have anything to do with.

'Until I'm dead myself of course.'

'Yes, but then someone else will deal with you and you won't know anything about it, will you?'

'No well, I'm just glad I'll be dead and won't have to.'

'Yes Marty, but if you were dead you wouldn't ... oh look, can we have this conversation another time, like in about twenty years, and get this bastard sorted?'

Morris slammed down the lid and locked it.

'There you go Mick, you're going to that great night-club in the sky now, via the municipal rubbish tip but ask me if we feel sorry about that.'

'Do we?'

'No Marty, we don't. Now just drive.'

He did, and fifteen minutes later they were at the council tip. Morris opened the back doors and was just pondering how they were going to get Mick and the freezer out separately without being seen when a familiar face appeared.

'Excuse me sir, is that a freezer?'

Morris thought he recognised something about this youth, but it could have been the yellow jacket. On the other hand it could be because he was the very same jobsworth who had stopped him coming in to dispose of Tinkerbelle that time. He had obviously been hanging around waiting for Morris to return ever since so he could pounce. Didn't his parents know he wasn't at school?

'Um, well, Marty, what do you think? Is it a freezer, or could it be a priceless piece of art that's just been exhibited at Tate Modern and when the exhibition was over they took all the other stuff away and left this by mistake because they thought it was rubbish and we've been asked to get rid of it?'

'No, Morris, it's a freezer.'

'Do you know, Marty, by golly, now I come to look at it more carefully, I do believe you're right.'

'Well, sir, you can't leave it here.'

Morris looked at the sign. 'It says Council Rubbish Tip. And this is rubbish, so excuse me, what exactly is the nature of this problem?'

'It's not rubbish.'

'I think you will find, on account of it being surplus to requirements, that that is exactly what it is.'

'No it's not.'

Morris was getting tired of this. 'Look sonny, why don't you go and bother someone else and leave us alone? Just let us be the judge of what's rubbish and what isn't, will you?'

'I'm sorry sir, I'm just doing my job. This isn't rubbish.'

Morris put his hands on his hips. The fact that there was a corpse inside and this was really not the right time or place to have an argument was a side issue now.

'OK, clever dick, if it's not rubbish what is it? Huh?'

'A freezer.'

'Do you know Marty, it's either deja vu or I have a distinct feeling we've been here before. OK, it's a freezer, I'll grant you that. But, and I think this is where we win, it's a freezer

184

we no longer want, and therefore, I think you are going to have to agree with me on this point, something you don't want is usually called rubbish.'

'Yes, sir.'

'Oh good.'

'Unless it's a freezer, or fridge, or any other appliance prohibited under the Disposal of Appliances bracket Waste Gases close bracket Act bracket nineteen ninety five close bracket.'

'What? Would you like to repeat that?'

'No sir. I think you got my meaning. You can't dump fridges or freezers because the gas in them has to be disposed of safely to save the planet.'

Marty drove out of the council tip with the freezer still in the back. Morris clutched a piece of paper with the address of the specialist dump for freezers under the Act. It was twenty miles away.

'Morris, that's twenty miles away.'

'Yes, I know. Look, I'm sorry about this.'

'You know, if you hadn't antagonised him it might not have happened.'

'Um, I don't think so. I mean, there's the planet to think of.'

'Yeh.'

They drove in silence until they got a flat tyre.

Shit. When is this ever going to end?

It was while Marty was looking for the jack that a police car pulled up. Well it wasn't going to end just yet, obviously.

'Good afternoon gentlemen. Having a problem?'

Well, we're just taking a freezer twenty miles to dump it with a body in it and now we've got a flat and my friend here seems to have omitted to stow a jack against this eventuality, but apart from that, no, but thank you for dropping by.

'Yes Constable. My friend here seems to have lost his jack. You, um couldn't lend us one, could you?'

'No sir.'

185

No, I had a funny feeling you were going to say that. And the reason for this lack of public service?

'You see sir, the force isn't insured.'

'Against what?'

'Well, sir, let's say you used my jack, or should I say the Constabulary's jack, and let's say at the very point where this van had no wheel the jack gave way and one of you was hurt? Well, you could sue the force couldn't you?'

'Yes, but we wouldn't, would we Marty? Honest, promise, we won't sue you. If all of that stuff happens.'

'Well sir, I believe you of course, but orders are orders. Are you a member of a motoring organisation, by any chance?'

'Are you, Marty?'

'No.'

No, well I knew you were going to say that.

But just at that very moment the god of fortunate coincidences woke from his afternoon nap and an AA van drove up. It was beginning to look like a roadside convention.

'Good afternoon, all. Can I be of any assistance? Are you a member of the AA sir?'

'No.'

'Well, if you were I could help you with that. That's a shame. On the other hand, if you were to join up now, I could then fix the wheel for you and you could be on your way. Would you like to do that?'

'How much?'

'Well, let me see. There's the roadside assistance policy, which is forty-nine pound fifty, then there's the home call-out policy, which is eighty-nine pound fifty, and then there is the comprehensive all singing all dancing policy which includes all the above plus towing home from anywhere in mainland Britain and travel and accommodation for up to four persons if that is necessitated for just a hundred and ten pounds. But before I forget, should you want European cover that will, I'm

186

afraid, be extra.'

'Well, Marty, what do you reckon? Do we need the European cover?'

'Well ...'

'No, quite. I don't suppose you do a now I'm here I could sort this out for a tenner policy?'

'That's right sir, we don't.'

'Well, it's the fifty quid job I suppose.' Mick was paying.

It was ten to four when they arrived at the dump.

'Come on Marty, they close in ten minutes. Let's just get this done and bugger off. I've had it.'

Ten to four was apparently a good time to dispose of bodies, because the staff were getting ready to go home. Marty backed the van as close as he could to a wall, and they got Mick out of the freezer and the freezer out of the van and Mick back in and safely locked away with no more mishaps.

As they drove home it dawned on Morris that this really was it. If no-one else died on him this was it, over. He said goodbye to Marty back at the flat, but not before he invited him out for an evening at his expense on the Friday.

There was a message on the answering machine.

'Morris, it's Angie. Have you seen Roger?'

'Angie, hullo, it's me. What do you mean have I seen Roger?'

'He's gone.'

'What do you mean gone? Gone from where? You don't live with him any more, or did you forget and go home to the wrong man?'

'No, silly, I had to go to the house to pick some things up and I deliberately went when he would be at work, but he wasn't there.'

'Angie, you're not making sense. Of course he wasn't there, he was at work.'

'Well yes, I know that, but I mean his things weren't there. His clothes, they've gone.'

'What, all of them?'

'Most of them. He's gone off somewhere.'

'Maybe he's gone on holiday.'

'I don't think so, not with that many things.'

'OK, maybe he's gone abroad for six months with his job.'

'Morris, Roger's a teacher, so unless his class have gone with him, that's not very likely, is it?'

'Well no, but ... well no. Anyway, hold on here, why are you worrying about where Roger is anyway? You left him, remember?'

'Now hang on, I didn't say I left him exactly.'

'Yes you did. There was a note. Something like Roger I've left you, if I remember.'

'Well yes but ... well yes.'

'Angie, this isn't like you. What's going on?'

'It's Peter.'

'What's Peter?'

'Well, he wanted me to leave Roger and come and and live with him but now he's not so sure.'

'Angie, how long have I known you?'

'Um, well about thirty odd years I suppose. What's that got to do with anything?'

'Well all our lives I've fibbed to you but you have always been scrupulously honest to me. It's a big difference between us. You have morals and I don't. I like morals in a woman. And now you're lying to me.'

'What do you mean?'

'You left Roger and you went to live with Peter Potter because that's what you wanted, not Peter. In fact he's never been sure.'

'How do you know that?'

'Well if you really want to know, he told me. He came round here one evening.'

'Oh. Morris, it's such a mess. What am I going to do?'

'You're not going to do anything. I'm coming round to the

house. Be there.'

28

He spent three hours talking to Angie, or rather listening to her, and at the end he tucked her up in bed, her own bed in her own house, and went home even more tired than usual, if that was possible. He couldn't sort out her problems, all he could do was be there for her. She was one mixed-up woman. He had always thought of his sister as the straight one whose life would always work properly, even if it was going to be boring, but now she was in the kind of mess he usually got into, and it was unsettling.

In the morning he was late for work. Just as he was leaving, Mr Crapovic turned up.

'Ah Mr Figg, very nice to see you. I can come in please?'

'Well yes, but will it take long?'

'No no, just take some measures please. Won't be long.'

And he proceeded to do what he had done only a few days before, only this time instead of committing the measurements to memory he wrote them down on a torn piece of paper. Then he got out a camera and took some shots of the flat.

'Mr Crapovic, what is going on? Are you sending pictures off to Ideal Home, because if you are I think you might have slightly the wrong end of the stick.'

'Yes, very good Mr Figg.'

Oh, I'll take that as a no then.

'Yes a very good flat. I think we can do something.'

Something? Something? Like what? And if you can't answer that question in English why don't you go away and leave me in peace?

And Mr Crapovic, as if he could read his thoughts, did just that. Morris stood in the doorway looking like someone who should be worried but isn't sure what to worry about. And since it was a riddle he couldn't answer, he closed the door behind him and went to work. On the bus, he pondered today's list of problems to be dealt with. Sell some funerals. Sort Angie's marriage out. Worry about when Rachel was going to ring. Still, at least he didn't have any bodies to dispose of. Actually, for an undertaker that is a worry.

Still, he wasn't an undertaker, was he? He was a caretaker. A caretaker undertaker. An understudy undertaker. An underpaid caretaker undertaker. He was so busy worrying about all of this he missed his stop, which made him even later.

'Ah, Mr Morris, I've been waiting for you to open.'

'Have you, Mrs Goggins? Why's that?'

'Well I was going to come and see you today, but I've got to go up to the hospital, it's my Cyril you see, so I was just waiting to tell you I won't be coming.'

Morris stood in the doorway and watched her shuffle down the road to the bus stop. He was trying to figure out if he needed to worry about Mrs Goggins, or he should put her in a compartment in his head along with Mr Crapovic and keep them both for a day when he ran out of other things to worry about.

He was surprised mid-morning when a man came in to ask about a funeral for his mother, and he was even more surprised when he booked. Well, maybe he really was an undertaker after all. Then just after lunch the man came back and cancelled on account of the Co-op giving double dividend on funerals this week and Morris said something rude to him, after he had left.

Then Rachel rang.

'Did you see me?'

'What, where?'

'On the telly.'

'Why were you on the telly?'

'Well they do that, on the news, you know, when a British athlete wins a silver medal at the Games.'

'Bloody hell. Did you? Oh my God, I didn't know. Rachel, I'm sorry, I wish I'd seen it.'

'Well never mind. Look, I've come back to barracks early. I'm shipping out in three days. They've brought it forward.'

'Oh God.'

'Can you get up here before I leave?'

'Yes, of course. I'll drive up tomorrow.'

'Great. I'll see you then. Bye.' And she was gone.

Which was when Morris thought of two more problems. First, he was supposed to be going out with Marty to say thank you. Second, he didn't have a driving licence. Come to that, three problems because he didn't have a car either.

The first was resolved when the god of nice timing got his act together and when Morris got home his licence was waiting for him in the post. He was now officially allowed to drive again. The others were resolved when he phoned Marty to apologise for postponing their night out and when he told Marty he didn't have a car to drive up to Catterick in, Marty said don't be silly of course you do, and Morris said I do?, and Marty said yes, the limo.

Well, it wasn't strictly speaking his, but on the other hand whose was it? It belonged to Widdlecombe and Tite but first of all he was Widdlecombe and Tite just now and second of all he was on company business, sort of, on account of him driving up to see Horace Tite's daughter, so on that reckoning he decided it was alright.

He phoned Angie before he left the next morning to ask if she was alright and she said no and he felt terrible about that, but there was nothing he could do. He would have loved to help his sister but he couldn't, not even if he had been around, which he wasn't.

When he got to Catterick it brought it home to him that Rachel's world really was very different from his and when he saw her in uniform his heart sank, not because she wasn't very attractive in it because she was in a funny kind of way, but she suddenly seemed out of reach. He couldn't make the leap between the scruffy world he inhabited and all this. She got changed and then she drove him into York and they booked into a little hotel and had dinner in a quiet Italian restaurant and she showed him her medal and he felt more and more inadequate but he tried not to show it. In any case, she assumed the way he reacted to her was something to do with her going abroad, which of course it was, because let's face it she said, six months is a long time and you hardly know me. Will you wait, she said. Will you come back, was what he replied. and she said don't be silly, of course I will, and it was all very emotional and when they got back to the hotel they lay in bed for a long time and somehow never got around to having sex and when they woke up on a bright sunny morning it felt wonderful but they both knew it wasn't going to feel like this again for a long time, if ever.

The last thing Rachel did when she gave him a final kiss through the open window of the limousine was to hand him an envelope. Don't read this until tomorrow, she said, after I've gone.

He drove back slowly, almost at funeral speed, trying to figure it all out. Rachel was doing things to his head no woman had ever done before, but the more he thought about her the less he could see them ever getting together. She was an athlete representing her country and she held a senior rank in the British Army. What was he? A useless layabout who just at the moment looked respectable because he held a junior position in a small firm of funeral directors. By the time he stopped at the services on the A1 for a cup of tea he had decided to open the letter, but such was his respect for Rachel that he resisted the temptation.

The next morning he woke early, with a feeling of dread, and he realised it was Rachel again. He felt bad when he stopped and considered that his thoughts were about himself, not her, She was the one going to some godforsaken place to do the bidding of an idiot government in a place where the natives didn't want her to be and were just as likely to take a potshot at her as not just because she was there. Morris had never been political, but when he thought these thoughts he started to be.

He sat in Horace's leather chair and as he watched the clock and it came to half past one and he knew her plane was taking off, with a mixture of eager anticipation and morbid dread he opened the letter.

Dear Morris

My first wish is that we had longer, to get to know each other before I go, but we don't, so I'm writing this to try to explain things to you. When I get back, if you still want to see me, well, we'll see.

I want you to know the things I'm going to tell you, because if you don't we won't have a future based on honesty, and I am going to tell you now that I want us to have a future.

Horace Tite is not my father. My parents were killed in a car crash when I was four, and I spent the next three years in an orphanage. I cannot begin to tell you what hell it was, and I'm not going to go into all that here. When I was seven, the Tites adopted me. They had a son, James, and Mrs Tite couldn't have any more children, I don't know why, but she had always wanted a daughter and so they chose me.

James never accepted me. I was always the child who came into his family and took attention away from him. It might have been different if I'd been his real sister, but I will never know that for sure, and anyway, it wouldn't change anything. Mrs Tite doted on me, which didn't help that situation, and James started being quite cruel to me, in small ways, but he never let me forget that I didn't belong there.

I ran away the first time when I was twelve. I was only gone for two days but it created havoc. They made a huge fuss about it and James gloated. I tried to tell them how I felt but somehow they never believed me. They wanted to believe I was their daughter and when I said I didn't feel like I was they thought that was something wrong with me, not them. I suppose they were right. After all, they did everything they could. Well, apart from dealing with James, and I couldn't really expect them to favour me over him, could I?

Things were better for a little while but when I was fourteen I got in with a bad lot of kids at school and started smoking and drinking. By the time I was sixteen I was taking other drugs and I had several convictions for drunk and disorderly behaviour and one for shoplifting. The Tites were starting to despair of me, and that was when she had a breakdown. She went away to some psychiatric hospital, they didn't tell me much about it, and she never came back. It was only years later when I traced her and she was still there, a little old woman out of her mind, and she didn't recognise me. I have always blamed myself.

Anyway, things just got worse after that and I ended up in a young offenders' institution. It was the best thing that could have happened to me. I could have gone the way of a lot of the kids and treated it like a college for junior criminals, but I didn't, and that was thanks to one person, a wonderful man called Bill Hardcastle, who was in charge of physical education. He pushed me to go to the gym every day because he could see it was what I needed. It was the discipline of that place, but especially the discipline Bill put me through, that turned me round, and made me what I am. Bill encouraged me to train hard and qualify for the junior English team that year at the Commonwealth Games. I knew I wasn't ready and I was right.

I came nowhere. But it made me even more determined to push myself further. The next year, Bill brought me some brochures for the Army, and I knew that was what I wanted to do. I joined as soon as I was old enough. My life since the first day at the institution has been one of unremitting discipline, and the Army was ideal for me because I had got to the point where I couldn't live without that. It has been what has defined me as a person ever since.

I advanced rapidly in the service, and then, when I was a sergeant, I married a corporal in the same company who I'd been giving lessons to, Freddie. It was a crazy marriage. Ask me now why I did it and I couldn't tell you. Freddie was a serial womaniser. He didn't know what marriage was for. The whole thing lasted two years, and Freddie left the army and I stayed and that was that. There hasn't really been anyone since. I'm not an easy woman, I know. I'm ashamed of my past, and I'm driven by that shame to succeed. What I need is a man who can tell me I don't need to keep driving myself. If that doesn't happen, one day I'm going to be an ex-soldier with a lot of medals and no children. It's not what I want. I don't know what it is about you, Morris, but my heart tells me you are a man who could change me, look after me, give me all that, including children.

I've probably gone much much too far. You don't know me, and here I am dumping all this on you. It's something to do with the posting. I know it's safe, well as safe as these things ever can be, but still, I want you to know that if I come back all right, which I will, that this is what I feel. You must decide in that time if you want anything to do with me. I'm a bit of a mess, I know, and most men don't want to get involved, but something about you says you are better than that.

Well, that's it. I know I'm going too fast but I can't help it.

Goodbye for now, and take care of yourself.

Love
Rachel

29

Morris sat and tried to take this in. A photograph of Horace Tite standing by a hearse came into view, and he tried to imagine what he had been through. He didn't know what was going on in the old man's head now, after the stroke, but Morris silently thanked him for looking after Rachel.

When the phone rang and it was her brother, he hadn't had time to work himself up into a froth of hatred for him. He just had to improvise.

'Hullo, is that Morris?'

'Yes.'

'Oh, hullo, this is James Tite.'

'Oh yes. James.' Morris could feel himself clenching his teeth.

'Well, I've rung to, um, let you know, we've decided to put the firm on the market after all.'

'Oh yes?'

'Yes, and we, er, wondered if you yourself would be interested.'

Well first of all, sonny Jim, who the hell is we, on account of your father being non compos mentis, and Rachel is thousands of miles away serving king and country, so I think, sonny, what you really mean is that now everyone is out of the way you have decided that yourself. Now come on, admit it.

'So, as I was saying, we would like to give you an opportunity to bid for it yourself.'

OK then, don't admit it.

'Because, well, we feel you should have first option as it were, what with you being on the spot and, well, you know, in control. As it were.'

Which, loosely translated, means you've hawked it round already and no-one else is interested, so you just thought you might have a chance of unloading it on poor dim old Morris.

Then he heard himself saying something he hadn't expected.

'Yes James, do you know I might just be interested in doing that. What sort of figure did you have in mind?'

If Morris was surprised by this answer, he wasn't as surprised as James.

'Oh, well, that's excellent.'

No it's not, it's a question.

'Well, let me see, we don't really have a figure in mind as such. I mean, perhaps you would like to sit down and think about it and get back to me, say in a few days time?'

'Yes James, I think I could do that. I shall have to speak with my accountant of course, and my solicitor.'

'Of course. Well, perhaps you would get back to me when you've had a chance to do that and put your bid together?'

'Yes James, why don't I do that?'

'Excellent, yes, jolly good. Well, cheerio for now.'

Did he just swallow all that bullshit?

Morris sat back in Horace's chair yet again and looked around him. Had he really just said he might buy all this? Surely there had been some misunderstanding. Still, he hadn't said anything he could be held to. Yes I might isn't a promise. And anyway, there was the small matter of the price. Where the hell, even assuming he wanted to buy the firm in the first place, would he find that kind of money? Anyway, what kind of money? How do you value an undertaker's? Anyway, even if he came up with a figure and James accepted it, no bank was going to entertain financing a business that was going downhill, let alone lending money to Morris Figg, well-known useless waste of time.

Anyway, who needed a bank? Tinkerbelle, bless her, had left the wherewithal to Morris in her will. Mick said so.

Hold on, hold on, first of all, who says it's a good idea, and second of all what about Rachel, she might not want it to be sold, but on the other hand does she have a say-so, and on the third hand who says thirteen thousand would be enough in any case?

Anyway, enough for what? Rachel said the premises were leased and that would expire in a couple of years so it couldn't be worth much and what else was there? The hearse and the limousine, both of which were about twenty years old. And the goodwill. Well, if the past few days had been anything to go by, there wasn't any.

Morris took some blank paper out of Horace's desk and wrote himself a list. He needed to ask some questions. What were the rent and rates and other overheads? Did the business have any debts? Lots of questions, like those, until they filled two sheets of A4. Then he took a red pen and wrote across the whole lot why the hell am I even thinking about this?

And then he did what Doris would have done in the circumstances. He put the kettle on and made a cup of tea.

He stopped thinking about James and started thinking about Rachel again, but he couldn't separate the two of them now. If he took over the firm, how was that going to affect their relationship? Did they even have one? All he knew was that he wanted her, now more than ever. The letter had sorted things out for him. He had put her on a pedestal and she had given him permission to take her off it. There was he wondering if he was good enough for her and all the time she was wondering if she was good enough for him, if her past mattered. He would have to tell her about his own past, and then they would be square. Well, some of it, anyway.

200

He needed to talk to someone about this, and there was only one person who could give him the answers. He shut the office and drove to the nursing home to see Horace.

Horace, of course, couldn't answer the questions, because he couldn't talk. Well, he could make noises which approximated to talking, at least they meant something to him, but he was locked in a world that Morris couldn't enter. He didn't even know why he was going, but still, Horace was the only connection he had with Rachel now.

A nurse showed him into Horace's room and left them.

'Mr Tite? Mr Tite, it's Morris, Morris Figg. Remember?'

Horace looked at him, which was a good sign, and then he looked away, which wasn't, but Morris took it as an invitation to sit down.

'Well it's like this Horace, you don't mind if I call you Horace do you, I need your opinion. First of all I want to tell you about me and Rachel. Look, I know about her not being your daughter and I know about your wife and I want to tell you I'm very sorry about what happened but you shouldn't think badly about her because really it wasn't her fault.'

Horace was looking straight into Morris's eyes now, and that's how Morris knew he could hear him. Tears had started to trickle down his cheeks.

'Look, I'm sorry to tell you all this just like that but if you can't talk to me I don't know how else to do it. I think you can understand what I'm saying, can't you?' Horace's face didn't move or change expression, but his eyes did, and Morris did something he never would have thought he would have been capable of. He put a hand on the old man's to let him know he knew, and with this physical connection between them he talked and talked, about Rachel and him, and James and the firm, and the old man sat there and he knew he was taking in every word. He told Horace that he loved Rachel too, and he knew, somehow, that he approved.

'So, the long and short of it is your son, who by the way I'm

201

sorry to say I have not taken a liking to, is trying to sell the firm. I don't think he's had much luck because he's even asked me if I would buy it and, well, I foolishly said I might. And before I go any further I wanted to come here and ask you what you thought, because you know I'm not all I make myself up to be, in fact I'm not much at all and I think you made a mistake when you took me on because frankly I wouldn't employ myself and that's not much of a reference is it? I only came along because the Jobcentre said I had to and I didn't mean to stay and, well, and this is the truth, I'm as surprised as anyone that, well, it kind of worked out. So when James offered to sell the firm to me something said yes, that might not be as stupid an idea as it sounded. So I want to know, if you understood all that, would you mind if I did that?'

He stopped talking and looked for an answer in the old man's eyes again. For a moment he could detect nothing, as if Horace was away somewhere, thinking about it, and Morris let him do that. He was in no hurry. Then he felt a stirring in the hand under his, and he tried again to read his eyes, and what they said, quite clearly, was yes, do it. Take over the firm and look after Rachel, and tell her I don't blame her for anything, never have, and that I love her like a real daughter, and ... and then his eyes closed and Morris panicked for a moment and he called the nurse but she just said don't worry, he's tired, he's fallen asleep. Morris squeezed his hand once more to say thank you and left him alone with his sleep and his memories.

When he got back to the office there were two messages. The first one was an enquiry about a funeral, which he took to be a good omen. Yes, buying the business suddenly seemed like a sensible thing to do. Yes, now he could see it all more clearly. He would change the name to ... to Tite and Figg, because he didn't think the late Mr Widdlecombe would mind. He rang back and the conversation went pretty well and to his amazement he convinced them, and arranged a meeting with the family for the following morning. He put the phone down and leaned back once again in dear old Horace's chair. Yes, all this could be his. His and Rachel's even.

Then he remembered there was a second message.

'Hullo, Morris, this is James Tite again. Look, since I spoke to you this morning we've had an unexpected offer for the business and, well I'm sure you'll understand, but I'm afraid we've accepted.'

OK James my old son, that's how it is, is it? Well why don't you just go and boil your head? Because you know, I don't care about your poxy little business. It's frankly not worth having. Without your father, it's nothing. Anyone who buys this needs their head examined. I hope you choke on the money, and I'm only sorry it's not my money you'll be choking on, except I'm glad it's not my money because it would be a waste of the stuff, and anyway you're the last person I would give it to anyway, so there. And anyway, what would your buyer say if they knew I was setting up my own firm, huh? A bit of competition for them, see how they like that. Yeh, if you think I can't run an undertaker's, you're making a big mistake. Oh yes, good ol' Morris Figg, Funeral Director, you wait.

He felt better after he thought all that, and more, and put the phone down without saying a word to James who just said Morris ... Morris ... are you there? He didn't feel better for long though. It was about the time he stopped feeling better that he realised what he had just been thinking. Morris Figg, Funeral Director? What the hell was that supposed to mean?

30

The next morning the alarm didn't wake him. At nine o'clock what woke him was a knock on the door.

'Good morning. Mr Figg?'

He wasn't awake enough yet to deny it. Anyway, this bloke didn't look dangerous.

'Atkins and Atkins, architects. My name's Julian.'

'Uhuh. That's nice Julian. And why exactly are you here?'

'Well Mr Figg, we have an instruction from the landlord, let me see, um ...' Julian fumbled ineffectually among his papers.

'I think you'll find, Julian, that it's Carol Crapovic.'

'Oh yes, quite. Well, Mr Crapovic has instructed my firm to draw up the plans for the extension.'

'What extension? He hasn't said anything to me.'

'Yes, no, well, I mean, I don't know anything about that. Look, would you like to see the letter?'

'No.'

'Oh.' Julian didn't know what that meant. He hadn't wanted to come to this horrid house in the first place. His speciality was barn conversions, only there hadn't been anyone else available for this job and against his better judgment he had agreed to come. He imagined the denizens of Tamworth Park to be only semi-civilised, and climbing up the worn-out stairs his heart had been filled with dread. Now this strange person was confusing him.

Morris sat on the worn-out sofa and picked up a copy of last week's Tamworth Free Advertiser, pretending not to notice Julian, and Julian took this to mean it was alright. He started in the bedroom, which was a mistake. Morris's bedroom was not a pretty sight at the best of times, let alone ten minutes after he'd got up. Julian tried to avoid seeing the unmade bed. It made him nauseous. Then, just when he thought the worst was done, he went into the bathroom. He hadn't realised anyone actually lived like this. In the kitchen there were several dishes containing leftover substances he could only assume had once been food, although he would have been hard pressed to say what. No, where Julian came from they didn't live like this.

He took a lot of measurements and even more photographs, stuffed his measure and camera into his leather briefcase, and fled. He would make his feelings known very strongly when he got back to the office. Yes, very strongly.

Morris, meanwhile, was trying to figure out what was going on. He poured some Frosties into the last clean bowl he could find. He had by this time remembered his bizarre idea yesterday of starting his own undertaker's, and now he was trying to get his head round Mr Crapovic's plan to do something he couldn't understand to his flat. There wasn't any milk. He briefly considered going down and pinching the bottle he knew would be waiting for the bakery man's return from work, but he had tried that one once too often and anyway it just didn't somehow seem right. So he sat and crunched dry Frosties while he pondered what was going on.

When he got to the office it somehow looked different. In the night, he now realised, he dreamed about it, with his name over the door, and now it was going to belong to someone else. He realised he minded, and he sat and tried to figure out why. Morris had never done anything useful in his life. Angie had tried to encourage him but he sank into a long-term state of apathy years ago and she had given up. Angie

205

believed in him; the problem was he had stopped believing in himself.

But now he wanted to own something, now he wanted his name over a door that said look at me I'm in business. Now he had the bit between his teeth. He didn't know how much it would cost to set up in competition to Widdlecombe and Tite, if thirteen thousand pounds was remotely enough, but he did know that he was going to work it out.

Funerals happen on someone else's premises, a church or the crematorium and the cemetery. All you need is a small office, somewhere to keep the bodies, and a hearse. The pallbearers are hired by the job. How much can that all cost? He wanted to talk it through with someone. His first choice would have been Rachel. He didn't really know her yet but she was tied up in all this. His second choice was Angie and he drove round there but she wasn't in. He wondered about going round to the vicarage in case she had gone back there but even if she had it was no place to talk, not if Peter Potter was around.

So he drove back to the office, only his route took him past Marty's warehouse and in desperation he stopped there.

'Morris, my old and valued friend. This is a surprise.'

'Yes Marty, it's a bit unexpected for me too.' Which was an oblique way of saying you weren't my first choice.

'Well, that's nice.'

It is?

'So Morris, what's today's problem? How can Marty help?'

'I don't think you can.'

'Oh, I'm sorry about that.'

And he looked it. Morris wondered why.

'No, look, I mean there's nothing wrong. I don't need any help.'

'Well, just a minute and I'll make a note in my diary. Tuesday the fourth, Morris didn't need anything. Apart, I guess, from a nice cup of tea.'

While he made it Morris wandered round the warehouse. The space where the freezers had been was occupied by an old wardrobe now, with two chairs piled on top of it, and a dining table on its side. He wondered if it had all been a dream. Then he wondered if Rachel had been a dream, and he fished the letter out of his pocket to reassure himself.

'So, how's the funeral business? Up and down I suppose?'

'Marty, if we're going to have that joke every time I come round I'm going to stop coming round. Anyway, there's one or two problems.'

And he sat and told his friend everything he had wanted to tell someone, and at first Marty told bad jokes but then he just listened, with nothing more than the odd uhuh and mm I see to interrupt. Then he asked a surprisingly sensible question.

'OK, so you need premises and a car, but there's something else you need, and that's customers. Do you think you can sell funerals?'

'I don't know. So far, no, I haven't been able to compete with the Co-op.'

'OK, what have they got that you haven't?'

'The divi.'

'Yes, but they haven't got Air Miles, have they?'

'No, I admit, probably they haven't. What's that got to do with anything?'

'Well, it's obvious. Offer your customers Air Miles.'

'Is that another bad joke?'

'It's not a joke at all mate. I'm being serious. Now, what are you going to call your firm?' Marty was getting into the spirit of it.

'I haven't got that far. Come on Marty, this is all pie in the sky. There isn't going to be a firm.'

'Tut tut, defeated already?'

'I don't know. I suppose just Morris Figg.'

'Figg Funeral Directors. Not sure about that. How about Figg and Figg, sounds a bit more like it.'

'But there aren't any other Figgs.'

'Morris, that's not how business works. Bloody hell, if you only told people the absolute truth, well, I mean, where would that get you?'

Morris had been telling lies all his life and that had got him precisely nowhere. No, it was no way to begin. Anyway, a name was hardly the most important decision. Premises were. And premises on the high street were going to cost, he knew that. And something told him that there was going to be more to competing with the Co-op than Air Miles.

'No, look, I've been thinking. There are only two ways for any business to compete. Either you offer something the other lot haven't got, or you compete on price.'

'OK, so what can you do that they don't?'

'To be honest mate, nothing. I mean funerals are funerals. Everyone does the same thing because that's all there is. Stick them in a box, shove it in the ground. The scope for being different is a bit limited.'

'Which leaves price.'

'Yeh, but if I've got to pay High Street rent and rates it's not going to be possible to undercut them, is it?'

'So don't have your premises on the High Street.'

'But if I don't, people won't find me.'

'Of course they will. People find me, and look at this place.'

'Yes, but they know you're here already.'

'That's true.'

'But hang on, how do they know you're here?'

'The leaflets. I go round houses leafleting, and then people call me.'

'Alright then, maybe that's the way to do it. Put leaflets through doors and have my premises any old place, like here.'

'What do you mean, like here?'

'I mean like here. Not here, obviously, I said like here. I mean, you couldn't have an undertaker's in a warehouse for second-hand furniture, obviously.'

'No, that's true. But you could if I moved the furniture down one end and built a partition wall.'

Morris got up and looked around. 'Well, you'd have to start here, and run it across over there, like this, so you've got the big double doors and I've got the small one for people to come in.'

'Yes, but you'd need to drive the hearse in.'

'That's true. What about if we .... hang on, Marty, what the hell are we talking about?'

'You setting up your firm here.'

'Are we?'

'I think so.'

'So how do you feel about that?'

'I don't know. Let me think about it. OK.'

'That was quick.'

'Yeh.'

So they started measuring up and making real plans and by the end of the afternoon they had made a definite decision, and then Morris went home and decided it was crazy, there was no way it would work, and he would phone Marty in the morning and tell him not to worry, he had realised it was foolishness and it wasn't going to happen. What he actually did was to phone him and ask if he had changed his mind, and when Marty said no he hadn't and asked him if he had he said no, of course not, which surprised him a bit. He was doing things he hadn't planned to do and he thought he ought to stop but he didn't and then he thought he ought to try harder to stop but he didn't do that either and so things just kind of happened.

So that afternoon Morris went round and agreed what rent he was going to pay, which suited Marty because business wasn't great and getting a regular income from part of the premises would suit him down to the ground. Having come to this momentous decision, they felt it was imperative that they go out and celebrate.

'Where shall we go?'

'Not the Pink Flamingo, that's for sure.'

'I'm with you there.'

'OK, look, I'll pick you up at eight o'clock. We'll have an Indian at the Golden Sunset Curry House only I don't think I'll be having the chips, and then we'll find a pub. I'll drive. We'll use the limo before the Co-op gets it.'

Morris turned up at eight in the hearse.

'What happened to the limo?'

'Flat battery, There was no choice.'

'I'm not sure about going out for the night in a hearse.'

'Come on, once we're in town we'll just park up and no-one will know.'

Which is what they did. Morris drank abstemiously. He had learned his lesson about drinking and driving. An undertaker who couldn't drive wasn't much use. It was a great night out. Marty picked up a girl at the Wig and Pistle and Morris declined her friend on account, he said, of him being engaged, to which Marty said are you I didn't know, and insisted they all have another drink, and at one o'clock he drove Marty and his girl home down the Oxford road.

It was singular bad luck that the god of unfortunate coincidences was also out that night and had been knocking them back, because Chalky White was at the wheel for his nightly alcohol-fuelled drive around the empty streets of the town, only they weren't empty. Morris was driving the hearse in a straight line and if Chalky had been doing the same with his Ford Zephyr everyone would have have got home safely but Chalky never drove in a straight line and tonight was no exception. He loomed out of a dark side street, straight across to the wrong side of the Oxford road, the side as it happened where Morris was minding his own business, and the two vehicles came to a grinding halt accompanied by the sound of buckling metal and the tinkle of breaking glass.

There really is only one thing you can say in those

circumstances.
    Shit.

31

The damage to the Daimler was one bent front bumper, a smashed headlight, and a nasty two-foot dent where the Zephyr had finally come to a halt. The damage to the Ford was rather more considerable but didn't interest Morris.

Still, there was an easy solution. James had asked him to produce an inventory of the firm's assets and he simply wrote one Daimler hearse, damaged. James rang him.

'I see the hearse has had a bump. Can you explain that?'

Yes sonny Jim, for you, anything.

'Yes, it was your father, I'm afraid.'

'Dad? He's an excellent driver. He's never had an accident in his life.'

'No, but then I don't suppose he's ever had a stroke in his life either.'

'What does that mean?'

It means, sonny, that you are just about to get stitched up.

'Well, you see, when it happened, the stroke I mean, we were just setting off to do a job. He put his foot on the accelerator and then it happened. He blacked out, the car lurched forward and hit the gate before I could stop it. I was more concerned about Mr Tite than the car, naturally.'

Which is more than can be said for you.

'I see. Have you had an estimate for repairs? There's no point claiming on the insurance.'

Yes. My mate Marty says, tut tut, that'll cost you a bomb.

That kind of estimate?'

'No, but it's a very old car. I don't know if they will be able to get the parts any more. What do you think?'

He could hear James's accountant mind doing the sums. The Co-op wasn't likely to be interested in a fully-functioning twenty-year-old hearse, let alone a bent one, which somewhat pushed the resale value down, which was where Morris wanted it. He could hear James dithering, and he let him sweat for exactly another fifteen seconds.

'On the other hand ...'

'Yes?'

'Well, I've got a friend who might be interested in buying it, for cash, as seen.'

'Really? Is he in the business?'

'No no, furniture. A hearse makes a good transport.'

'Really? Oh, well. Um, cash, you say?'

'Yep.'

'Um, how much do you think?'

'Oh, I've no idea. What do I know about these things? What would you suggest?' He could tell that suggesting was about the last thing James wanted to do.

'I know less than you probably. What would you say? Five?'

'Hundred?'

'No. Thousand.'

It's a good technique. James was now trying to talk him up from hundreds, which even Morris knew was silly, but he was on the defensive. Morris was prepared to go up to three and a half. James gave in at three. Morris almost felt sorry for him. Almost.

By the time he had had the alterations done at the warehouse and the signwriting over the door, he was down another two and a half, but so far Tinkerbelle's money was holding up nicely. Morris and Marty stood back to admire the new front. The signwriter had, they thought, done a good job,

213

even if Marty had some reservations about the name Morris had chosen.

The Coffin Shop, Funerals to Die For. Prop. Morris Figg.

'You don't think it's a bit, you know ...?'

'Cheap?'

'Yes, that's the word I was looking for.'

'Yes. Cheap is good. Cheap is how we compete, and I want people to know.'

'Anyway, what's a prop?'

'A prop? Oh, that's me. You're a prop too.'

'I am?'

'Yes, but don't worry about it. Now come in and tell me what you think.'

Inside, the furniture consisted of a second-hand desk from Marty's side, plus some second-hand chairs and a second-hand filing cabinet, also supplied by Marty, and on the walls hung the various pictures from Widdlecombe and Tite which of course the Co-op hadn't wanted. In fact they didn't want anything. They had closed Widdlecombe and Tite down, to eliminate the competition. Well, now they had Morris to contend with.

The chapel of rest consisted of a second-hand walk-in fridge behind a curtain. Several sprays of plastic flowers completed the decor. They gave the place a certain funereal, if cheap, look.

'Yes, yes, very nice.' Marty didn't sound sure. 'Well, all you need now is some customers.'

And the first one walked through the door.

'Hullo? Are you open?'

'Yes, yes, do come in. I'm Morris Figg, proprietor. This is our decorator. He's just leaving. How can I help you?'

Morris managed to refrain, with some difficulty, from doing the full impersonation of a Victorian undertaker, but even so he noticed he was wringing his hands.

'Well, my name's Cyril Goggins.'

Cyril Goggins? Cyril Goggins? No, surely not.

'Yes, it's about my late mother.'

'Late, you say? Mrs Goggins?'

'Yes. Is there anything wrong?'

Well, obviously there is, with her.

'Oh no. It's just that I used to know Mrs Goggins and, well, I'm shocked to learn of her death. She has died, hasn't she?'

'Oh yes. That's why I'm here. She left a note, said she wanted Widdlecombe and Tite to bury her, only I went there and it's closed down so I didn't know what to do. Then I got a leaflet through my door.'

Oh, the wonderful power of advertising.

'Yes, Mum said she wanted Mr Figg to do her, and here you are, even if you're not Widdlecombe and Tite, so I reckon that will be OK. Would you take on the job? Money isn't a problem.'

'It isn't?' Morris was genuinely puzzled.

'Oh no. I said she should take out a funeral plan but she didn't need to, she was already insured, you see.'

'Yes, I see. Well, that's excellent, excellent.' Morris realised he was sounding like Horace Tite and tried to make himself stop. 'Well, Mr Goggins, why don't you sit here and I'll explain everything to you and you can decide which option you want for your mother.'

'Righto.'

'Well, there's the Economy Package, the Super-Economy Package and, for those whose finances are, shall we say, limited even by the standards of the economy funeral profession, of which The Coffin Shop is the leading exponent in this area, there is the Dead Cheap Option.'

'The Dead Cheap Option?'

'Yes, a recycled cardboard coffin and instead of a hearse we wheel the body down to the cemetery on a gurney made from two Tesco trolleys welded together.'

'I see. No, I don't think Mum would have wanted that. I

think we can afford the best you've got.'

'The Economy Package, then?'

'Yes please.'

'Excellent, excellent. Well if I could just take some details and get your signature we'll have the old girl, I mean the departed, at rest in no time, no time at all.'

Morris did wonder, after Cyril had left, if perhaps he hadn't overdone it. Still, it was his very first customer. He would learn. Encouraged by the result of his first advertising, he spent the next three hours tramping the streets delivering more leaflets, and he came back to check if anyone had rung. No-one had. It was a bit disappointing, but it was his first day and he had a sale, so there was reason only to celebrate.

He didn't want to do that with Marty tonight, so he shut up shop and went home to spend some time on his own. He wished he could tell Rachel all about it. And lo and behold, on account of the god of good timing being on the ball, there was a letter from her waiting for him. It was full of chatty news, as if they had known each other for years, and it was of course a love letter as well. He read it three times before he put his fish fingers under the grill, and then again while they cooked. There was so much he wanted to say to her. Part of him worried that the magic would somehow vanish before he had the chance to do that.

He settled down with one of his now infrequent smokes and a beer, and the phone rang.

'Hullo, is that Mr Morris Figg?'

'Yes.'

'Hullo sir, my name is Captain Henderson. I'm the Welfare Officer for the Second Battalion, the Devonshire Regiment. I am afraid I have some bad news for you.'

32

Rachel's Land Rover had been blown on its side by a mine. She had two broken legs but not much other damage. She was, as Captain Henderson had said, a lucky girl. She shouldn't apparently have been on the road at all, but had volunteered to visit a Company that was holed up in the desert, to boost their morale. She had undergone surgery at the Army's field hospital and now they were airlifting her back to the UK. From the airbase she would be taken by ambulance to the military hospital in Portsmouth. Would Morris like to visit her there?

He could just get to Portsmouth and back before Mrs Goggins's funeral. He gave Wally full instructions, met Peter Potter to go through the service, and hit the road in Marty's van. His only transport was a hearse, and he didn't want to turn up at a hospital in that.

Captain Henderson's estimate of Rachel's injuries had been a little on the optimistic side. In addition to two legs in plaster, she had a bandaged head from a piece of shrapnel that had just missed her eye, and several large dressings covering burns to her arms and torso. She didn't look good, and Morris was shocked.

'So, do you still love me then?'

'Did I say I loved you before?'

'No.'

'Well that was a mistake.' He couldn't have said in all

honesty if it was love or pity he felt, but whatever it was it was strong, stronger than he remembered feeling ever before. Then he knew what it was. A want to take care of her. And that was certainly something he had never felt for a woman before.

He didn't know which bit of her face to kiss so he just sat by her bedside and felt foolish.

'So tell me, which part of PT instructing involves getting blown up?'

'Well, there's a first and last time for everything, and this is definitely the last time. Anyway, there's no more soldiering for me now, not with this lot. I'm out.'

'Of the Army?'

'Yep.'

Morris wanted to know how she felt about that and from the tear trickling down her cheek he had a fair idea.

'Anyway, tell me what's been happening to you since I left you to look after yourself.'

'No, let's talk about you.'

'I don't want to talk about me, I'm a bit tired of me just now, so really, can we do that another time and talk about you instead? And if you don't want to do that I want you to tell me how Pops is doing.'

'Oh him. Well, I've been to see him a couple of times.'

'Really? Have you read my letter?'

'Of course, a hundred times. I've talked to him about it.'

'Really? Is he able to talk?'

'Well, no, I did the talking and he listened. Look, I'm certain he can hear and understand. He just can't reply.'

'And what did you say to him?'

'About the business, naturally. And us.'

'Us? Is there an us?'

'As far as I'm concerned there is. If you want there to be.'

'Morris, look at me.'

'Yes? I'm looking. What do you want me to say?'

'Well for a start I want you to tell me where we go from here. I'm finished. You know that?'

Morris thought about this before answering. He knew the next thing he said was going to matter a lot.

'Now look here Rachel. OK, you're finished as an athlete and a soldier.'

'Yes. And what does that leave?'

'You really don't know the answer to that?'

'No.' She was raising her voice. The nurse peered through the door to check and closed it behind her.

'You don't think you exist outside of the super-fit Rachel da Souza, the girl in uniform with the silver medal, do you?'

'No, I don't.'

'Then, my girl, you've got a pretty poor opinion of yourself.'

'That's right. That's exactly right. I was nothing before I became what I am now. It was martial arts and the Army that made me. I don't exist without them.'

Now it was Morris's turn to get angry.

'Rachel, I didn't fall in love with you because you broke Mick's fingers, or because of your uniform. What I see is a person, a lovely one, a woman I want to be with and that's got nothing to do with the things you're talking about.'

'Yes, but that's just you. Don't be offended but you know what I mean.'

'Yes, and you're wrong. You've fought so long and hard to become what you are that it's all you can see. You're the soldier and medal winner, but think about this, who created that person? The Army? Your trainer? No, I don't think so. You can't create someone from nothing. You're a success not because of them but because of you, because you had it in you to do those things. The real heroine is you, not the cardboard cut-out that people see.'

Rachel was crying openly now. She sat sobbing, and the nurse heard and came in.

'Mr Figg, really I won't have this upset. I must ask you to

leave.'

Rachel looked up from her hands and glared at her. 'Corporal, he's staying. And that's an order.'

He sat quietly now and held her hand. She needed time to think about all the things he'd said, and he let her doze. The nurse crept in apologetically with a cup of tea for him. Finally, Rachel woke and smiled at him weakly, but she didn't continue the conversation.

'So tell me about Pops.'

'Yeh, he's OK, no change really as far as I know. The firm has been sold though.'

'What? How is that possible? If he can't sign anything ...'

'James. He has power of attorney, apparently. He got an offer from the Co-operative Funeral Service and it's all gone through.'

'James? He's a nasty piece of work. But what about you, I mean your job?'

'I'm a prop now.'

'What, you mean you're playing rugby?'

'Huh? No, I've started a business of my own.'

'No kidding. Doing what?'

'Burying. I've launched my own funeral firm.'

'No. Really? Bloody hell. How? Where? Why?'

'In reverse order, because I had to do something and even though the Co-op took over the old firm they closed it down so they are still the only competition, in my friend Marty's warehouse round the back of Hinckley Street, and with some money I, um, inherited.'

'Wow, that's dynamic. Morris Figg, Undertaker.'

'Well no, not exactly.'

'What's it called then?'

'The Coffin Shop.'

'Morris, you're winding me up.'

'Would I do that to a woman in your condition?'

He sat there and talked like he had known her all his life.

She dozed off sometimes but he just sat and watched her sleeping. The sun went down and the room got dark but he didn't want to put the light on. She came out of her doze from time to time and smiled at him.

'You still here?'

'I can go if you want.'

'No, don't.'

But the nurse came in and said yes, do, and he had no choice. Orders are orders. He found a cheap bed and breakfast not far from the hospital, slept the sleep of the dead, and was back first thing in the morning. He arranged to pick Rachel's car up from Catterick and drive down, then he could visit her regularly until she was ready to go home. Wherever that was now.

Meanwhile he had to get home himself. There was work to do, people to bury.

He got back to town late, but instead of driving back to the flat he went to see Angie. She wasn't at the house though.

'Roger.'

'Yes? You look surprised Morris.'

'Um, well, I mean I thought Angie ...'

'What? Might have come back? No.'

'But you have, I mean you're here.'

'That's because I live here. Morris, you look confused. Which surprises me, since it's all over the front page of the local paper.'

If Roger thought he was confused before, now he really was. 'Roger, what the hell are you talking about? What is? Has something happened to Angie?'

His brother-in-law went through to the kitchen and Morris followed him. Roger handed him The Barton & Tidbury Sentinel. It was, as he said, all over the front page.

'Vicarage Love Nest Minister says I Won't Resign. Jesus. That's Peter Potter. Hang on, The Reverend Peter Potter has received an ultimatum from the church authorities to resign his position and vacate the vicarage of St Elmo's Church but has said he won't give in. Mrs Angela Brotherton, his 39 year-old lover ... bloody hell, they haven't even got her age right. Mind you, it's not a bad photo.'

'Is that all you've got to say? It's not a bad photo? Who gives a flying fuck how old she is? The stupid cow has gone and got her name all over the front page of the paper. Do you realise everyone at school is talking about this? I'm the joke of the year. The sixth formers have been going round wearing dog collars.'

'Is that all you're worried about? What about Angie?'

'What about Angie? Do you really think I give a shit about her after this?'

'Um, no, well, I can see your point. You know, I'm beginning to think my sister really is a silly cow. Mind you, that Peter Potter, I never thought he had it in him. Holy shit.'

'For once, Morris, in your inimitable way, you have just about hit the nail on the head. Now, if you don't mind ...'

'Hang on, I just want to read the rest of this. Continued on page 2, hold on, there's more.'

'Morris, come on, it's late ...'

'Bloody hell. No, it can't be. Oh shit.'

'What now?'

'Roger, I need this. Got to go. Bye.'

And he was in the van driving hell for leather for home. Ten seconds after crashing through his front door he was on the phone.

'Marty?'

'Morris, what is it? Do you mind, I've got Mavis here.'

'Fuck Mavis.'

'Yes, well, it's funny you should say that.'

'Marty, I'm deadly serious. Get rid of her, and get over here. Now.'

'Morris old friend, you're not making sense. What the hell are you talking about?'

'Haven't you seen The Sentinel?'

'No, never read it. What is it?'

'Not what, who. Mick.'

'What? You mean the Mick we ...?'

'Yeh, that one. He's on page two.'

'Oh shit. I'll be there in half an hour.'

An hour later he ran breathless up the stairs.

'Sorry about that. You've got the van, remember, so I had to ask Mavis for a lift and she wouldn't bring me 'til I'd given her what she came for. Where is it?'

Morris handed him the paper.

'Body of club boss found in freezer. Oh bugger, bugger bugger bugger.'

'Yes, that's what I thought.'

'Shit, Morris, what are we going to do?'

'Well, for a start we're not going to panic.'

'Not going to panic? What the hell are you talking about? The police have found the body we dumped in the municipal freezer recycling centre and you're saying don't panic. If you're not panicking, then you bloody well should be.'

'Look, think about it. What is there to connect the body with us?'

'Well, there's the freezer, for a start.'

'Yes, but what is there to connect that with us?'

'Er, nothing. No, shit, hang on, it'll have our fingerprints all over it.'

'Oh, shit. No, hang on, I was wearing gloves, because the body was frozen.'

'Oh, that's all right then. There's nothing to worry about then is there? Except I wasn't.'

'Oh. But look, OK, it's got your fingerprints on it. But even if they manage to lift them, what's that going to mean to them? They only connect fingerprints with villains they already suspect, you know, people whose prints are already on their computer system.'

'Like mine, on account of me having been arrested, if you remember, in connection with drug pushing.'

'Shit.'

33

Marty was on a ferry for Dublin the next morning. He left Morris in charge of the warehouse, and made him promise to ring and keep him informed of developments. Morris was worried for his own sake too, because the police might trace the freezer back to Marty, because PC Penny might remember Morris's frozen chip business. Well, it was a chance he would have to take. He had more pressing problems than something that might not happen. He made a list of them in his head. Get out there and sell funerals. Bury Mrs Goggins. Find out what the hell Carol Crapovic was up to with the flat, and then try to get his head round whatever it was Angie thought she was doing. And do whatever he could to help Rachel to see her future differently.

Mrs Goggins's funeral went without a hitch, apart from Wally smelling distinctly of alcohol and Morris having to have strong words with him and him saying ooh, now you're giving orders you're getting like Horace Tite, and Morris saying look, this is a serious business even if it doesn't look like it in this warehouse, and if I'm paying you you need to think about that, and Wally saying ooh again, once too often, and Morris saying that's it, after this job you can shove off, I'll find other pallbearers.

So problem number six, or was it seven, was to do that.

Since The Coffin Shop didn't yet offer a twenty-four hour service, Morris could take the weekends off. After the

Goggins job there was a cremation for another family who had dealt with Widdlecombe and Tite before, and on the Friday night he set off for Portsmouth in high spirits. It hadn't been a bad week. If you ignored the Mick business. And the fact that he was hiring three of Carol Crapovic's Croatian labourers as pallbearers, and they didn't speak English, but still, who has ever heard of a pallbearer having to say anything at a funeral?

It came about when he went round to see his landlord to find out about the extension.

'Ah, yes, Mr Figg. Very good. Your flat is too big.'

'Too big? Mr Crapovic, if you make it any smaller I'll have to sleep with my feet on the landing.'

'Yes, yes, very good, sure, but Carol Crapovic didn't get where he is today, no, you see Mr Figg we are going to build up from the flat roof of Mrs Diggle's kitchen and make whole new flat. Julian says all we need is your bathroom.'

'Oh, is that all? Well, that's fine then.'

'Very good. Glad you see it like that Mr Figg.'

'Mr Crapovic, I was being sarcastic.'

'Very good Mr Figg, I like that.'

And so on, and so on, until Morris knew he had lost, and he swapped his bathroom for three illegal immigrants so he didn't come away completely empty-handed. He could always go to the toilet when he got to work.

So first thing Saturday morning he arrived at the military hospital and went to Rachel's room, only she wasn't there. He panicked.

'Don't worry dear, Sergeant-Major da Souza has gone to the operating theatre. You can wait here for her.'

'Thank you nurse.'

'Corporal.'

Whatever. Two hours later he was fast asleep on the bed when they brought her back.

'Er, excuse me, mind if she has the bed?'

'Oh, sorry. How is she?'

'Oh, the surgeons say she'll be fine.'

'What about her legs?'

'Yep, she's still got them both. She's lucky.'

That hadn't exactly been what Morris meant, but he decided to wait and ask Rachel when she came round from the anaesthetic.

'Hullo soldier. How do you feel?'

'Been better, but that seems like a long time ago.'

'What do the medics say?'

'You know, the usual sort of thing. Good morning and how are we today, stuff like that.'

'I see. They should have surgically removed that pathetic sense of humour of yours while they had you under.'

'Shut up and give me a kiss.'

Which he did.

'Now, tell me everything. What was the operation for?'

'Well, they had to reset both legs. It was done in the field hospital but in a bit of a hurry. You know how these things are.'

'No, but I can imagine. What do they say about, you know, when you'll be able to walk?'

'Oh that? Well, sure, I'll walk again.'

'And?'

'And I'll walk again. What else is there?'

'Life, Rachel, life.'

'Oh yes, that.'

And so the conversation went on, all that day and the next, and Morris struggled to say anything light-hearted, and finally he left for the long drive home in a much worse mood that he'd driven down in. He hadn't known what to say to her, and why should he? They were new to each other, and Rachel had a long history which he had only an inkling of. How was he supposed to help her see a future when he didn't understand her past, and that meant he didn't really know her at all? If everything had gone the way these things usually do she would have come back to England and they would have got to know each other at the proper speed but now she was depending on him to get her through this, right now, because there was no-one else. He felt out of his depth. He needed some help.

Back at work again, he went out every day for a couple of hours stuffing leaflets through doors and he didn't know why but people started phoning. He picked up another job that week and he was so busy he forgot he had meant to go round to the vicarage to see Angie. He went on the pretext of arranging a funeral with Peter Potter.

'Morris.'

'Hullo Angie.'

'I wondered when you would turn up.'

'I can go away again, if that's what you want.'

'Stay where you are kiddo. I could do with the company.'

'Got yourself into a bit of a mess haven't you? That's usually my line.'

'Well, I must take after you. I'm a late developer.'

'So, what's it all about?'

'Dunno. I can't remember why I'm doing this. It's all got out of hand and now I can't seem to stop.'

'But you left and went back to Roger.'

'Well, not strictly, because if you remember he wasn't there when I got back.'

'No but he is now.'

'Yes, but before he got back I came back here.'

'Look, Angie, I'm sure there's some kind of explanation for all this but if there is it's too complicated for me.'

'No it's not. You see Peter didn't want me here and I went back to Roger, who wasn't there, and I stayed in the house for a few days until I wasn't sure what going back to Roger meant if he wasn't there and I got lonely and I came round to get the rest of my things and kind of stayed. Peter meanwhile decided that he did want me after all. You know, he's not such a wimp as I thought. Once he gets the bit between his teeth, well, look what's happened. The church people say he's got to resign but he won't. He says he'll fight for his rights.'

'Has he got any?'

'No, I don't think so, but on the other hand his solicitor says they can't fire him because he hasn't actually done anything wrong, so at least he's got the right to stay here as long as it takes them to find a better solicitor than his.'

'Doesn't shacking up with a married woman qualify as something wrong?'

'Well, they don't like it, but it's not enough to get fired for, and there are laws about these things these days apparently. And his union is supporting him.'

'His union? I didn't know vicars had a union.'

'No, neither did I. There's a lot I didn't know about vicars, but I'm learning fast.'

'Anyway, where is God's gift to women? I need to arrange a funeral at St Elmo's.'

'He'll be back soon. Do you want to wait for him?'

'Would you feel bad if I chickened out and ask you to get him to call me?'

'Yes, but it's what I would expect.'

'I'm a coward, aren't I?'

'Yep, but I still love you.'

'Do you? I didn't know you ever did.'

'Slip of the tongue, kiddo. I didn't mean it.'

'That's alright then.'

Morris went straight from the vicarage to the nursing home. Horace was sitting by a large window, apparently soaking up the sun, and when Morris sat down next to him the old man put his hand on his and kept it there while they spoke. Morris told him about Rachel and then he said he had an important question to ask him, was he ready for that, and with a little pressure from his hand Horace said yes, and then Morris asked him the question and the old man turned his head towards the sun while he thought for a moment, and then with his hand he said yes, yes, yes.

34

The next week nothing went wrong, so by Friday Morris was starting to get nervous. He knew Rachel was alright, because he spoke to her on the phone every day. He knew Marty was alright, because the police hadn't been round looking for him and there was nothing more about Mick in The Sentinel, and he rang and told him no news is good news. He knew Angie was alright, because she said she was, even if he didn't really believe her. The Coffin Shop was alright, because they were taking enquiries every day now and some people were a bit shocked by the economy funeral approach but a lot weren't and by the end of the week he had booked an interment on the Friday morning and a cremation for early the following week. The only business he turned away was weekend jobs. Rachel was more important.

So after the Friday job he went home and got changed, drove over to the nursing home to pick Horace up in Rachel's car, stowed his wheelchair in the boot, and set off south.

Horace dozed a lot of the way for which Morris was grateful. It's hard to have a conversation with a man who can only whisper a few words while you're driving. He was impatient, Morris knew, but it was late when they arrived and Morris drove instead to the nursing home he had booked them into and told him they would go first thing in the morning.

By nine o'clock they were at the hospital, and as Morris

pushed the old man's wheelchair into Rachel's room he wondered if this was a good idea, or at least if he should have told her.

Rachel wasn't in her bed. She was on crutches. She looked at Horace, and then she looked at Morris, and then she got confused and nearly fell off her crutches so Morris wheeled the old man over to the bed and without saying a word he left them to it and went outside for a smoke. He finished that and wondered how long he should leave them and was about to go back in when the nurse came out and rolled up a cigarette.

'Got a light?'

'Sure. Here.'

'Thanks. What's with the old man?'

'Oh, he had a stroke.'

'Sorry about that. Hard for her. You can see the likeness, can't you?'

'What?'

'Yeh, no mistaking it. She's just like him.'

Morris needed to think about this, but try as he might he couldn't figure out why Rachel would look like a man she wasn't related to. When he looked at them he tried to see it but he couldn't, which left two possibilities, that the nurse was on something, or she was completely barmy.

It occurred to him as he drove back to Barton the next day with Horace what the connection was, which meant she wasn't barmy after all. It wasn't a family resemblance, it was a personality one. Horace and Rachel were like minds, hard-headed types with a soft centre. It explained not only why the nurse thought they looked alike but why they were so close. They needed each other, and Morris knew he had done the right thing.

He knew that even more in the days and weeks that followed. Horace's condition improved in leaps and bounds, and he knew it was Rachel's influence that was making the difference. By the time she came up to Barton to convalesce

232

he was talking again. OK, a lot of what he said was unintelligible, but that didn't put him off and Morris encouraged him to say anything he wanted, and it wasn't long before the old man was telling him to get his hair cut and then Morris knew he was going to be alright.

He never regained the use of his legs though. Morris knew there was only one way he and Rachel would cope at the house, even with the nurse who came to visit every day, and that was if he moved in himself to look after them both. He moved his stuff out of the flat and let Mr Crapovic take the bathroom.

The Coffin Shop was doing well. He went out most days to deliver leaflets but soon there were so many calls coming in that he had to employ a boy to do that so he could be in the office. Marty was still in hiding in Ireland so he tended to spread himself out at the warehouse in his absence. Mr Crapovic's men came round regularly to work and Morris started to teach them some English.

Morris rang Marty.

'Morris my old friend.'

'Hi Marty. How's it going over there?'

'Well, you know.'

'No, that's why I asked.'

'Well, it's boring. I get up about ten and have me breakfast and then I go to the pub for me lunch and then I come back about four for me tea and then I go round to Auntie Maire's for me supper and then I go back to the pub and have another couple of pints and then I come back here and go to bed. Then I get up about ten and have ...'

'Yes, thank you Marty, I've got the picture. So why don't you come back? I could do with your help.'

'Oh, are you selling lots of stuff? That's great.'

'No, not exactly. I sold that sideboard for a tenner ...'

'A tenner! Bloody hell, Morris, that was worth fifty quid.'

'Oh, sorry. Anyway, some bloke came in and bought the

table with the broken leg ...'

'Hang on, I didn't have a table with a broken leg.'

'Well he said it was broken. I didn't look too closely to be honest. I let him have it cheap.'

'Look Morris, I think I'd better come back before I go out of business.'

'Excellent. See you soon.'

Morris took the table without the broken leg and the sideboard round to the tip. It was worth the money to get Marty back. On the way back he decided to pay Angie a visit. At the door to the vicarage he bumped into a journalist from The Sentinel.

'Excuse me sir, are you connected with the vicar by any chance?'

'What do you mean, connected?'

'Well, can you give the paper another angle on the story? You know, can you say anything our readers would like to hear?'

'Yes, bugger off.'

Angie opened the door just enough for Morris to slip in.

'Bloody hell, Angie, what's with The Sentinel? How big a story can this be?'

'Dunno. Well, you see it's got a bit bigger than last time you were here.'

'Like what?'

'Well, first there was the union, and they've got a rep coming round here every other day to advise Peter, and then there's the parish council, which Peter sits on of course but they've passed a motion of something or other which means they don't want him at their meetings, and then the Sunday school teachers refused to come to Sunday school as long as this carries on.'

'So why is it carrying on?'

'Oh I don't know. I offered to leave but he won't hear of it now. Says it's nobody's business what he does.'

'I think he's probably wrong there, from what you say. It seems a lot of people think it's their business. Is anyone on his side? I mean apart from you?'

'Well, apart from me and the union, there's the boy scouts. They're all in favour of keeping up with modern trends apparently. The scoutmaster objected, said it wasn't in keeping with Baden Powell's teaching or something but they burned him on their campfire and elected a new scoutmaster.'

'Really?'

'Well, possibly not the bit about the campfire. And then there's the mother and toddler group.'

'Oh yeh, and what's their angle?'

'They think Peter should have a wife.'

'Even if it's someone else's?'

'I think they think I'm going to get divorced and marry him.'

'Are you?'

'No, yes, well, no, oh I don't know.'

'Look Sis, trust me on this one. You married Roger and if you don't mind me saying so that wasn't one of the best ideas you've ever had, so I suggest you think long and hard about Peter Potter, and then when you've done that you walk away from this.'

'Uhuh, and since when are you an expert on relationships?'

'OK, fair question. Yes, a very fair question. OK, I give in, I'm rubbish, take no notice of me.'

'Oh come on Kiddo, you're not as bad as all that.'

'Yes I am.'

'Well, yes, I suppose you are.'

'Except for Rachel.'

'Oh yes? Tell me more.'

And he did. He was still talking when Peter Potter came in.

'That bloody reporter ... oh, Morris, I didn't know you were here.'

Apparently.

Morris got away from the vicarage as soon as he could, and drove back to the shop. There he found his three Croatian pallbearers gathered round a newspaper. On inspection this turned out to be the Daily Telegraph and he not unnaturally wondered what they were finding so interesting, on account of their command of English extending to yes, no, please and piss off, the last an expression learned apparently from Mr Crapovic, and not much else.

Goran was their spokesman when it came to communicating with Morris, not because he had any more English than his friends but because he spoke German, the logic of which was lost on Morris but still.

'Herr Figg, please ...' and he thrust the paper in Morris's face, the meaning of which was obviously that the latter should read something.

'What? Let me see that. Um, Election in Turkey?' Three heads shook in unison. 'No, well how about this one? No, nothing to do with Saudi Arabia then. Um, Australia? No. That just leaves this. Body of British SOE soldier repatriated. This one?' He pointed at the picture, and all three men smiled hugely and nodded vigorously.

'Yes, Herr Figg, please.' And Goran gesticulated something that obviously meant please read it in Croatian, well, not read it in Croatian but read it, in Croatian.

'OK. It says the body of Sergeant Frederick Figg has been located ... bloody hell, Great Uncle Fred? No, it can't be. Hang on. Sergeant Figg, attached to the Special Operations Executive, was parachuted into Yugoslavia in 1944 to organise a unit of Tito's partisans but was betrayed by the Chetniks, whoever they were, and was believed to have been shot by the Germans. His body was never recovered, but a farmer ploughing a field in the village of, no, can't pronounce it, turned up his identification tag and informed the local police, who contacted the British Embassy, who arranged to have the body dug up and sent back to Britain for formal identification. No shit. Uncle Fred. Thanks boys.'

Then he wondered something.

'Um, hold on, how did you know what this said?'

They didn't know what he meant, but they guessed. Goran pointed to another picture alongside Great Uncle Fred.

'Crapovic.'

Morris peered closely at the picture. It showed a man of indeterminate age with a long rough beard, dressed in the skins of an animal with long shaggy hair, and he was carrying a rifle which even Morris could tell was of pre-world war one vintage. The only thing he had in common with Carol Crapovic was an evil leer.

'No, I don't think so. No, look, not Carol Crapovic.' He spoke loudly and shook his head. 'This man, look, too long ago, not Carol Crapovic.'

Goran said yes, yes and Morris said no no and then Goran made him look at the caption.

'Igor Crapovic, the local partisan leader, whose body was also found with Sergeant Figg. No shit.'

Morris folded the newspaper carefully, jumped in the car, and drove back to the vicarage to tell Angie about Great Uncle Fred. When he got there, though, there were two police cars in the drive and Peter Potter was just getting into one of them.

'Bloody hell Angie, what's going on now?'

'It's Peter.'

'Yes, I can see that. I mean what's he done?'

'He hit the reporter from The Sentinel. They got into an argument and Peter lost his temper and lashed out at him. They've just taken the reporter away in an ambulance and now they've arrested Peter.'

'Yes, I saw the ambulance as I came up the road. Good God, I never knew he had it in him. Your reverend is a bit of a dark horse, isn't he?'

'He's more than that, he's an idiot. What the hell was he

thinking of? What am I going to do?'

'You? I don't see it matters what you do. It's got nothing to do with you.'

'Well the paper's going to send someone else now and they're going to want to ask me all sorts of questions and I'm on my own. Morris, you couldn't be a big brave older brother and stay here for a few days could you?'

'Um, let me see. I've got an old man who's had a stroke and a girlfriend with two broken legs back at the house, so let me see, no.'

'Oh.'

'Well, OK, just for a day or two, till this blows over.'

'Great, thanks. I can't even get to work because they know my car.'

'Don't worry about that, we'll use the hearse. They won't think of looking in that.'

'The hearse?'

'Yeh, I'll put an empty coffin in and you can lie in that.'

'Morris, tell me you're not serious.'

'Actually I am. Can you think of a better way of getting you past the Press?'

'Bloody hell. That bloody Peter. I could hit him myself.'

'Well, while you're at it, give him one for me.'

35

Peter Potter came up before the Barton Magistrates' Court the next morning, after an uncomfortable night in a police cell. Morris took Angie and they sat at the back to avoid her being recognised. The court was full. Word had, it seemed, got around. Peter looked about how you would expect of a vicar who's been in a punch up and then slept in a cell. Rough.

He didn't deny the charge and it was all over in twenty minutes. Bound over to keep the peace. Morris drove them both back to the vicarage. When they got there a crowd had gathered on the front lawn and up the drive. A small group of parishioners were sitting in a circle on the grass singing hymns to a guitar. The first banners they spotted bore the legends Free the Vicar and Peter Potter is Innocent.

'Well first of all, mate, you're obviously not innocent on account of having a criminal record, and secondly you are free so that one's a bit uncalled for.'

'Oh dear, it's all a bit unnecessary, don't you think?'

'Yes, well, hitting that poor bloke from the paper some might say was unnecessary.'

Angie sat in the back with her eyes shut tight. She was trying to pretend this wasn't happening. It was something that clearly ran in the family, hoping that something you can't see might not be there when you open your eyes again. Only, as ever, it was.

There was a bang on the side of the car and a large man looking like an old testament prophet loomed over the windscreen carrying a banner which read something to do with the wrath of God.

'They're not all friendly. Do you want a blanket over your head when we go in?'

Angie was coming out of her stupor. 'Don't be daft, Morris, they know who he is. Let's just get this over with.'

Morris parked as close as he could and two police officers held the crowd back while they made a dash for the front door. Peter put the key in the lock, and nothing happened. He tried again, and nothing happened again.

'Come on, get on with it, I don't want to hang about out here.'

'It's the key. It's not working.'

Angie took it from him. 'For God's sake Peter, don't be such a wuss. Give it here.'

But a key that doesn't want to work for the vicar isn't likely to suddenly change its mind and work for his mistress. Then a man spoke up. They hadn't noticed him standing by the door.

'I think you will find sir, that the barrel has been changed. By me. Bill Bailey, your local bailiff. I've changed the lock on instructions from the church authorities, I have the letter here if you would like to see it.'

Peter grabbed it. 'The bastards. They haven't wasted much time, have they? Got an injunction while I was banged up, I'm not allowed inside.'

'That's right sir. One person is permitted to go in to fetch your belongings. Who would you like to nominate?'

Angie volunteered, since her belongings were also inside, and she carried out as much as they were likely to fit in the car for a first trip, while the bailiff looked on and the police stood there expressionless and the crowd stood there in awe at the sight of their vicar being evicted and several press photographers not only from The Barton Sentinel but the nationals as well snapped away gleefully.

There was only one possible place Morris could take them, and he drove back to Horace's house. Horace himself was hardly going to object, and he hoped Rachel would understand. She did. She and Morris were sharing a bedroom, which normally Horace wouldn't have allowed but they had taken advantage of his condition. Under the circumstances though, Morris felt it would be pushing things to suggest his married sister share a room with the vicar of St Elmo's.

Horace recognised Peter, which was a good sign as far as his recuperation was concerned, but unhelpful in every other way. They didn't feel it was necessary to go into the whole story, so they told the truth about him being fired and evicted, but they didn't tell him why. Which left Angie to be explained, but Morris just said her husband had come out as a raging transvestite and he had had to rescue her, a story sufficiently far fetched to obviate discussion, even if Horace had been able to do that. It wasn't perfect, but it got everyone sorted out for now. Horace looked vaguely worried about all these people with strange stories in his house, but still, it was nice to have company.

The next morning, Morris gave Peter Potter a strict warning about going out, or even standing by a window at the front of the house. He didn't want a repeat of the scenes at the vicarage at Horace's house. Then he left Angie in charge of housekeeping and went to work. He was, it seemed, the only person who had anything purposeful to do, which when he thought about it was a big change from how things used to be.

Marty was back.

'So Morris, tis grand to see you, oh yes, for sure.'

Morris was reminded that Marty always came back a lot more Irish than when he went.

241

'So tell me, what's been happening?'

Oh, not a lot. 'Well, there's no more news about Mick, so I reckon we're in the clear.'

'You're in the clear anyway. It's me they'll be coming after.'

'Well they haven't, so I reckon they won't. My guess is the rain we had after we dumped the freezer washed your fingerprints off.'

'Well why didn't you say that before? I could have saved all that hanging about back home.'

'Would you have believed me if I had said it?'

'Well, no, since you ask, I wouldn't.'

'That's why I didn't say it. Anyway, at least you've had a holiday. I've been up to my ears in stuff.'

'Well Uncle Marty is here now boy, so just you relax.'

Morris somehow didn't find that very reassuring. Marty looked around at the warehouse. 'Now all I've got to do is sell some of this gear and earn some money.'

'Oh yes, I wanted to talk to you about that.'

'What, you want to buy it?'

'No, I want to talk to you about earning money.'

'Well, my old friend, I'm afraid dere's not much chance of me giving you any work for a while. Ting's looks pretty bad, what with me being away and all.'

'No Marty, I don't want to work for you. I want you to work for me.'

'What, in the burial business?'

'No, I'm thinking of converting this place into a theatre and getting you to do the choreography for my first ballet.'

'Are you? I'll have to tink about that.'

'No Marty, I promise you, I'm not really.'

'You mean it was a joke, like?'

'Yes, something like that. Anyway, look, things are hotting up here and I need someone else on the team.'

'Doing what, exactly?' Marty looked suspicious. He wasn't too keen on bodies.

'Everything. Pallbearing, driving the hearse, the whole lot really. Someone who speaks English would make a change.' No, on second thoughts, skip that last bit. 'Well, what do you think?'

'Mm, how much does it pay?'

'Well, how about what you used to pay me when I worked for you?'

'But that's terrible.'

'Yes, I know. It's all I can afford though.'

And so Marty joined the staff of The Coffin Shop. It wasn't long before the firm grew and needed more space, and Marty's business was now defunct and didn't need any, so he sold all the stock as a job lot to a second-hand dealer the other side of town and he and Morris turned the whole warehouse into a funeral director's, with a proper chapel of rest and mortuary now, and a proper office too, and things went so well Morris even took to having fresh flowers. Well, not that fresh. He got Marty to go back to the church after each service and liberate any wreaths the relatives hadn't taken. The temporary vicar at St Elmo's didn't seem to notice.

Meanwhile, he had quite forgotten about Great Uncle Fred, but one day Carol Crapovic turned up at the warehouse.

'Ah, Mr Figg, this is very good. Yes, very good indeed. How my men helping you? Working hard?'

'Oh yes, now I've taught them left and right we're more or less getting the coffins in the right place.'

'That is very good, Mr Figg.'

'Yes, I think so. Anyway, it's nice to see you but I have a feeling this isn't a social visit.'

'Oh dear, Mr Figg, I am so glad to see you I hope too you are glad to see me.'

This was obviously going to take some time. Hurrying Carol Crapovic was like trying to get a kettle to boil by wishful thinking. Morris gave up.

'I have come here today to talk to you about a thing of great important.'

He hesitated, looking for the anticipation in Morris's face which wasn't there.

'I see. Well, I have today had letter from Croatian embassy.'

'Really, the Croatian embassy? Well I never.'

'No Mr Figg, I don't think you have. On the other, I have. I think I said this already, no?'

OK, cut the sarcasm, it doesn't translate. Morris asked his former landlord to sit down and offered him a cup of tea. There was no point in trying to hurry this. It was going to take as long as it was going to take.

'Biscuit, Mr Crapovic?'

'Oh no, thank you. I must be careful of this.' He patted his ample belly. Anyone could have told him it was about twenty years too late to worry about his figure. 'Well, perhaps just one.'

'So, you wanted to tell me something.'

'Yes, yes, the important thing. You see, Mr Figg, I have had letter from Croatian embassy.'

Yes, we did that bit. Do get a move on on account of I've got the rest of my life to sort out and about ten other people's too so ...

'And they say they have found body of my grandfather.'

'Oh, I'm sorry. How did it happen?'

'Well, a farmer dig him up.'

'What? No, I mean how did he die?'

'The Germans.' Mr Crapovic hissed this bit of information, and it was while Morris was trying to figure out what the hell he was talking about that it all came back, the newspaper article, Great Uncle Fred.

'Yes, the bastards kill him. My grandfather, Igor Crapovic, he was great partisan leader in Croatia, only some people call it Yugoslavia then. He killed lot of Germans, and of course

Croatians.'

'What? Why did your grandfather kill Croatians?'

'My grandfather was good Croatian, they were bad Croatians, Chetniks.'

Yes well, I must have been off the day we did modern Balkan history. 'So, your grandfather was a partisan leader and he was executed by the ...', and here Morris looked around in case any might by some bizarre chance be hanging around and overhear him, '... by the Germans?'

Mr Crapovic beamed. 'Yes, yes, very good. And Frederick Figg. Same name as you, no?'

'Yes. None other than my Great Uncle Fred.'

'Oh, he was great man also?'

'Yes, well, no, not that kind of great. Great Uncle.'

'He was a great uncle?'

Morris hesitated before trying to sort out the confusion, and decided on his experience so far it would probably only create more.

'Yes. Do carry on, Mr Crapovic.' Morris was getting into this. Now, it wasn't a waste of time.

'Well, Grandfather Igor is coming to England.'

'I thought he was dead.'

'Yes, body coming to be buried. By you, please.'

'Yes, of course, it will be a pleasure.'

'And Uncle Fred. Read, please.' He handed Morris the letter.

'Um, this is in a foreign language.'

'Oh, sorry, of course. I translate please. Yes, yes, uhuh, ah, here it is. The remains of Sergeant Frederick Figg have been sent to the British Embassy, who are arranging for shippings to the United Kingdom for military burial. Very good, yes?'

'Yes, very good. But, well, why is your grandfather coming all the way to England for burial? Why not bury him in his own country?'

Mr Crapovic put an arm round Morris and spoke from the

heart. 'Mr Figg, did you have grandfather?'

'Probably. Why?'

'Well, I am his only relative living. I would like him here with me. Can you understand this?'

No. 'Yes.'

'Very good, Mr Figg, very good. Now I leave you. Goodbye.'

Mr Crapovic left Morris to his thoughts, which were interrupted by a knock on the door.

'Hullo, Mr Morris Figg?'

'Yes.' His days of denying it were well and truly over.

'Hullo, Mr Figg. My name's Baz Chaudhuri. I'm from The Barton & Tidbury Sentinel.'

36

'Yes, Mr Figg, I've come to talk to you about your uncle, Sergeant Frederick Figg.'

'Oh, not um ...'

'Not what?'

'No, nothing. Well, Great Uncle Fred, eh?'

'Yes, we've had the information from the Ministry of Defence. It's a great local story, you know, War Hero's Remains Return to Barton.'

'Well you know more than I do.'

'Yes, that's my job. Now, I wondered if you would be able to fill me in with family history, photographs, you know, that sort of thing.'

'Um, well, I don't know, I'd have to talk about that with my sis ... , um anyway, I didn't even know he was a war hero.'

'No, well, all returning soldiers are war heroes for the headlines.'

'Even dead ones?'

'Especially dead ones. Anyway, he probably was a genuine hero, I mean parachuting behind enemy lines and all that.'

Bas looked about twelve to Morris. What he knew about the war was probably nothing.

'Well look Mr Chaudhuri ...'

'Baz, please.'

'Baz, look, leave it with me and I'll see what I can find for you. Now, I'm afraid, work calls.'

'Yes, well I'm sorry to take up so much of your time. Here's my card. Call me.'

The rest of the day was uneventful and Morris went home, as he now called it, at six. Peter Potter was in the kitchen eating a cold chicken sandwich. Morris had noticed he had a cavernous appetite. Angie said it was his nerves.

'Ah Peter, just the man I want to talk to. That journalist you thumped. His name wasn't Chaudhuri, was it?'

'Yes, why?'

'Well, he's been to see me, about something completely different, but he looked like he might have recognised me, you know, Angie's brother.'

'Do you think he's looking for me?'

'Hard to tell. I'm going to keep an eye on him. He wants to know about my Great Uncle Fred, don't worry about why. Anyway, there's something else I wanted to talk to you about.'

Peter stuffed another wedge of chicken sandwich into his mouth. 'Uhuh?'

'Yes. Look, you and Angie are living in Horace's house rent free, which is OK, and Angie's paying her way billswise because she's working but well, you're not. Don't you think you ought to look for something?'

'Like what? My days in the ministry are over.'

'I know, but come on, there must be plenty of things you can do. Do you have any qualifications?'

'Yes, I've got a degree.'

'Great. What in?'

'Divinity.'

'Oh. Well, you can't go on here for ever eating like that without contributing. At least go and sign on.'

'Sign on what?'

'At the Jobcentre, you know, for unemployment benefit.'

Peter choked on his sandwich. 'What? How can I do that?'

'Easy, you just get the number seven bus, it takes you straight past.'

'Morris, I don't think you appreciate my position.'

'Yes I do. You're unemployed and living in someone else's house and eating food other people are paying for. Have I missed anything?' Morris knew he was being cruel but he wasn't in a being kind mood.

And so Peter signed on for Jobseeker's Allowance at the Barton Jobcentre. They knew exactly who he was and at first they were a bit embarrassed but when they got the measure of him they insisted he take the first job that came along. He went back and told Morris he wouldn't do it and Morris, who everyone seemed to accept was now the head of the house, said oh yes you will, and so the Reverend Potter went to work on the fish counter at Tesco.

You can run but you can't hide. The next Friday there was a picture of him on the front page of The Sentinel, standing with a salmon in each hand, and some bright spark had digitally added a dog collar to his Tesco uniform. The headline ran, inevitably, Is Love-nest Vicar Up To Something Fishy? The byline on the piece was Baz Chaudhuri. Baz, it seemed, was now running a vendetta.

Peter was back at the Jobcentre on Monday. They sent him to work in an insurance company out of town where no-one would know who he was, which they didn't but he turned out to be so inept at office work he was back at the Jobcentre a week later. His last job was at a call centre but there were complaints when instead of saying goodbye he said God be with you. This went on for another month until even Morris had to concede he had tried.

Horace was improving daily, but he seemed to accept that Morris was running the household. Morris took Rachel out for a walk every evening, at first on crutches but after a few weeks she was walking just with a stick. Morris encouraged her constantly, but he could see she wasn't coming to terms with her new situation. She had by now been pensioned off by the Army, but she didn't want their money, she wanted to belong.

He took her to the Wig and Pistle one evening, bought her a large drink and tried to find the right words.

'So, how's Pops?'

'You know. You see him every day, like I do.'

'Yeh. I think he's coming along great.'

'If you call being in a wheelchair great, I might concede that.'

'But at his age, I mean ...'

'Oh sure, he's had a good innings, fair dos and all that, yes I know what you mean, but look, he's always been active and I talk to him a lot and I know he hasn't come to terms with his new situation. And before you lead smoothly into well have you come to terms with your situation let's get to the point of coming to the pub, no I haven't and nor will I.'

Morris looked down at the table and played with a beermat. He just didn't know what to say.

'Look Morris, none of this is your problem. You don't, you know ...'

'Have to stay?'

'Yes.'

'Oh yes I do girlie.'

He ducked just in time. She was blazing. 'You just remember what happened to the last man who called me that Morris Figg.'

'Excellent. Well, we've established that you haven't lost your fighting spirit.'

'Very clever. OK, so I've still got a temper, but it's a bit hard to kick the shit out of your opponent when you can't actually stand up for more than thirty seconds at a time. Look, I know you mean well but ...'

She didn't know but what. Neither did he. They didn't know where this was going. It was time for Morris to play his trump card. He put an envelope on the table. Angie hesitated.

'What's this?'

'An envelope.'

'Very funny. What's in it?'

'Well, you'll find out if you open it.'

She did, and she read in a puzzled tone.

'Leopard's Gym, annual membership, Ms Rachel da Souza. What's it mean?'

'I think you'll find it means that Rachel da Souza has an annual membership at Leopard's Gym.'

'What am I going to do with this? In case it had escaped your notice, I'm crippled. You've wasted your money.'

Now it was Morris's turn to get angry.

'First of all, it wasn't my money. It was my idea, but your father paid for it. And secondly, you are not crippled. Crippled people don't walk to the pub. You have an injury which has totally trashed your chance of participating in the Olympics, yes, I'll be the first to admit that, and your Army career is over too....'

'Oh, is that all?'

'Yes, that's all, because what that does, Rachel, is make you the same as the rest of us poor mortals, able-bodied. In a few months you will be as fit as I am. OK, that's not saying much ...'

'No, it's not ...'

'Well you don't have to agree with me so enthusiastically. As I was saying, you've come down to the level of the rest of us, I know that, I know it hurts, but that's life, it hurts sometimes, so at the risk of upsetting you I'm going to tell you to stop feeling sorry for yourself and get over to Leopard's and use their facilities to start building up your strength. That's why we did it. Not because there's any chance you're going to compete again, but because you can get back your self-respect through exercise.'

'I see. And is that it? Have you said everything you wanted to say?'

'Um, yes, yes, I think I have.'

251

'Fine. Well, thank for your interference. When I want your help I'll ask for it.'

And with that, she picked up her stick and hobbled off as angrily as she could without actually falling over. Morris sat downhearted. It had seemed like a brilliant idea, Horace had agreed readily, but it wasn't, it was a miserable failure. Until, that was, he noticed she had taken the envelope with her.

Rachel said nothing more about the gym, but every morning she disappeared about nine o'clock and didn't come back until lunchtime. Morris was at work but Angie reported back to him.

They noticed the colour coming back into Rachel's face, and now where her eyes had looked defeated they had a sparkle in them. Even Horace noticed it, and in the quiet night-time talks he had taken to having with Morris after the house had fallen silent he mentioned it. They knew now they had been right.

The proof of this was that where before she had given in to Morris's sexual needs rather than participating, now she seemed to have got her appetite back. Some nights he was so tired he had to fight her off.

The weeks passed and while Rachel got back her strength and her will to live, Morris beavered away at The Coffin Factory, Angie worked at the Infirmary, and Peter Potter did nothing. Morris worried about it, not least for Angie, because he could see she wasn't happy about having a partner who was conspicuously not being useful. Peter didn't seem to worry about it. He just carried on eating. He didn't even do any housework while everyone was out. He'd had a housekeeper before and he didn't seem to know about these things.

And things came to a head. Morris, in his role as paterfamilias, asked Peter to come and see him in the kitchen.

'Sit down Peter.'

'No, it's OK, I'll just get myself a sandwich.'

'No, I want you to sit down.'

'No, really ...'

'SIT DOWN.' Morris rarely spoke in capital letters but Peter was trying his patience.

'Oh, well, if you really want me to.'

'Yes, I do. Thank you. Now Peter, we've had this discussion before but tonight we're going to have it again, only with variations.'

'Oh yes?'

'Yes. It is, in case you had any doubt, about your situation here. I accept you're finding it hard to adjust to the world the rest of us inhabit workwise, and I took your point the other day about working for me but to be honest that wouldn't go down well with the new vicar at St Elmo's and in any case what you can bring to the firm is somewhat limited.'

'Well, that's that then.'

'No it's not. I'm talking about housework here.'

'Housework?'

'Yes. Don't pretend you don't know what that means. This, and I want you to look round you carefully, is a house, and in order to keep it running smoothly, with I might say rather more people than is normal, it requires a certain amount of work.'

'But the women ...'

'I hope, Peter, that you are not going to say the women can do it. Are you?'

'Um, no.'

'Excellent. Now, Rachel, as you know, is recovering from wounds received saving her country from foreign hordes, and in any case is in receipt of funds and contributes financially. You don't. Angie works and she too contributes financially. You, however, are not and you don't. I work, and while I don't earn a lot of money I bring in what I can. If we leave Horace out of this, and I do hope you will have the grace to do that, that leaves, let me see, oh yes, you. You don't work. You don't pay anything into the kitty. And you do, excuse my language, bugger all around here. Well, OK, you don't earn so you can't pay. What you can do is get off your backside and clean the house, organise the laundry, do the shopping, and provide us all with a hot meal at the end of the day.'

Peter gulped. He visibly flushed. Everything Morris was saying, he knew, was true. He hated him saying it, he just couldn't argue with it. So, it had come to this. The Reverend Peter Potter dirtying his hands.

'Well, Morris. I want to thank you for your frankness.'

'You're welcome.'

'And you have my assurance that I shall, um, from now on, yes, I shall from now on ...'

'Yes?'

'Help.'

'Help? Is that it?'

'Well ...'

'Peter, I want you to think back thirty seconds and remind me of the list of jobs I just gave you.'

'Um, well, alright. Er, shopping?'

'Yes, good. And?'

'Cooking? Look, I'm really not much of a cook. You might prefer ...'

'No we wouldn't.'

'Oh.'

'And? Come on.'

'Um, cleaning?'

'Yes, that's the one. Cleaning. We'll show you where all the cleaning materials are kept and you can get started tomorrow.'

'Fine. Alright. Fine. Well, I think that just about covers it, so ...'

'No, I think you will find that's not quite true chum. Now, I want you to think very hard, and tell me what the other thing was, and I'm going to give you a clue, watch my eyes.'

And Morris's eyes wandered across the kitchen to the washing machine. Peter followed them and looked at it in horror.

'That's the washing machine.'

'Er yes, that's not bad. Now, your starter for five, what is it we do with a washing machine?'

'Look Morris, there's no reason to rub my nose in it. I know what a washing machine is for. I just don't know how to use one. They're horrible complicated things and only women can understand them.'

'Peter, Peter, that's a terribly defeatist attitude, and in some way I don't comprehend it's sexist too. Come now, who do you think designs washing machines?'

'Men?'

'I shouldn't be at all surprised. So, if a man can design one, my guess is a man can figure out how to use one. And, and here I may be going out on a limb but I'm prepared to take the risk, I have a shrewd feeling that this particular piece of equipment comes with a book called an instruction manual, and whilst you may have no experience of laundry I happen to know you have a degree in divinity and my further guess is that in order to get that you required a certain level of literacy, so you can read it. And here, my son, endeth the first lesson.'

The next morning Morris left for work in the sincere belief that when he returned Peter Potter would have got to grips with the house. He left Rachel with instructions that she was allowed to bully him if necessary, but she was to stop at breaking his fingers, on account of he wouldn't be able to cook with bandages on his hands.

Marty was in before him.

'Ah, Morris, and a very fine morning to you.'

'Marty, I know I'm the boss but come on, how long have we known each other, you don't need to lick my boots.'

'OK. Look here shithead ...'

'On the other hand, this is a respectable firm and we have standards to keep up. Bloody hell, I'm starting to sound like Horace Tite. No, it's worse than that. I'm starting to be Horace Tite. Shit, I've got to swear a bit more. Anyway, what's on today?'

'Well, there's the Maguire family coming in this afternoon to finalise the cremation, and we've got to go over to the Infirmary this morning to collect the last mortal remains of, let me see, oh yes, Montague Balsam.'

'Marty, we don't really say the last mortal remains, you know, at least you don't, at least not on the pitiful wage I pay you.'

'OK boss, there's a stiff to pick up at the slaughterhouse.'

'Yes, well, remind me sometime ....'

There was a knock on the door.

'Ah, Mr Crapovic, come in, come in. I expect you've called to make the arrangements for the two war heroes?'

'Good morning Mr Figg, and Mr Finnigan. Yes, indeed, I have. And, Mr Figg, I want to say something.'

'Yes?'

'Yes.'

'Well?'

'Oh, yes, I want to say that I, Carol Crapovic, will pay not only for the funeral of the great partisan leader Igor Crapovic, but also of his comrade in arms, your great Uncle Fred Figg.'

He beamed munificently.

'Oh well, that's very generous of you but, after all, he's my uncle. In any case, I've had a letter from the Ministry. They pay, apparently.'

Mr Crapovic looked deflated.

'But it was, nevertheless, a magnificent gesture. I tell you what, if you really want to, you can pay for the reception.'

'Oh, will that cost much?'

'Less than the burial.'

257

'Ah, very good, yes, I agree. I like you, Mr Figg.'

'Yes, I know. So, what date are we talking about?'

'Are we talking about? I don't think so.'

'No, you don't understand. I mean what date would you like to arrange for the funerals?'

'Ah, very good. The fourteenth, please.'

'Let me see. Yes, that will be fine, as long as the bodies are delivered in time.'

'They will be, Mr Figg. Carol Crapovic arrange everything, not to worry you. Day before, I deliver two coffins, you will see. Very good, yes?'

'Yes. Well, we'll see you then.'

As Mr Crapovic left the shop Morris had a distinct feeling he should be worrying. He couldn't put his finger on why, but his instincts told him, as a man who knew a thing or two about pulling a fast one, that something smelled not entirely kosher about all of this. Carol Crapovic was just a bit too keen to complete the arrangements.

'Marty, do you smell anything?'

'Well, Morris, on account of this being a funeral parlour, I mean it always smells a bit, don't you think?'

'No, I don't mean that. I mean Mr Crapovic.'

'Him? Can't understand anything he says.'

'Oh, that's helpful. Well, let's get over to the slaughterhouse, I mean the hospital.'

But before they could do that there was another knock on the door. It was Baz Chaudhuri.

'Ah, Mr Figg, I'm glad I caught you.'

'You did?'

'Sorry? Well, if you've got a moment, I wondered if you have managed to dig anything up for me.'

'What, like a corpse? Sorry, undertaker's joke. Actually, I have.' He rummaged in the drawer of his desk. 'Here's an old family portrait of Uncle Fred in uniform. You will return it, won't you?'

'Oh, absolutely.'

He left clutching the precious photograph.

'Marty, I know I've asked you this question once already this morning, but do you smell anything? And please don't say what you said before.'

'OK, yes.'

'So do I. It seems to be a day for untrustworthy people.'

'You mean like us?'

'No Marty, I do not mean like us. You and I are now respectable business people, upstanding members of this community. Alright, I'll be the first to admit we've got a past, both of us, but the past is, by definition, the past, and the future is, well, the future, and ... oh shit, come on, let's go get the stiff.'

38

It was a long day for Morris. He got back to the house tired and for a moment he forgot that Peter was cooking the dinner. Or at least he was supposed to be. A smell of burning greeted him as he came through the door, along with Rachel, who always welcomed him home.

'Rachel, is that burning I smell?'

'Uhuh.'

'Tell me it's the boy scouts roasting Peter Potter and you will make me a happy man.'

'What? Morris, have you been drinking?'

'Me, drinking? It's the Devil's own brew. Not a drop shall pass my lips.'

'You're starting to sound like Pops. No, come to think of it, you're starting to look like him too. Get changed out of that gear will you and I might feel like giving you a hug. Or more.'

'A hug will do for now my dear. Anyway, what's for dinner?'

'Fish and chips I'm afraid.'

'So Peter's first venture into the kitchen wasn't a success then?'

'No. Angie wanted to go in and help him but I wouldn't let her.'

'That's my girl. Well, it's only day one. How about the cleaning?'

'Bad news on that front too. He's been in the kitchen all day so there hasn't been time for anything else.'

'OK, well, tomorrow is another day. Maybe he'll get the hang of it. Anyway, how are you? How was the gym?'

'Oh, I didn't go.'

'No? Why not?'

'Look, Morris, I want to talk to you ...'

And as usual the god of bad timing put his twopenn'orth in and Angie wandered out of the living room.

'Aha, the happy couple. And a smell of burning. Don't tell me, Peter?'

'Sadly not, just the dinner.'

'Fish and chips tonight?'

'Yep.'

Peter came out of the kitchen, wearing a rather fetching apron.

'Ah Peter, yes, suits you. I understand your first culinary experiment has not been a success.'

'Morris, now look here. You knew perfectly well I don't have any experience but did that make any difference?'

'No.'

'Actually, it was a rhetorical question. Anyway, I have been slaving over a hot stove all day, as well as running around after Horace, you don't know what it's like.'

Angie objected to that. 'Actually, Peter, I think you will find I do, and I expect Rachel does too.'

'Oh Angela, I thought you might be a bit more supportive. I am trying.'

His bottom lip was starting to wobble and Angie was afraid he might be about to cry. She regretted what she had said, not because she thought it was wrong but because she couldn't stand the embarrassment of her man blubbing in front of other people. 'Look, come on Peter, get your pinny off. We're going out to get fish and chips. And after that I'll come in and teach you the basics.'

They sat and ate together, but Rachel didn't join in the conversation. Morris could tell she had something on her mind but there was no possibility of asking her what it was until bedtime. First, though, Peter Potter had some news.

He cleared his throat, which usually presaged an announcement in church. Angela looked round the room to see if anyone was listening.

'Excuse me people, Peter wants to say something.'

'If it's about dinner, the less said the better.'

'Well it's not, actually. What Angela means is that I have an important announcement to make, and I should like to take the opportunity of having the household gathered on this occasion of ... of ...'

'Fish and chips.'

'Yes, well, I suppose it's not really an occasion.'

'Come on Peter, spit it out.'

'Oh, yes, well. Well, what I wanted to say is that Angela and I will be leaving you.'

He looked around to see if he had everyone's attention. He did. Even Horace was looking at him, though it would be hard to say if it was with the same hope that Morris had in his face.

'Have you got a job then?'

'Yes. Well, no, not exactly a job.'

'You're going to prison for hitting Baz Chaudhuri.'

'Certainly not. No, I am pleased to say I have in fact been offered an excellent opportunity to continue my work in the ministry.'

'Oh yes? Which ministry's that then?'

'The Church, of course.'

'I see. You've been offered another parish.'

'No, well, yes, I suppose you could say that, in a way.'

'Peter, why is it that every time I ask you a question I have to guess what the answer is myself?'

'This morning I received a letter from the Word of Jesus Gospel Society.'

'That's nice.'

262

'African Department.'

If he didn't have people's full attention before he certainly had it now.

Angie couldn't stand the suspense. 'What Peter is saying is that we will be going out to Nigeria with the WJGS as part of their programme of Christian outreach in Africa. It's a wonderful opportunity and I think Peter has done marvellously to get the offer.'

'And are you going with him?'

'Yes, of course, Morris.'

'Oh, right.'

It was Angie's normal habit to look her brother straight in the eye when she spoke to him. He searched her face but she refused to make contact. Something on the floor apparently was more interesting. He wanted to say something else but Rachel cleared her throat in the way people have of letting you know not to and he got the message.

'Well, Peter, I think I speak for everyone here when I say congratulations, we're all very pleased for you. If only so we can get some decent grub. No, Angie, put that knife down, it was a joke.'

Morris insisted on helping Angie with the washing up.

'OK, Sis, tell me what the hell is actually going on here.'

'What do you mean? It's pretty simple, isn't it?'

'No, actually, it isn't. OK, the bit about Peter going to Nigeria is, I grant you that, on account of him being a reverend and all that, but come on, you're not even married, no I take that back because let's face it there's something more important, which is that you are married, to Roger, so apart from anything else, and I assure you there's lots else but I'm keeping this simple, how have you convinced the Society of Spreading Religious Claptrap in Foreign Countries that you're going as a couple?'

'They didn't ask us to prove we're married, naturally.'

'Oh, I see, so there isn't a moral issue about lying to the

society then? Very Christian, don't you think?'

'Look ... look ... oh sod it Morris, it's none of your bloody business, is it? What makes you concerned about any of this anyway? Let's face it, you'll be getting rid of Peter.'

Morris did something he never thought he would do. He put his arms round his sister.

'Angie, you are stupid aren't you? Doesn't it occur to you that I don't want to get rid of you?'

Angie said nothing and just cried into his shirt and he said nothing and just felt his shoulder getting damp. He couldn't have spoken anyway, because his little sister would have known he was crying too. Rachel came in, did a smart about turn, and went out again.

It was in bed later that Morris talked to her for an hour about him and Angie, how their father had left them when he was ten and Angie was only six and their mother had had a hard time bringing them up, and when he was about fourteen she married an American soldier called Hank and moved to South Carolina and left the children in the care of their Aunt Janice, but Aunt Janice died when Angie was still only seventeen and the two of them set up home together so Morris could look after her but two years later she met Roger and married him and ever since then they had been close but had never been able to talk about things. Now he was going to miss her like hell.

Rachel listened to him as he lay in her arms and she knew how he felt. They were silent for a while, but then Morris remembered she had been trying to tell him something.

'So you were saying, about a year ago, you didn't go to the gym. Not up to it?'

'No, well, I went to see Doctor Jarvis.'

'Uhuh. Legs bothering you?'

'No, it was to get a test result.'

Morris propped himself up on an elbow. 'Rachel, what's wrong? You should have told me before, not waited all this time. What is it?'

'We're going to have a baby.'

39

Morris spent the next week in a daze. Rachel worried how he was going to take the news but she needn't have. He wasn't sure himself how he felt because it wasn't something he had ever really contemplated in his life but now he was presented with it he found he was deliriously happy. He felt closer to Rachel as a result, and that made him happy as well. Rachel had mixed feelings.

Meanwhile, there was Angie to worry about, not to mention the business. Two coffins arrived a week later, accompanied by a beaming Mr Crapovic.

'Ah, Mr Figg, well, as you see Carol Crapovic keep his word. Two coffins, on the dot as we say, ready for the funerals. This one your great uncle and this one with flag is famous partisan leader Igor Crapovic.'

It seemed that Morris's misgivings about all of this were, after all, unfounded. Which just goes to show how wrong you can be, because once the delivery people left Mr Crapovic closed the door.

'Mr Figg, you have a key for this door?'

'Yes, why?'

'You lock this, please. Quickly, for there is no time to spare.'

'Mr Crapovic, would you mind telling me what the hell is going on?'

'Yes indeed, after locking the door.'

'Alright, alright. There, now.'

And now what happened was that Mr Crapovic produced a

large screwdriver and proceeded to undo the lid of the coffin with the Croatian flag. Morris wanted to say something but the only thing he could think of to say was what the hell are you doing that for and he had a strong feeling he was about to find out.

When all the screws were out Mr Crapovic said help with this Mr Figg and he did as he was told. He didn't know what someone looked like when they had been buried in a field for fifty years but he had a shrewd idea there wasn't going to be a lot to see, which just goes to show again how wrong you can be, because Mr Crapovic removed from the coffin an oxygen cylinder and mask, asked Morris to hold them and then he put his hands into the coffin and then, with some effort, he pulled out a man, a man moreover, who was to all appearances not only not dead for half a century but who wasn't dead at all.

'Quick, Mr Figg, help me please, he is very weak.'

Well, what do you do in that situation? Morris helped the man out and got him stretched out on the floor. Mr Crapovic put the oxygen mask back over his face and the man muttered something weakly.

'Yes, I think he is going to be OK.'

'Mr Crapovic, who is this man exactly, and if you tell me he's your grandfather, the great partisan leader Igor Crapovic, I have to tell you I'm not going to believe it.'

'No, no, of course not. He is Milan Stankovic.'

'Oh good, well that explains a lot. But not, I'm afraid, enough. Who exactly is Milan Stankovic?'

'He is rich farmer from Croatia who wants to live in England.'

'You mean we have just imported an illegal immigrant in a coffin under the noses of the authorities?'

'Probably.'

Morris found he had to sit down. 'Look, first of all, is he going to live? He doesn't look too good if you ask me.'

'Well, if he lives, that is good for him, and if he dies, well, then we bury him in this coffin, yes?'

'Mr Crapovic, I'm afraid it's not as simple as all that. There are laws you know. You can't just go burying people who aren't who you say they are.'

It was while Morris heard himself saying this that he realised how far he come in a short space of time. Still, that was then and this was now, and what's more The Coffin Shop was his own business and he wasn't prepared to risk it for his one-time landlord. Then something else occurred to him.

'Mr Crapovic, does this man speak any English?'

'No, why?'

'Well, I want to ask you something. Given that Croatia is part of the European Union, he didn't need to enter the country illegally. He could have flown into Heathrow and walked through passport control.'

'Yes, this is true. You know this and I know this, but a farmer who speaks only Croatian does not know this.'

'You mean you've swindled him, as well as breaking about fifteen different laws?'

'Well, Mr Figg, if you are going to speak to me like that I will ...'

'Yes, you will what? And anyway, while we're discussing the matter, what about Igor, where is he in all this?'

'Oh Igor, don't worry, he is safe.'

'Yes, but where safe?'

'In Croatia. This man buried him again on his farm.'

'This is the farmer who found the bodies, isn't it?'

'Yes. When he find out the bodies are coming here, he asks for my help. You see, I just try to help people.'

'For money. Well, let me think about this. OK, I tell you what we're going to do. All I care about is not getting done for this, so Mr Thingovic here is getting in your car and disappearing. We've got two coffins, so you leave it to me and a load of sand will be buried tomorrow with full military

268

honours. And that, I hope, is the last time I am ever going to see you. Do I make myself clear?'

The Army sent a military burial party the next morning and the funerals went ahead as planned. Well, not exactly as planned, but only Morris knew that, like only Morris knew a lot of things. Rachel wore her uniform for the last time and joined the honour guard. The Barton and Tidbury Sentinel sent a photographer. Quite a crowd turned up and Morris suspected he spotted Mr Crapovic standing to attention at the back as the Last Post was played.

Morris could tell that Peter Potter would have liked to conduct the service, but there was no way the new vicar of St Elmo's would have countenanced that, so he pushed the wheelchair for Horace, who came not because he knew who Great Uncle Fred was but just for old times' sake.

'You're Morris Figg, I think?'

'And you, I think, are Rachel da Souza, and this is how we met. How romantic.'

'It seems like a long time ago. A lot has changed.'

'Look, Rachel we never get time to talk do we? We need to take some time out for this, you know, the baby. This isn't the place.'

'You can say that again.'

'This isn't the place. So, how does it feel to be back in uniform?'

'Great. And sad. But thanks for letting me.'

'Listen, I'm just the undertaker.'

'No, he was your great uncle, too.'

'That's true. Rachel ...? '

'Uhuh? '

'Look, let's go out for dinner tonight.'

'Why, Peter's cooking getting too much for you? I'm a soldier, don't forget, we can eat anything as long as it's dead.'

'No, it's not that. It's just that there are so many people in the house and we always seem to be up late ...'

'No, you stay up late, talking to Pops. I don't know how you two find so much to discuss. Anyone would think he was your father.'

'So how about it?'

'What here, behind that big gravestone?'

'Rachel, you're not being serious.'

'Ooh, Morris Figg, you've come over all deep and mysterious. Sorry, my love, it's the old me, what with the uniform, no of course, let's do that.'

And they did. Morris took her to the Chinese restaurant they went to the first time they met, and there he proposed to her.

And like the first time, they kept the waiters waiting to close up, talking about all the things, now they were going to be married, that really needed to be settled between them, not least the baby. But there was something Rachel needed to say beside that, about the gym, and where all that was going, because being a mother was going to be great, she suddenly felt that, now they were going to be married, but what still wasn't great was her frustration. She needed more than going and doing a workout every day. It was good while she was there but every day when she came home for lunch she was left with the feeling that there wasn't any purpose to it. It made her feel good, but only as long as she did it. She needed a better reason for exercise, a goal, something that would at least help to replace what she had lost. The baby would be a part of that, of course, because motherhood, she already knew, was going to help her redefine herself, but there was still something missing.

Morris listened, but he didn't know what to say, so he said nothing and they went home to make an official announcement. Angie was ecstatic, Horace, who had been polite about the baby, was now able to give them his blessing at last. He knew Morris wasn't exactly what he would have wanted, he had sussed him out the first day he walked into

Widdlecombe and Tite, but still, there had always been something and he had changed since then, and he trusted him to look after Rachel.

Horace, they knew, would not consider anything but a church wedding. The obvious choice was St Elmo's but there were two problems, the first of which was that neither of them was a churchgoer and the new vicar was a stickler for that kind of thing so persuading him to officiate was going to be tricky, and the second was that they knew Peter Potter would want to do it, and Angie asked them if he could and Morris didn't like to say no.

'OK, but if he does it where does he do it if it can't be St Elmo's?'

'Don't know, kiddo. Can we do it here?'

'I don't know if that's allowed. Anyway, Horace wants a church wedding, so we're going round in circles.'

Just then Peter walked in with a tray of biscuits. They smelled good.

'Do you know Reverend, I do believe you're getting the hang of this cooking thing. We couldn't persuade you to change your mind about Nigeria?'

It was only a joke but Morris glanced at Angie and she looked, he thought, a bit wistful.

'Sorry old chap. It's all arranged.'

'Well, we've got a problem, and we wondered if you can help.'

'Oh yes?'

'Well, we want to get married in church, OK Horace wants us to and we want to do what he wants, and none of the other churches in Barton know us but the new vicar at St Elmo's isn't likely to welcome us and, well, we know you would like to officiate, and that's as far as we've got.'

'Well, I don't see the problem.'

'You don't? Well, at the risk of boring the others, we want to be married in church ...'

271

'No, no, Morris, Morris, you misunderstand me.'

'That wouldn't be unusual.'

'You said you want me to officiate.'

Not particularly. 'Yes.'

'And you want to get married at St Elmo's.'

'Spot on.'

'Then, my good people, that is what you shall do.'

'No, Peter, listen, that's not possible, on account of, in case you've forgotten, you are no longer the minister there and you got locked out. Where are you going?'

Peter disappeared but was back in half a minute.

'Morris, you are right, but you are also wrong.'

'That's the story of my life, but in this particular case what do you mean?'

'Well, you said I got locked out, really locked out because they changed the barrels.'

'Yes.'

'At the vicarage.'

'Yes.'

'But not, dear congregation, at the church.' And here he brandished a large, old-fashioned key in triumph. It was, after recent weeks, his moment of glory.

40

Angie and Peter were due to depart for Nigeria on the twenty first, and on the Wednesday before that, at midnight, which Morris thought was a bit over-dramatic but Peter, who was getting very much into the mood for this, insisted on, a small group of people filed into the side door of St Elmo's church. Once safely in, they locked the doors and lit the large candles on the altar. Angie went round and distributed some of the candles they had brought with them around the empty pews, and the church looked like it might have done in the early Victorian days when it was built. It was all most satisfactory.

Rachel fixed another candle over the back of Horace's wheelchair and from the front it looked like he had a halo.

Marty was best man but Rachel had to forego bridesmaids. Bride and groom both carried a candle up the aisle and Rachel's train, made from satin coffin lining, trailed behind her into the darkness. Peter Potter was in full regalia and he did them proud. Morris wore his undertaker's tailcoat, which Rachel at first objected to, but she agreed in the end that it wasn't worth spending money on a suit that no-one would see in the gloom.

When Peter got to the bit about if anyone has any just cause why these two should not be married there was silence while they peered into the depths of the church as if someone might materialise and do just that but of course they didn't

273

and Angie was heard to sigh with relief and accidentally blew her candle out and they all laughed and then Morris put the ring on his bride's finger and Peter said he could kiss her, which Morris knew already, and he did and so Rachel became Mrs Figg and Morris became a happy man.

After the ceremony Rachel wanted to put the candles out but Peter, in a last defiant act against the church authorities, insisted they leave them burning where they were. When they were found by the verger in the morning it was to become the start of a mystery that people talked about for many years after that. In fact it became an annual ritual that congregants gathered during the night on that date and lit candles. Some said it was to welcome St Elmo with a ring of fire, others said don't be daft it wasn't even his feast day, and the vicar invariably said stuff and nonsense it's all superstitious mumbo jumbo, which depending on your view of these things might safely be said about why the church was there in the first place.

Peter not only officiated at the wedding but he was also chief caterer for the reception, which they held back at the house at one o'clock in the morning. Then they all went to bed and when they finally surfaced the next morning they wondered if it had been a dream, but they couldn't all have had the same dream, and in any case Rachel now wore a wedding ring. They went down to the Registry Office to make the marriage legal, and then they went back for a wedding breakfast of Frosties for Morris and leftover midnight feast for everyone else.

Two days later Peter and Angie were packed and ready for an early drive to the airport the next morning. Horace always retired after everyone else, but on this occasion Angie and Morris waited for him to go to bed and then they sat in the kitchen over a last cup of tea together and talked.

'Well, Kiddo, this is it.'

'I was hoping you weren't going to talk in clichés.'

'Sorry. On the other hand, it really is. Morris, promise me something.'

'What?'

'You won't try to persuade me to change my mind.'

'Look, I know you better than that. OK, I admit I don't know why you're doing this. I mean, fair enough, Peter has shown a different side recently and even I have to admit he's not such a bad bloke and he can even cook, after a fashion, and maybe that's why you're doing it, but anyway it's too late to go back now.'

Angie wasn't sure herself why she was doing it and she was grateful to Morris for not insisting that she justify her decision. Or maybe she wasn't.

'Look, you've got Rachel now, and the baby coming, and your business, so I don't need to worry about you any more, do I?'

'No, but maybe I still need to worry about you.'

'Nah, I'm a big girl. I can look after myself.'

'You're falling back on clichés again. That's a bit telling isn't it?'

'What do you want me to say? Look, we've said it all over the past few weeks. I will be alright, I promise you.'

'OK, but I want you to promise me something else.'

'Fair enough. I asked you the same thing.'

'Well this is a bit more serious. I want you to promise me that if you ever change your mind you won't stay out there being afraid to come home and admit you got it wrong. You're a stubborn woman and you stuck it out with Roger longer than you needed to. No-one is going to think any the worse of you for admitting it was a bad idea, if it was I mean, and sorting it out.'

'But aren't you assuming it's all going to go wrong?'

'No, well, I'm assuming it might, that's all. I don't want it to, you know that, but I just want you to be happy, and I promise you that if, for any reason at all, you do come back on your own, I'll be here for you. Now stop arguing with me or I'll come over all sentimental.'

'Too late, you already have. Come here, you great lump.'

And she took him in her arms and they held each other close for a long time, thinking their own thoughts, afraid to let go, but in the end of course they did and that was that.

The next morning Morris drove them to the airport in Rachel's car because Angie refused to turn up at Heathrow in a hearse, and there they hugged for a long time again and then Morris said something to Peter about looking after his sister and if he didn't he would have him to answer to, more clichés but Morris was so troubled he could only think in clichés now, and then he drove home in sombre mood. Would he ever see her again?

At ten o'clock that night there was a knock on the door.

'Angie.'

'Morris.'

'Angie.'

'Morris. We could keep this up all night but to be honest I'm knackered and I don't really want to stand out here all night with my suitcases saying Morris, so would you mind if I come in?'

He helped her in with her luggage and then he went out and looked around.

'Where's Peter?'

'He should be landing in Lagos any time now.'

'Without you?'

'I always thought you had great powers of observation Morris, but on this occasion you have excelled yourself. Now, are you going to put the kettle on or do I have to die of thirst standing here in the hallway?'

At that moment Rachel came out.

'Good God, I thought I heard a familiar voice. Angie.'

'Yes, and I say Rachel and you say Angie and then I say oh for heaven's sake stop. Yes, it's me. No, Peter's not here, he got on the plane, which as you can probably tell I didn't, not unless I parachuted out halfway over the south of England, which I can tell you now I didn't. And, that, I think, about explains it.'

Rachel made them all tea and then she left Morris and his sister in the kitchen to talk.

'Well, look Morris, you made me promise.'

'I did?'

'Yes, God you've got a short memory. You said I was to come home if ever I thought I had done the wrong thing.'

'Yes, but I thought you might give it a week or two, or even a year or two. Bloody hell, what happened between leaving here this morning and getting on the plane?'

'Well, we were sitting in the departures lounge and it was a long wait and I looked at Peter and I thought about Roger ...'

'Bloody hell, you're not going back to him?'

'Don't be an ass. No, I just started thinking, that's all, about what you've been saying, you know, about making wrong decisions, and I realised it was the wrong decision, well not wrong exactly but hasty. I still don't know Peter and suddenly, sitting there, I grew up and I realised that the safest thing to do when you're not sure is to do nothing. So here I am.'

'And what did Peter say?'

'I don't know.'

'What do you mean, you don't know?'

'I chickened out. While he went to the toilet I left him a note.'

'Shit. Angie, that's terrible.'

'I know, and I feel every bit as terrible as I should so you don't need to make it any worse.'

'No, I meant it was terrible leaving his luggage unattended, when they're always warning you not to do that.'

'Oh yeh. Quick thinking, Morris, but thanks.'

'Anyway, what about work? What will you do?'

'Oh, that won't be a problem. The hospital's desperate for

physios. They'll have me back like a shot. I might have to give my leaving present back though, but since that was a watch from Argos that stopped working before we got to the airport, I don't think I mind too much.'

And so the household went back to how it was before except for Peter's absence. Morris prayed daily that he wouldn't turn up on the doorstep as well but he didn't and as the weeks passed the fear receded, then they got a postcard, or more accurately Angie got a postcard, from him. He sent it to the house, he said, because he reckoned she would go back to her brother. Actually, there wasn't room for anything else after he wrote that so they just had to guess why he sent it, and what they guessed was it was his way of telling Angie he had forgiven her, for which she was grateful. Years later Morris read in the paper that Peter became Bishop of Lagos, which was, he thought, very satisfying, just before Moslem fundamentalists burned down the Anglican cathedral in the capital, which was less satisfactory, but typical Peter Potter.

Rachel continued going to the gym every day but as time passed her exercise regime became strictly curtailed by her pregnancy. Morris could tell, as much as she was happy about the baby, that she was less happy not to be able to work out. Rachel was still unable to let go of that part of her life, and Morris didn't know how to help her.

The Coffin Shop prospered in a modest way but the god of sticking his finger in where it's not wanted must have been bored one morning because Marty came to Morris with a problem.

'Ah, Morris my old friend and boss, what a fine morning it is to be sure, to be sure, yes, a fine morning indeed.'

'Marty, what's wrong?'

'Wrong, Morris, why should anything be wrong?'

'Because you're talking like a leprechaun, and that always means there's something wrong.'

'Well, since you ask, there is. Well, there might be.'

'Yes? And are you going to elucidate or am I going to have to extract it from you surgically?'

'Well, it's like this.'

'Yes, yes, like what?'

'Um, well, there may be a problem.'

'Yes, yes, we've done that bit. Now can we get on to the bit about the kind of problem there might be?'

'With the police.'

'Shit. Marty, what have you been up to, first, and second, does it in any way involve me, and third, could you leave to join Peter Potter in Nigeria before the shit hits the fan?'

'What? Would you mind running through those options again?'

'Yes I would. For God's sake Marty, spit it out or I promise you I am going to have you embalmed alive, I am going to stick a straw up your nose and suck your brains out, although that might be difficult on account of I would have to locate them first. In short, Marty, what the fuck is the problem?'

'Well, you remember Mick from the Pink Flamingo?'

'What? No, that's not possible. It's been ages.'

'Oh no, nothing like that. It's just that one of Mick's, shall we say, business activities, was the provision of certain recreational substances.'

'Bloody hell, Marty, you got done for that before. Didn't that teach you anything?'

'No.'

'Well, that's honest if nothing else. So?'

'So I kind of took over that line.'

'But don't I pay you enough here?'

'No, you pay me peanuts.'

'And look at the monkey I got. Shit, what's happened? Have they found out?'

'Well, sort of. They know there's a big shipment in the area, but they don't know who's involved yet or where it's stashed.'

'When you say big, what are we talking about here?'

'About half a ton.'

'What? No, you're having me on. Half a ton? Shit. OK, look, you're on their list of prime suspects and they're bound to come looking for you, so I suggest you get the hell out of here, and I mean right now. And where's the stuff stashed?'

'Well ... you don't use all of the warehouse do you?'

41

There was, stacked in an old wardrobe Marty had never sold, wedged behind a partition wall, enough cannabis to keep the citizens of Barton high for a week. Morris thought he was in control of his life but now he realised, as he felt himself sliding into irreversible panic, that was a delusion.

He told Marty he had to get rid of it, and get rid of it now, not tomorrow or even in an hour's time but now, but then the phone rang and it was one of Marty's friends to tell him there were three police cars travelling towards the warehouse at speed. Now it was Marty's turn to panic and this had the strange effect of helping Morris to think clearly. They had two bodies in the chapel of rest, and they got the lids off, the entire stash stowed away and the bodies put back on top just as blue flashing lights filled the warehouse with the urgent message that time was up. Morris was just tightening the last screw when all hell broke loose.

'Good heavens, Sergeant Crump isn't it? There seems to be some sort of emergency.'

'Yes sir, there is. I have here a warrant to search these premises.'

'What are you looking for? Don't tell me - a dead body.'

'No sir. I can see that would be somewhat amusing but on this occasion we're looking for a large quantity of cannabis believed to be hidden in this warehouse. So if you will stand aside please, and allow my men to do their job.'

'By all means, Sergeant. Marty, would you be kind enough to show these officers all the various hiding places we usually secrete the drugs in.'

'But Morris ...'

'Yes, Marty, I see your problem, since this is a funeral director's and not an underground criminal organisation.'

Sergeant Crump had heard more of this than he had patience for and his men were fanning out across the warehouse with large torches and, which was bad news, a sniffer dog, an attractive brown and white spaniel which wagged its tail furiously as it sniffed at Marty's trouser legs. Then it cocked its leg and pissed all over them and while Marty stood there too scared to move Morris almost wet himself laughing.

They looked everywhere. In the chapel of rest, the office, the mortuary, they took Morris's desk apart and then they took the hearse apart. The spaniel got excited when it came to the wardrobe but since there was nothing in it they had to accept it was a false trail.

That just left the coffins.

'Well, sir, that just leaves the coffins.'

'Surely, sergeant, you don't intend to profane the sacred trust we hold to look after the deceased?'

Sergeant Crump was hoping Morris would say something like that. He was hoping he wouldn't have to look in the coffins, on account of him having a mortal dread of bodies. The police pathologist thought it was funny, the whole station thought it was funny, but the sight of blood made him come over all faint.

'Constable Penny will examine the coffins, sir, if you don't mind.'

'And do you have a warrant to do that?'

Sergeant Crump wasn't sure about that. It said premises, it didn't say coffins. He was wondering if he could get away with saying no, you're quite right, we can't examine the coffins but

282

PC Penny, who had no such qualms, was already undoing the screws. There was no backing down now.

The god of opening the right coffin must have been smiling on Morris that day because there were two bodies, a little old lady, Miss Grimshaw, who had died peacefully in her sleep, in one and in the other were the various bits of Carlo Castelli, who had ridden his Harley Davidson, for reasons best known to himself, under a thirty-eight tonne lorry and come out the other side in a number of parts. PC Penny peered inside, went an interesting shade of green, though Marty afterwards described it as grey but it could have been the light, and fainted.

That was enough for Sergeant Penny. A minute later the yard was empty of police cars and Morris and Marty could breathe again.

'You are, my son, one very lucky man. How we got away with that I will never know, but we did. Now, what are you going to do with this stuff?'

'I don't know. Sell it?'

'Oh yes, very bright, I'm sure. Go straight to jail, do not pass go, do not collect your pension. Try again.'

'Um dunno.'

Morris sighed. Why, oh why, did he have to sort out everyone's problems? Right, here we go again.

'OK, I'll tell you what we're going to do, we're going to bury it. Look, I've got to go and see Father Leary. You get Miss Grimshaw here in with Carlo and put all the stuff in her coffin. She's going first at St Saviour's this afternoon, so all that lot will be out of here before Sergeant Crump gets a less gormless dog and comes back for another sniff around.'

Nothing, to his amazement, went wrong. Miss Grimshaw, AKA half a ton of cannabis, received a solemn Catholic burial and Morris went home exhausted but relieved. It had been a close run thing.

There was a hastily-scribbled note from Rachel in the

283

kitchen. Horace had had another stroke.

He got straight back in the car and rushed over to the Infirmary. Angie had been on duty and she was there in her uniform, looking after Rachel. Horace was stable, and he was constitutionally strong, but the doctors warned them he was never going to be the same again. And another stroke would probably finish him off. They wouldn't be letting him go home until they were as sure as they could be that that wasn't going to happen just yet.

Morris said he and Angie should take it in turns to be there and Rachel should go home and get some rest but she said he was after all her father so she couldn't let them do that. Angie made up a bed in her department and they took it in turns to get an hour or so of sleep. By the morning Horace was improving, but they all looked like death warmed up. Morris had to go home and have a shower and shave before Carlo's funeral. He left the girls reluctantly but with no choice.

They got the coffin with Carlo and Miss Grimshaw to the crematorium with a minute to spare. Morris was so tired he couldn't for a moment remember whose funeral this was supposed to be. He called Mrs Castelli Mrs Grimshaw but fortunately Mrs Castelli didn't speak much English so the damage was minimal.

Morris and Marty sat way at the back of the crematorium. They could have gone back to the office but Morris was too tired to move. It was as the piped music started up and the curtains parted for the coffin to slide into the furnace that he happened to remark to Marty something about Carlo.

'Yes, it's a good job they don't know he's not really in there.'

'No Marty, you've got it wrong. They are in there, aren't they? That's Carlo, isn't it? Well, him and Miss Grimshaw.'

'What are you talking about, we buried them yesterday.'

'No we didn't, we buried the stuff yesterday, remember?'

Marty thought about this. 'No Morris, look, you're tired. Remember, you said put them in one coffin and the stuff in the other?'

'Yes, we buried the stuff at St Saviour's, and this is them.'

Marty thought again. 'No, I don't think so. This looks very much to me like the one I put the stuff in.'

'Well it can't be.'

'Well I'm sorry to argue with you, Morris, because I know you're the boss and normally when you're less tired you would be right, but I have to tell you I think it is.'

'No Marty, it can't be, and I'll tell you why. Because if half a ton of cannabis went into that furnace the consequences would be unthinkable.'

'Oh shit.'

Morris found he was suddenly wide awake and on his feet. The congregation looked round in surprise as the pair of them rushed outside, and there it was, the world's biggest spliff, a crematorium chimney belching out a great cloud of cannabis smoke. The cloud stopped for a moment, as if deciding which direction to move in, and Morris sank to his knees and prayed for an east wind to take it away from the town centre, and the god of wind direction heard his prayer, and laughed. A stiff westerly breeze came up from nowhere and the cloud moved vigorously in the direction of Barton town centre, where the wind suddenly dropped and deposited the fix on the innocent shoppers and the office workers out for their usual lunchtime air.

It would go down in the anals of history as Barton's finest hour. The traffic ground to a halt but no-one seemed to mind. Drivers got out of their cars and smiled dreamily at each other. Stallholders on Barton market gave away fruit to children and at the library staff handed out books to passers-by. A local burglar gave himself in at the police station but they were so far gone they forgot to lock the cell door and he wandered off again and gave himself up to the Salvation Army instead. A traffic warden walked down the high street taking her uniform off and issuing tickets to parking meters. Her bra

285

was later used in the magistrate's court as evidence.

The national news media got wind of what was going on and rushed photographers and reporters and film crews to the town but by the time they arrived it was all over, and none of the locals knew what all the fuss was about and the photographers and the film crews went home shaking their heads.

As long as it lasted, though, everyone was so happy you wouldn't have thought anything could go wrong. But of course it did, because when the town came to its senses the police came to theirs and something, they knew, had to be done, even if they weren't exactly sure what it was had happened and what should be done. It didn't take Sergeant Crump long to put two and two together, though, and come up with Marty Finnigan.

By six o'clock they had both him and Morris in custody.

Rachel and Baz Chaudhuri arrived at the police station at the same time, Rachel phoned by Morris and Baz alerted by his mole in the force. Baz, it seemed, knew pretty well everything that went on in Barton. Well, it's no more than you would expect. OK, he never got to the bottom of the business with Peter Potter and he held a grudge for a long time about that, but an opportunity presented itself now to claim some satisfaction and settle some old scores.

The headline in The Sentinel the next day read Barton Undertaker Introduces Happy Hour and, apart from getting his age wrong, Baz had all the details. Sergeant Crump allowed him to accompany his officers while they systematically took The Coffin Shop apart and there was a photograph of Morris next to a picture of The Wardrobe where forensic scientists from Divisional Headquarters found traces of cannabis, and the paper printed an insert picture of a bag of the stuff they got from a picture library, in case any reader should want to know what a bag of cannabis looks like.

Rachel was particularly upset that The Sentinel made it all

out to be Morris's doing and omitted to mention Marty, and when the pair of them came up before Barton Magistrates the next morning things didn't look good for Morris. Marty, though, came through. He confessed to the whole thing and insisted that Morris knew nothing about it. The panel was disinclined to believe him because the Stipendiary Magistrate, Mrs Ollernshaw, remembered Morris from the days when he used to shoplift from Tesco and she never forgot a face or forgave a sin. Mrs Ollernshaw was a lay preacher at the Truth of God Pentecostal Church, and she knew a thing or two about sin. Her colleagues, however, persuaded her that the evidence against Morris was thin if not non-existent and in the light of Marty's confession it would be nigh-on impossible to convict him. Mrs Ollernshaw gave way, reluctantly, but her price for this concession was that Marty be sent to the Crown Court for trial, where he was likely to receive a stiffer sentence, if he was convicted of course, but in the light of his admission of guilt she knew that was a foregone conclusion, and she went home to her cats that evening a satisfied woman.

Morris was released while Marty was bundled into a black van with small windows and driven off. It was a miracle, Morris realised, that in all the fuss no-one had thought to ask if the coffin that was burned at the crematorium only had cannabis in it, where was the body it was supposed to contain? It was one of those fortuitous happenings that have the ability to lighten the darkest moment.

Morris felt sorry for Marty, but on account of it being his own fault and what's more on account of him causing Morris a great deal of grief, not that sorry. He felt a great deal less sorry for him when he and Rachel got back to The Coffin Shop from the court and saw what the police had done. They had stripped it back to the original warehouse. You wouldn't have known there had been a funeral director's there at all, apart from the sorry pile of detritus piled up on the floor. Curtains had been torn down and the linings ripped away.

The stuffing of the chairs was pulled out and left in piles. A few dying flowers gasped their last on the carpet. It hadn't taken them long to turn a business into trash. Morris was angry, very angry, and it was beyond Rachel's ability, in her present condition, to prevent him from smashing up what was left, so with a heavy heart she left him to it.

42

Morris finally came home after midnight. He was drunk. Angie was asleep but Rachel was sitting up in the kitchen.

'So, got it out of your system yet?'

'No. If I ever catch up with that piss artist ...'

'Well you won't, will you? He's going away for at least a year and I don't expect he'll show his face around here when he gets out, so put Marty Finnigan out of your mind and do something useful with your anger instead.'

'Oh, right. Come on Rachel, haven't you ever wanted to kill someone?'

'Yes, but the difference is, my love that you are never going to do that and I have.'

Morris blinked in incomprehension. He wasn't sure he had heard what he thought he had heard.

'Rachel, did you just say what I think you said?'

'Yes.'

'OK, do you think you should talk to me about this?'

'Well, I've never felt the need to do that before, but now you're asking me, yes. It was on the deployment, the day of the explosion. The bomb went off and the Landrover went over on its side and I was trapped. For a moment I couldn't figure out what had happened. I was in a daze, and there was a lot of noise in my ears. The driver was dead and there was no sign of the only other man, and then I saw two militants coming towards me through the smoke. They were grinning at me and waving AK47s around and shouting something I couldn't understand and I was frightened.'

'So what happened?'

'Well they were pointing their weapons at me and shouting and for some reason I will never understand I stopped being scared and I got angry.'

'What did you do?'

'I pulled out my 9mm and killed them both with a single round to the head.'

'Bloody hell.' Morris was sober now. 'Bloody hell.'

'Yes, my thoughts exactly.'

'But you never told me.'

'No, well, it's not something I'm particularly happy about. I didn't join up to kill people, and I've been trying to figure it all out ever since. Don't forget, we didn't really know each other very well, and I didn't want to bring that into our relationship. Anyway, now you know.'

'Is there anything else I should know?'

'Isn't that enough?'

'Yeh. Does Pops know?'

'No. Are you going to tell him?'

'Not if you don't want me to. Anyway, I'm sorry, you've had him to worry about as well as me. How's he doing?'

'Oh, you know him, as strong as an ox. He's not ready to hand in his notice just yet. Comes from burying so many other people, I expect.'

'You know, Rachel, he's going to die one day, and that might not be as far off as you think. The doctor said ...'

'Yes, I know what she said. I've put that bit of information in a box in my head marked do not open until absolutely necessary.'

'Is that a good idea?'

'Probably not, but I don't have any other way of dealing with it.'

'Well, I'm just glad he won't know anything about this latest fiasco.'

'No. So, what do you reckon, time for bed?'

Morris was exhausted and he fell asleep as his head hit the pillow. Rachel lay there and listened to him breathing heavily and knew how much she loved him. Then she closed her eyes and made herself sleep, in the hope that when she woke all of this would be different.

In the morning it was all depressingly exactly the same. They drove over to the Infirmary to see Horace and he at least was a small ray of hope, although to look at him lying there you wouldn't have said he was much of one but the doctor said actually he was doing well and they would be able to take him to the nursing home in a few days.

Then they drove to the warehouse, as they had quickly taken to calling it again, to try and figure out what could be done. Rachel was more hopeful than Morris.

'OK, let's look at this rationally. It's a mess ...'

'Yes, so far I'm not going to disagree with you.'

'Quite. Well, look, there's nothing that can't be sorted out though, is there?'

'No, fair enough, but there's more to a business than premises. After the paper have finished with us who do you think is ever going to trust us to bury their loved ones now?'

Morris was right. Baz Chaudhuri had kept the story on the front page of The Sentinel every day. He was squeezing every last drop of blood out of this.

'Alright, but come on, what have you got to lose by trying? At least go over to St Elmo's and talk to Reverend Smylie.'

Morris didn't need to do that though, because the god of unwanted coincidences hadn't given up on him yet and at that precise moment there was a knock on the door and, yes, it was Reverend Smylie.

'Ah Mr Figg, Mrs Figg, how are you? Dear me, this is a mess. Who did this?'

'The police.'

'Really? Surely not? Well anyway, look, I've come over, I'm afraid, as the bearer of bad tidings. Are you, I mean, have you ... look, is it your intention to continue offering a funeral service in the town?'

'We were just discussing that.'

'Well, I may have something to say on the matter myself. It is my sad duty to inform you that, um, my colleagues in the Anglican Church have asked me to inform you that, well, how can I put this, that under the circumstances of this unfortunate publicity they are unable to work with your firm any longer. I'm so sorry, but I am sure you see the necessity for this painful decision.'

'I see. Oh well, that just leaves the other lot.'

'Ah, I believe Father Leary is on his way to see you this afternoon.'

'Right. Well, thank you for that, Reverend. Unless there's anything else?'

'Um, no, no. Well good day to you both. And if I may offer some words of consolation ...'

'No thank you.'

'Oh.'

Morris closed the door behind the vicar in the knowledge that it wasn't going to open for business again. He was, however, as so often, wrong, because no sooner had he turned the key than there was another knock. It wasn't a strong one, and at first he wasn't sure he had heard it at all, but he opened the door to check and there stood Mrs Diggle, his erstwhile neighbour.

'Good God, Mrs Diggle.'

Mrs Diggle had a new hearing aid. It wasn't perfect, but it was enough.

'Mr Figg. I'm so glad you are open. It's Tiddles.'

'What's Tiddles, Mrs Diggle?'

'Here.' And she proffered him a cardboard box marked Heinz Baked Beans, 12 x 300 gm. 'I want you to bury him for me.'

'Oh no, not Tiddles?'

'Yes, I'm afraid so.'

'But how did it happen?' By now Rachel was standing by his side looking sympathetic.

'I don't want to talk about it.'

'Oh, alright.'

'Well, if you insist. It was that nasty man downstairs. He brought some rat poison back from the bakery and Tiddles got it and, oh, Mr Figg, would you mind if I sit down?'

Morris found an upturned chair without its stuffing. He put a piece of wood across it and sat her down.

'There you go dear. Now, as you can see, things are a bit topsy turvy here at the moment.'

'Yes, I do see. Got the decorators in, have you?'

'Um, yes, sort of. Anyway, about Tiddles. Look, I'm afraid, well, it's not normal for a funeral director to arrange for the burial of pets. However, there is a special section at St Elmo's and ...' and here he hesitated and thought about Reverend Smylie, 'no, don't you worry, Mrs Diggle, I'll take care of everything.'

'Thank you so much Mr Figg. You're such a good man. Um, will it cost much?'

Morris looked at Rachel and he could see what she was thinking.

'No, Mrs Diggle, in fact it won't cost anything.'

And, without any further ado, they went straight round to St Elmo's where Rachel kept Reverend Smylie talking in the vicarage while Morris gave Tiddles the last funeral he was ever going to perform.

Rachel drove Mrs Diggle home and Morris went back to the warehouse to retrieve some important papers he was going to need to wind the business up. There was another knock on the door. If it was another funeral, he decided, the answer was no.

293

'Excuse me, are you Morris Figg?'

Well, why deny it? 'Yes. Can I help you?'

'Well, I do hope so. You see I'm looking for Rachel da Souza.'

'Sorry, no-one here of that name. Unless you mean my wife, Rachel Figg.'

'Do you know, I believe I do, yes, now you mention it I was aware she had married, I apologise for my mistake. May I offer my congratulations?'

'You can if you like. Are you a friend of hers?'

'Yes, a very old friend. My name is Bill Hardcastle.'

43

Rachel was overwhelmed to see her mentor again. She made him explain, over dinner and a bottle of wine, how he came to be in Barton.

'Well, I read about your injuries in the paper. I keep all the cuttings I find about my proteges, but none more than you Rachel. It was just sad to have bad news, especially after your silver medal. That article has pride of place in my collection. I don't suppose I could see it?'

Rachel went off and found the medal.

'Yes, yes, lovely. You have made me a proud man my girl. Well, as I was saying, I read about you and it came into my mind that it would be great to look you up, but that wasn't so easy. And then I had personal matters that got in the way ...'

Bill stopped talking.

'Do you want to tell me about them?'

'I might as well. You remember my wife, Juliet?'

'Uhuh. Don't tell me she died, please'

'That would, I hate to say it, have been easier to bear. No, she left me.'

'For another man?'

'Woman.'

'Oh, I never knew.'

'No, well neither did I, obviously, but afterwards I thought about all the years we hadn't had children and I started to see things more clearly. I was so busy helping other people's children I had forgotten I didn't have any of my own.'

'Bill, I'm really sorry.'

'Don't be, that's life. So anyway, where was I up to? Oh yes, Juliet went off and I was busy and put you to the back of my mind but then an amazing thing happened.'

'What was that?'

'I was at the airport, waiting for a flight to Brisbane, and I got talking to this man who claimed to be a vicar. If you ask me it was a pretty unlikely story. He was in a bit of a state, said his girlfriend had just walked out on him. Hell's bells, I thought he was going to start crying right there in the terminal, not much of a minister if you ask me. So I sat and listened to his story while my flight was delayed, again, and he said he had been staying in Barton at the home of Horace Tite, a name I didn't recognise at first but then your husband here came into the story and one way and another I discovered that you were here too because it was the so-called vicar who claimed to have married you two.'

Angie had been quiet up until now but felt she had to confess. 'Actually, he really was a vicar and he really did marry them and I, I'm afraid, am the girlfriend who walked out on him.'

Bill leaned over to her in a confidential sort of way. 'If I may say so, my dear, I spent half an hour with your vicar, and I would say you made the right decision.'

Angie blushed but still, she was pleased with that vote of confidence from a complete stranger.

'Anyway, a most happy coincidence it all was and I decided there and then I would come and visit when I got back to the UK.'

Morris had taken to Bill Hardcastle. He would have done that anyway, on account of what he had done for Rachel, but now he met him in the flesh he could see why she was so fond of him. He was pleased, too, that he had been so nice to Angie. He was a short, bluff, no-nonsense ex-paratrooper and

Morris knew that when you got to know him he would be a friend for life.

They all insisted he change his plan to book into a hotel and stay with them instead. They talked on into the night, Bill regaling Morris and Angie with stories about Rachel mostly, and his time in the Paras, and by the time Morris went to sleep later he had almost forgotten his troubles.

The next morning Rachel took Bill to the gym and despite the pregnancy put herself through an exercise routine that impressed him.

'Mm, not much sign of the injuries, is there?'

'Maybe not, but you know I'll never compete again.'

'Mm, perhaps not, but you're in good shape, my girl, if you'll forgive the expression.' He smiled and patted her bump, which showed more in a leotard than it had last night.

She wanted to do more but Bill wouldn't let her. He was like Morris. He fussed over her, as if no woman had ever had a baby before.

They went home for lunch and Bill quizzed Morris. He wanted to know everything about him. Morris told him the lot, well everything that was good to tell because you can take the spilling the beans thing too far.

'So, that's about it. We've got Horace going into a nursing home, Rachel here having a baby and fretting that she can't complete in the Olympic Games at the same time, and my business gone up in smoke. That about sums it up, really. Angie is the only one who does a normal day's work and gets paid for it. Without Rachel's pension and the fact that we're living in Horace's house rent free, we'd be in trouble.'

He wondered why he was telling this man all this stuff. Because he asked, probably. Bill Hardcastle, he was learning, was that kind of man, the kind who asked you anything he wanted to know and expected you to tell him, and once you'd done that he had the ability to make you feel good about it. He wasn't that much older than Morris but Morris already

297

looked up to him. Well, from where he was looking up was about the only direction.

It was a relief to tell someone in any case. He hadn't realised until he did just how guilty he felt for not having the means to support Rachel, instead of which she was now supporting him, not to mention that the house they were, as he told Bill, living in free of charge was her father's. Until recently he would have thought he was on to a good thing, but it didn't feel good. His life had changed too much to think like that any more.

Having nothing much to do, Morris found himself going for walks in the mornings while Rachel was at the gym, and the next day he just happened to find himself walking past St Elmo's. Without knowing why he went into the graveyard to check up on Tiddles. Then he wandered around looking at old gravestones and some not-so-old ones he had done the funerals for himself and thus it was that he found himself in front of one with Doris's name on it. He sat down cross-legged on the ground, and wondered how she and Tinkerbelle were getting on. So much had happened in such a short time, he could hardly recognise himself. Here he was, married, expecting a child of his own, OK he didn't have a job, but maybe an answer to that would materialise, just like it had before. Yes, maybe Tinkerbelle would have the answer for him.

'So, this is where you come.'

He stood up awkwardly. 'Bill, I didn't hear you coming.'

'No, it's the training, you're not supposed to.'

He was smiling and Morris wasn't sure if he was being serious.

'So who's Doris Fosdyke?'

'A very old woman who helped me out of a serious mess once. I thought if I come here she might help me again, if you see what I mean.'

'Uhuh. Do you want me to leave you two alone?'

'No no, let's walk.'

They did that, and Morris pointed out to Bill the graves he knew professionally and Bill asked him what it was like being an undertaker and Morris said he wasn't any more but while he had been it had been oddly satisfying.

'Is that because you like burying people or you like being in business?'

'Dunno. I've never actually thought about it.'

'Well think about it now.'

It sounded like an order. 'Now you ask, I think it was because I like being in control. I was out of control before. Rachel wouldn't have liked me then.'

'You might not have liked her. How much do you know about her past?'

'Everything. She told me right at the beginning. Thought I should have the chance to walk away from her.'

'That's typical Rachel. You've found a gem there, you know.'

'Yeh, but I don't know where we go from here. It's not just that I need to have an income for us and the baby, but to be honest before all this blew up Rachel was having a tough time anyway.'

'Her injuries?'

'Yes, well not them as such because she's made a huge improvement, but, well, you would know more about this than me, she can't come to terms with the fact that she's no longer a Sergeant Major and Olympic hopeful.'

'No, that's why I came.'

'Is it?'

'I knew she would struggle with it. You see, Rachel defines herself by her achievements, not who she is. She has a poor opinion of herself as a person. Take away the uniform and medals and she falls over.'

'I'd noticed. What do I do about that?' He somehow trusted Bill to have an answer, to have come to Barton

299

bearing gifts.

'OK, Morris, let's look at the situation. What assets do you have?'

'D'you mean money? Not a lot, a few thousand.'

'OK, money, but no, I don't really mean that. I mean, what can you bring to a new situation? OK, you don't understand, well let me help you. You've got Rachel. She may be feeling sorry for herself just now but after the baby's born I can tell you she will not want to hang around. That girl's got real drive, and two broken legs and a kid aren't going to get in her way. You will have to find something she can put that energy into, not just so she doesn't drive you crazy but because without a goal she won't find a new way to define herself.'

Morris was putty in Bill's hands. He was ready to do anything he asked.

'So much for Rachel, but what about you? What have you got?'

'Er, nothing. What you see is what you get, and I would be the first to admit it's not very impressive.'

Bill laughed. 'You don't have much self-confidence either, do you?'

'No, and in my case that's for a good reason.'

'Well, we'll come to that. What else is there?'

'What do you mean?'

'Morris, I want you to do me a favour.'

'Uhuh?'

'Will you show me your premises?'

'The warehouse?'

'Yes.'

'But it's just an empty building.'

'Do you have a lease on it?'

'Yes.'

'Then I want to see it.'

44

They walked round to what used to be The Coffin Shop and was now a rather unprepossessing warehouse. Morris suddenly saw it through the eyes of a stranger and what he saw was pretty shabby. He wondered how he had got away with running a funeral director's there at all, even an economy one.

The first thing they saw when Morris unlocked the door was the gurney made from two Tesco trolleys welded together. It made him ashamed that Bill was seeing all this. Bill, though, wasn't looking at any of that. He was walking round looking up.

'Mm, not bad. Not quite as big as I imagined, but I think it will do.'

'Do? Do what? Bill, would you like to tell me exactly what we're doing here?'

'Yes I would. I don't suppose there's such a thing as a chair?'

Morris improvised, and they sat, and Bill came clean about the Walter G Leatham Foundation. This, he explained, was funded by the eponymous Walter, who, Bill informed Morris in case he was ignorant of the matter, was the chairman of Leatham Industries of Australia. He had left Britain when he was nineteen after he got out of Borstal, and made his way to the other side of the world with the clothes on his back and a burning hatred of authority, but instead of getting into trouble, like he had here, he turned his energies to business, and the rest is history. Now, he was one of the ten wealthiest men in Australia, with business interests in the US and Britain as well.

Bill met Walter four years ago, sitting on some committee or other, and the two men had got on immediately. Walter invited Bill to his ranch in Queensland where he had some youngsters from deprived areas of Sydney doing some training. It was a small project he had dreamed up, but what he wanted was someone who could build it into a proper scheme for young people who had got themselves into trouble. Well, it was an offer Bill couldn't refuse. The scheme was going well now, with kids from all over Queensland getting sent there as an alternative to incarceration by the courts, and Bill had set up similar facilities in New South Wales and Western Australia too.

Morris listened attentively. It was a fascinating story, but it didn't occur to him that it had anything to do with him.

'So, Morris, there you have it. The Foundation has become my life in those four years. I live, eat and dream it. It's the best thing that ever happened to me, for sure.'

'It sounds brilliant. But what's it got to do with Rachel and me?'

'I'm here because Walter asked me to come. He knows about Rachel, about her past, just like the kids we work with over there, and he sees her as a shining example of what can be achieved. On my say so he wants her to head up the Foundation in the UK.'

'Shit.'

'Not, under the circumstances, a surprising reaction.'

'But hold on, that's great, for Rachel I mean, but um, please don't think I'm being selfish but I have to find something while she's doing all that, or is the idea that I stay at home and look after the baby?'

'No. Look, Morris, I've been looking at you since I arrived. You don't rate yourself very highly, do you?'

'No, we've been into that.'

'Well listen, I have some experience in judging people. Don't forget, it's my job. Your problem isn't that you're no good, it's that life hasn't given you the opportunity to see if you are good or not, so you have always assumed the worst. I hear from Angie that she and you had a rough start in life. Well, so did I and so did a lot of people, but that's the past and the past has nothing to do with the future, not of you don't want it to. Rachel defines herself by her successes but if you don't mind me saying so you have learned to define yourself by your failures, and now you believe in failure but what I'm looking at isn't what you have or have not achieved but who you are. And you are going to have to trust me on this one because I'm telling you, and I am, don't forget, something of an authority on these things, you're OK.'

The only sound in the warehouse was the slow drip of a tap in the kitchen. Bill knew a lot of things, and one of them was, like all good salesmen, when to stop talking.

'You're not just buttering me up so I give Rachel my blessing on this?'

Bill looked him straight in the eye. 'Morris, buttering up is something I don't do.'

'No, I don't suppose so.'

'So we'll pretend you didn't say that, shall we?'

'OK. Have you talked to her about this?'

'Not yet.'

'Why? Why talk to me first?'

'Because, and this is going to surprise you, I have a nagging worry your wife might say no.'

'You're kidding. Why would she do that? It's the opportunity of a lifetime.'

'Yes it is. But I know the woman and I've been looking at the two of you together and I can tell you she is going to worry about you, about the kudos that comes to her leaving you out in the cold.'

'I see. So in fact this is about her, not me.'

'Look Morris, I know it sounds like that, and I admit that was the first thing I thought of when I arrived, but don't forget if I hadn't seen how important you are to her I wouldn't need to persuade you, would I? You two come as a couple, and the Foundation wants both of you.'

Morris thought about this. Bill wasn't stupid. It was time for him to stop being stupid as well.

'Bill, are you ever wrong about anything?'

'Yes, frequently. It's a condition of life and I'm no different from anyone else. But at the risk of philosophising, the people who don't learn end up in the shit and the people who do don't always win but they have a bloody good chance of it, and I decided a long time ago to think about everything I do before I do it and the result is that everything I have ever done has been well and truly thought through and tends, therefore, to work. Now we're talking about me and that wasn't my intention.'

'In that case you're not as smart as you think you are. I needed to hear that before I said yes.'

'Does that mean you are saying yes?'

'Yes.'

So they went back to the house to talk to Rachel.

The pregnancy was too far advanced for them to fly out to Australia to meet Walter Leatham, so he combined various bits of business and came to Barton to see them. He treated Rachel like a war hero and Morris basked in the reflected glory. And he treated Morris with respect and that went down very well not just with Morris but with Rachel too.

Mrs Leatham turned out to be a formidable woman who was in large part responsible for her husband's success in life. She took to Rachel immediately and insisted on taking her and Angie to London to buy baby clothes even though Rachel insisted they had all they needed. Her husband was a sports fan on a huge scale. In a week he insisted that Morris and Bill accompany him to a rugby match at Twickenham, the European gymnastics championships at the NEC and another rugby match, this time in Paris, because France was playing Australia. When his home team won, nothing would suffice but to spend a night in the city attempting to drink it dry, after which Bill and Morris had terrible hangovers and Walter was stone cold sober.

Then they returned to Barton and got down to business. Walter offered Morris and Rachel a contract to run the UK Foundation and its sports centres. Morris asked if he meant to say that in the plural and Walter said of course, did he think he had come all this way for one poxy gym, and Morris said no of course not and they signed.

Walter looked at the warehouse and tutted, which Morris could understand. It was a dump. Walter asked if he could recommend an architect and he didn't know if Atkins and Atkins were any good but they were the only firm he knew so a week later Julian was tramping round the warehouse taking measurements. It wasn't a barn conversion, but the firm got the job because Morris asked especially for him and as a result he was made a partner.

Everything went well, until the planning application went to the council. Julian had done his work faultlessly. The planning committee, though, turned them down. Morris was furious. He stamped around the house in a huge strop and no-one could go near him.

'OK Rachel, now look, I want you to go down to the council and break the planning committee chairman's fingers one by one until he gives in, got that?'

'Morris, my love, it's a nice idea and terribly tempting but not in my condition, so do you have a Plan B instead?'

'But what reason did they give? What does Julian say?'

'Apparently they were worried about the washroom facilities. Too small, or too big or something.'

'What? You're joking. Who's the chairman? Call Julian will

you and ask him.'

'Only if you promise not to go to the town hall and threaten him.'

She rang Julian.

'Morris, you're not going to like this.'

'OK, who is he?'

'He isn't. It's a she. Mrs Ollernshaw, JP.'

'Hang on, isn't she the magistrate who ...'

'That's her.'

'The cow. She's done this because of me. Hang on, though, how could she have known I'm even involved? The application's in the name of the Foundation.'

'There's more, I'm afraid. Julian said there was a reporter at the committee meeting, from The Barton and Tidbury Sentinel.'

'Don't tell me.'

'I must. Baz Chaudhuri.'

It was all she and Angie could do to stop Morris going over to The Sentinel's offices. He calmed down eventually, but it took the rest of the evening.

Bill was due back from Australia the next day. He stayed with them now as a matter of course. It was convenient, and everyone had come to like him. He and Angie wheeled Horace round the garden. And it was Horace who resolved the problem. His speech was limited and Angie was the only one who could understand him. Since he had come back from the nursing home she had become the one who spent time with him. Rachel was due in three weeks, and with the Foundation as well she was grateful for Angie's support.

Angie found Morris in the kitchen nursing a cup of tea.

'Well Kiddo, I think I've got some good news for you.'

'Uhuh? You're going to go and break the old bag's fingers?'

'Morris, I've known you for a long time but I never realised you have a violent streak. No, it's Horace.'

'I see. You're going to wheel him down to the council and

he's going to break her fingers?'

'Not quite, but the first bit was right. I am going to take him to the Town Hall.'

'For the purpose of?'

'For the purpose of him talking to the old bag.'

'That's nice. And he's going to persuade her to change her mind, I suppose?'

'Yes.'

'Uhuh. On account of?'

'On account, Kiddo, of the old bag and Horace once had a thing.'

'Thing? What kind of thing?'

'You know, a thing.'

'Shit. No. Not really?'

'Yep, apparently. It came out just now in the garden. The old man's obviously been thinking about it and he told me he wants to help. He reckons he can persuade her.'

'Well if it meant getting the application through I would seduce the old bag myself, but if Horace is available that would be better.'

'Well, you might have got slightly the wrong idea. I don't think he's planning to have it off with her on the floor of the council chamber.'

'Whatever. Just get him down there.'

And she did. And four weeks later they had their planning permission for the Walter G Leatham Sports Centre.

Which just left Baz Chaudhuri to deal with. It took Morris a while to figure it out but the idea came to him in one of his rare moments of mental clarity. He called some friends who owed him a favour, and then he made an anonymous telephone call to The Sentinel to say Peter Potter had been spotted in Tidbury. The paper sent their ace reporter, the very same Baz Chaudhuri, over there, and he found some carefully-placed evidence that Peter had been there but had since travelled on to Birmingham. Determined to track his prey down, Baz called his editor and got his permission to follow. From there he went to Leicester and when he called his editor again he was told to come home but he couldn't do that. From Leicester he tracked Peter to Cambridge, and from there the trail led to Ipswich and the last time Baz was seen he was on the ferry to Holland. By the time he landed the paper had fired him.

45

Three weeks later, on the due date, Rachel gave birth to a son, Timothy William Figg.

They put together a Board of Governors for the UK branch of the Foundation, and invited Mrs Ollernshaw to be its chairman. She insisted on being called the chair, which both Bill and Morris thought was hilarious. Bill said she had cabriole legs but Rachel thought that was unkind, if funny. She brought Timmy to board meetings and insisted on breastfeeding him on demand, Rachel that is, not Mrs Ollernshaw, the latter looking askance at first but eventually she was won over and demanded to be allowed to rock the baby to sleep while she chaired meetings.

Sergeant Crump represented the constabulary on the board and the rest of the membership was made up by the headmaster of a sink school in the area and other local worthies.

The building work proceeded apace and every time Morris visited the site it got harder to remember Marty's warehouse let alone The Coffin Shop. There were tradesmen of every description working on every part of the building, including some he didn't know existed. They used the famous wardrobe to keep their brewing up things in.

By the time they had ripped the floor up and removed the entire roof and all the windows, Morris wondered what the point was. Wouldn't it have been cheaper to just pull it down and start from scratch? Still, Julian came round once a week to check up and he said everything was proceeding according to plan, and the Foundation had a large bank account from which the Board disbursed regular payments and it was in every respect a respectable business. The Sentinel did a big piece on it, with an artist's impression of the finished sports centre and Morris had to admit he was highly impressed with it all, if a little scared. He couldn't quite figure out how he, Morris Figg, well known layabout, had come to be entrusted with this great and worthy enterprise. He expressed his worries to Rachel in bed and she just laughed. She was enjoying every minute of this. Motherhood had changed her in some miraculous way and Morris thought that even without the Foundation she had found some new way to define herself. And then there was Timmy. Morris couldn't understand how that had happened. Well, he knew how it had happened but what he couldn't figure out was why him, why was he blessed with this gorgeous wife and beautiful son? Maybe it was right, what Bill had said that time, that actually he deserved all this, as long as he let himself believe he did.

Angie gave her notice in again at the hospital, and this time she asked specifically that there was no whip round for a watch from Argos, she would be happy with a couple of drinks at the pub to say goodbye. Horace was taking up more and more of her time and she found that more satisfying than being at work, and she also found she could get paid by the Department of Giving Money Away as a carer. In any case, Morris and Rachel were on good salaries now and on top of that what with it being Horace's house and the mortgage was paid off years ago the outgoings were pretty low. Morris said she should set up a sports physiotherapy department at the Centre and she said she would think about it, but the god of mucking about with your plans had other ideas.

'Angie.'

'Morris. How's it going?'

'Fine. It all seems to be happening without me, but I go down there and make it look like I'm earning my pay.'

'It'll all change once it opens. You know, you've surprised me, I'll admit it. You've turned into an ace at making things happen. The Foundation needs you.'

'Well, sister of mine, thank you for that vote of confidence. Anyway, I'm glad you're going to be working with us.'

'Ah.'

'Ah?'

'Yes, ah.'

'You're going to say something, aren't you.'

'I shouldn't be surprised.'

'I mean like ah but. Come on, admit it, there's a but coming up, isn't there?'

'Yes Kiddo, I'm afraid there is. It looks like I'm going to be letting you down.'

'Oh yes? Had a better offer have you?'

'Yes.'

'Angie, I wasn't serious. What are you talking about? Who's given you a better offer?'

'Bill.'

'But hang on, we need you here. What does he want you for?'

'To marry him.'

'Yes but ... hang on, say that again.'

'Bill has asked me to marry him.'

'Bloody hell. When did this happen?'

'Yesterday.'

'No, I don't mean the marrying bit, I mean the bit that comes before it, you know, the going to the pictures followed by the going out for dinner and saying I love you and saying I love you too and darling I can't live without you bit. When did all that happen?'

'Oh, over the past few months.'

'Months! How come I didn't know anything about it?'

'Well my dearest brother, it never occurred to me to give you a running commentary on our relationship.'

'But ... but ...'

'OK, that's two buts. Do you want to be more specific?'

'Um, OK, how about the fact that you're still married to Roger, huh?'

'I think you'll find that can be sorted out. It's called divorce.'

'Divorce? That's a bit final isn't it?'

'Uhuh, that's the idea.'

'Oh. Anyway, look, if you don't mind me mentioning it, I mean, well, Bill, isn't he just a bit old for you?'

'He's ten years older than me. I don't consider that's an issue.'

'Alright Angie, I haven't wanted to do this but you force me to. Do you love him?'

'Yes.'

'Really?'

'Look, Morris, I'm thirty five. Ask me if I can define love and I have to say I won't know the answer to that as long as I live. Ask me if I feel good about Bill and I have no trouble at all. Yes. I feel safe with him, and that's something I haven't felt for a long time. You told me once not to rush into another relationship with my eyes closed, well, look, they're wide open. OK, I can't promise you it's going to work because I don't know, but we both feel right about this. Don't forget it's taken a lot of trust on Bill's part to open up to a woman again. And I have to say I think his wife was a bloody fool. Bill is that rare commodity in my experience, but one that your Rachel, if I may say so, has found. A good man.'

Morris sat and pondered this. He looked into his sister's eyes and found what he was looking for. This was for real, and suddenly he knew she was right. Bill Hardcastle was a good man, he already knew that, he was a man he would trust with his sister. Suddenly, Morris felt a great surge of relief, and it showed in his face. Angie came and kissed him.

'Thanks Morris. I love you.'

'Oh.'

'Morris?'

'Yeh?'

'Do you love me?'

'Yes, of course I do.'

'Well, I believe you since you put it so nicely.'

'Angie?'

'What?'

'Well, you're not pregnant, are you?'

'Morris, just because you and Rachel did it that way round. No, I'm not. But as it happens it's something Bill and I are both agreed on, we want to start a family as soon as possible.'

'Um, Angie, something else occurs to me. Where are you going to live?'

'Sydney.'

'Bloody hell, Sydney?'

'Uhuh. I know it's a long way but look, you've got all this now. You don't need me, do you?'

Morris thought about that. No, he didn't.

'Anyway, come on, we'll be back so often you'll wonder if we ever went.'

'Angie?'

'Yes?'

'Have I been a good brother to you?'

'No, you've been a pain in the neck. Don't ask me again or I'll start crying. Anyway, who ever said I was your responsibility?'

'I dunno. Someone must have. Or else I just thought they did. That's what big brothers are for, isn't it?'

'Yes, kiddo. But I'm going to have a husband now and you really don't need to be my big brother any more.'

'Not even if I want to?'

Angie thought about that, and then she put a big sister's arm round him.

313

'As long as you want, Morris, as long as you want.'

Found a mistake?

It doesn't matter how many times a manuscript is proof-read, some of the little blighters manage to hide until after publication. If you spot an error, do please let me know, at:

robert@brynin.com

Printed in Great Britain
by Amazon

80827112R00180